Peace of Me

Peace of Me

T.N. Williams

URBAN CHRISTIAN

Urban Books, LLC
78 East Industry Court
Deer Park, NY 11729

ISBN 13: 978-1-61664-947-0
ISBN 10: 1-60162-881-1

Printed in the United States of America

DEDICATION

To the newest addition of the family, Jeremiah. You have just entered this world, but the joy you bring is indescribable. May you grow to do marvelous things and continue to be a blessing.
Love you with my whole heart, Nana's son.

ACKNOWLEDGMENTS

Let me first thank God. Lord, you keep using me and loving me despite myself. I see your plan for my life and pray that I will honor you by doing your will.

To my children, Jackie, Jordan, and Xavier. You constantly encourage me to excel as your role model. You are my motivation. To my parents, Cynthia Phillips and Greg Williams, I thank you for giving me life and continuing to be my biggest and best supporters. To my extended family, I love each and every one of you. To LaSherise Simpson, Torrie Evans, Lora Blackmon, and all my coworkers at DSS, I must say that we work well under pressure. Our positions have humbled me and you keep me laughing when things get intense. May God continue to help us help others. To Monte Neal, Eugene Jones, Omar Friday, and Charles Jones; you are the best male friends a woman could ask for. Thank you for lending your time, your ears, and your input when I need you most. I have tremendous respect for all of you. To the man with the best marketing and entrepreneurial advice, Kirkland Oliver, I must say I appreciate your pushing me to focus and challenging me like nobody else could. May you continue to prosper. To Pastor Bryan and First Lady Debra Pierce of Bethel Baptist Church, you have blessed me so much. I love your beautiful spirits.

To my executive editor, Joylynn Jossel, Lord knows I test your

Acknowledgments

editing abilities, and without fail, you always help me deliver a beautiful story. I am forever in your gratitude. To authors, Nikita Nichols, Pat Simmons, and Rhonda McKnight; thank you for entertaining my e-mail insanity and sharing your creative minds with me. This has been a season of trials for me, and I have needed to vent on more than one occasion. I don't know what I would do without you. For the entire Urban Christian family, may we place a positive, permanent imprint on this world with our written words.

Lastly, to all the readers, reviewers, and book clubs, I hope you are enlightened by the words I captured on paper. Please visit me at my Web site www.tnwilliams.com. I would love to hear from you. Be blessed!

CHAPTER ONE

ME

Desiree Monaya Potts
Age: 17
Born: November 8, 1991
Missing since: October 12, 2006
Flint, MI

"Missing? Oh . . . my . . . God," I exclaimed in disbelief.

It took all of thirteen seconds for me to recognize Desiree on the flyer. In that amount of time, I realized her slender, dark brown face was also in my condo. Her picture was stashed away in a metal box. It was amongst other images of young girls. Photos with no name or identity. The pictures were taken of children with gleeful smiles, dressed in just enough clothing to pass as sweet and innocent. They were copies of photos that my ex-husband, Khalil, had cherished. A sick joy realized by only him until right before he went to prison three years ago for molesting our daughter.

An agitated sigh escaped my lips.

I had been unquestionably naive about Khalil; about who he was, what he was.

The pictures were found in a box that I would have never known existed if a ficus tree in our old house had not gotten knocked over after the sale of the property. It was kicked over by my son, Caleb, as he tried to squeeze past two men hauling an armoire through a narrow doorway. Another surprise left behind by the man I married. How ironic that Khalil would place his dirt amongst dirt.

His choice for a hiding place had made me shudder. I remembered how my heart beat a tap dance against my ribcage on that day I picked the ficus plant up off the floor. I remembered my shock as I removed the metal box from the broken clay pot. I had anxiety before I knew what the contents were.

My deranged ex-husband with his hideous secrets. Who would have thought that underneath the façade of that sensual man would be such a perverted mind?

That he was nicely dressed up on the outside in polo shirts dashed in Tabarome Creed cologne while his inside reeked of a disgusting nature.

Khalil, the ever faithful husband and adoring father, who had women in our church congregation whispering that they wished their spouses were more like mine.

Before I knew what kind of man I married, I proudly accepted every compliment. I use to glow just looking at him. I had loved and trusted my husband unconditionally. Khalil made it easy for me to be clueless. His unassuming, sweet personality and handsome appearance made it easy for his treasures to stay hidden. Heck, he had everybody fooled. His lies flowed like fluid from his lips constantly and consistently deceiving. And I must admit that he mastered his disguise of ordinary. But . . . Khalil was anything but ordinary.

Desiree's picture and that collection of other photos were part of his sickness. At least that's what I tried to convince myself. I hoped that would lessen the pain, humiliation, and anger.There were even some days that I could acknowledge Khalil's deeds as a disease.I prayed for some kind of healing of the man I once loved. Only God could deliver someone from that level of insanity. Then there were some days that I could not. *Pedophilia* is what Kaleia's therapist called it when I had my daughter in counseling.I thought we could simply make the problems go away.As if saying that word 'pedophilia' would lessen the damage done.As if I'd ever forget how he turned our world upside down.

An icy blast coursed down my vertebrae, rattled my tail bone like a debilitating frostbite from being pushed head first into the Antarctic Ocean.Abruptly, I tried to shake it off. I buttoned the collar of my wool coat and rubbed my gloved hands together, but the inside of me was chilled.

Caught in a daydream that felt as raw as the frigid March breeze, I took off one glove and brushed my fingers against the cold glass window. The ends of the picture were frayed where the tape held them in place. The flyer had been up for quite some time. The ebony-toned teenager with a crescent moon scar above the right eyebrow had a smile adorning her thin face, a grin peeking upward to high cheekbones.No cares or concerns. Her eyes were as bright as her smile, and both embodied a carefree-ness that only a child could have. Should have.

"See, I knew that I had money on my card. That little clerk didn't know what she was doing. Trying to act like something was wrong with my credit.Pul-lease." My identical twin sister, Alicia's, irritation cut into my thoughts.

I glanced at her, blinked twice, as she stomped toward me while zipping up her purse. Physically, Alicia looked exactly like me. From our caramel toned skin to our chocolate dipped almond-shaped eyes to our slender figures, we matched. But our personalities were as different as tropical punch Kool-Aid and Barolo red wine.

Alicia and I had been at the shopping plaza picking up items for both our daughters' sweet sixteen party scheduled for the next weekend. Her debit card had been denied. An obviously overworked clerk with an attitude swiped the card three times. I had noticed the smug twitch of the clerk's lips when it declined and the embarrassment on Alicia's face.

I saw the fury coming. My sister often snapped easily, especially when tested or humiliated, which she seemed to be both at the time. She nearly had a full blown fit before I offered to pay for the party decorations. Public scenes didn't bother Alicia, but they were three touches beyond tolerable for me. I had suggested we make it to her bank before it closed. I had been used to her temper since we were small children. I tried to keep her as calm as possible. Alicia didn't want to go to a bank and decided to walk to the grocery, four stores down to check an ATM machine for her balance.

It was as we walked down the short path of strip mall that the flyer inside a Dollar-Do-Ya window caught my attention. Alicia kept walking and didn't notice me stop. Probably didn't notice anything until after she checked her account.

I stared at Desiree's pretty, chocolate face on the flyer. I half listened as Alicia continued complaining about the clerk.

"Oh, I have a mind to take this stuff back, get a refund, and make her ring it back up again. It's not like she has anything better to do. She doesn't know who she's messing with. Trying to throw attitude. I can show her attitude."

"I'm sure that there was an error with the store machine. Don't let yourself get riled up for nothing," I encouraged her even as a knot of emotions ate through my insides.

"How is it my fault that the woman doesn't make over

minimum wage? She probably declined it on purpose trying
to be funny. That clerk had me out here looking like a fool.It's
a good thing nobody else was in that store; otherwise I would
have cussed her behind out. She just doesn't know how close
she came to a good cussing out." Alicia's heated words could
have melted the snow covered parking lot behind us.

My sister continued talking, but I no longer heard her voice.
Her rant had faded into the background until I'd completely
tuned her out. I stared at the date on the flyer, then back at
the face.Desiree went missing several weeks before Khalil was
arrested.Somebody's child vanished into thin air.

When she disappeared she had been fourteen years old.Two
years younger than my daughter was now.I couldn't imagine that
being Kaleia. I couldn't imagine sleeping at night without
believing she was safe. Without believing either Kaleia or
my other child, Caleb, were safe and sound. Not knowing
whether one of my children was dead or alive seemed tragically
incomprehensible. There couldn't be a worse feeling for a parent.

Thinking about Desiree's face, I was transported back to
discovering her picture in that box. The hardened soil had
made it difficult for me to pull the lid up, but I had tugged.
Finally it gave and rose with an eerie squeak. On that moving
day, three years ago, I knew I'd found something sinister.

Pulling myself from past to present, I read the scant details on
the missing poster, and my suspicion was validated. I instinctively
thought about foul play. I rubbed my abdomen and tried to
calm my nerves.

Alicia finally realized I wasn't paying her any attention.
"Why are we standing here?" she asked as she placed a hand
upon her hip.

"I know her." I pointed to the poster, touching the cold
glass again. "I mean, I don't personally know her.Khalil knew

her. Remember . . . I told you when I gave the police pictures of her and the others. They were supposed to help those girls. She's not supposed to be missing." That churning in my stomach was growing larger.

Alicia worked at that Detroit Police precinct and knew everything. "Oh."

The churning continued growing and building, until my insides felt like they were about to burst outward.

In that moment I knew. I knew without any factual evidence that Khalil would forever be linked to that young girl's face. I knew that his evil doings had rocked more than just my family.

"Hmm. Your twisted ex. That man is like diarrhea. He keeps giving you the runs long after you think you're cured." Alicia pursed her lips momentarily. She stared at the missing date before adding, "October of 2006. I would be the first to blame him for wrongdoing, but during that time he was stalking you. You don't think he also had something to do with her disappearance?"

I feverishly nodded.

Khalil was capable of anything.

CHAPTER TWO

KALEIA

Kaleia Alexander dropped her book bag below the fire alarm case on the third floor of Montgomery Christian High. She clamped the personalized mint green invitation between her thumb and forefinger as she waited. Under her breath she recited the words she planned to say, but nothing sounded right. She didn't know why she was nervous.

The timing had to be exact after watching his routine all last week. That Monday morning, as she saw Tevin approach, she took a deep breath, while tapping the invite against the skirt of her school uniform. Before he passed her by, Kaleia thrust the invitation in front of him. Tevin's hazel eyes broke from the text message he was sending and locked with hers, but there was little recognition. Kaleia wasn't the least bit surprised by his confused gaze. Tevin probably never noticed her at the basketball games or in the cafeteria. He had no clue that she saw him score twenty-eight points in the defeat against St. Mary's Catholic or that she knew he only ate Subway sandwiches with his three main friends during lunch period. Kaleia also knew that Tevin used to sell Xanax bars and marijuana laced with crystal meth to a few select students in the school bathroom before he changed locations because one of the teachers started getting suspicious. Kaleia knew more than enough about Tevin Jameson.

She had to make the conversation quick. The bell would be sounding in a few minutes.

"There is a party this weekend. I really want you to come." Kaleia tried to seem confident. Flirting was not something that came naturally. She had never talked to a boy like that. Kaleia knew that she wasn't the only girl vying for his attention, and she didn't want to sound dumb.

He opened the invite and read her name. "Kaleia. I don't think we know each other."

She quickly explained, "I come to all your basketball games, and I like how you play. It would make me very happy to have you come to my sweet sixteen party."

"You want *me* at your sweet sixteen? Is this an extra special invitation?" A grin developed as he flirted back.

"Yes. You could consider it an extra special invitation." Kaleia could see the obvious amusement that was playing off the green and brown specks of his eyes. She continued talking. "Also, D-Boyz will be performing. You know that they are the best in local rappers. Think about it." She didn't wait for a response as she walked past him and headed up the hall.

Her walk stayed steady until she made it outside to the courtyard. Black penny loafers immediately slapped against the pavement, barely grazing the cracked cement as Kaleia dashed across the school grounds. The arm of Kaleia's lavender book bag, decorated with hearts, danced to the beat of the wind.

Kaleia ran as fast as her legs would allow, praying that she wouldn't get a detention pass. Ms. Denison, her third hour teacher, had a very limited tolerance for tardiness. But sometimes Ms. Denison's tolerance depended on her mood. Kaleia knew the risk involved when she decided to approach Tevin.

A straggly tree branch snapped against her thigh as Kaleia made a sharp turn around the main building. The late bell rang just as she burst through heavy wooden doors. Kaleia leapt up the steps two at a time and didn't stop until she reached the first room on the right. Kaleia's assigned desk was in the third row. Ms. Denison's eyes followed her until she reached her seat, sat down, and retrieved her text book out of her bag.

"Ms. Alexander, how nice of you to join us today." Ms. Denison's syrupy voice met Kaleia as she entered Biblical Theologies class.

Kaleia let out a loud sigh when Ms. Denison brought her attention back to the class.

"We were just about to discuss family secrets. Namely David's family secrets. David was a man after God's own heart, but he had a lot of skeletons in his closet. He was marred by a family legacy that he created. Could somebody tell me what those secrets were?" Ms. Denison asked.

Tim Tancred, a student who sat directly in front of Kaleia, spoke. "David had a soldier killed because he was sleeping with the man's wife and got her pregnant. Eventually the baby died, but King David created the gangster-style. "

"Hmm. I would've never equated David's actions as gangster." Ms. Denison's eyes perused the room, her bird-like neck turning left to right. "Anyone else?"

When no response came from any of the students, Ms. Denison spoke. "That was indeed one of the secrets, but David somehow also created the ultimate dysfunctional family. If you read Second Samuel, you will find that David mistreated his children, who turned around and mistreated each other. David's son, Ammon, had an infatuation with his half-sister, Tamar, and when Ammon faked illness to get Tamar into his room, David didn't question the actions. David failed to help Tamar after she was raped by her own brother. Tamar eventually confided in her other brother, Absalom, and he killed Ammon, but swore Tamar to secrecy about the rape. Now *that* was scandalous."

The classroom discussion became electric as if a current flowed to each desk.

Paula lifted an alabaster hand in the air. "I have issue with somebody like that being God's right hand man. Pervertedness is inherited."

Jack eagerly added, "Yeah, for all we know, King David might have been watching from another room like it was an X-rated video."

A mousy haired Lisa grimaced at Jack from two seats over. "That is a terrible thing to say. Poor Tamar. She was wronged by all three men in her family. She was probably messed up in the head for the rest of her life."

Those comments hit home. Kaleia could feel herself shrink inside her own skin. She anxiously shifted in her chair. Kaleia wondered if Tamar felt as terrible back then as she did now about keeping family secrets. She could feel the accusations without an eye on her. It made her feel guilty. When her father, Khalil, was arrested, the news spread all over the city. Classmates started to treat her like she had leprosy. Kaleia wished that she was able to keep her family secret, a secret. Talking about it not only confined her father to a prison cell, it also left her to live a life full of misery and guilt.

If Tamar was vowed to secrecy, Kaleia wondered who told the secret that would be held against her father, David, in a Bible for all time.

Kaleia crushed the ink pen she held into the pad of her hand. She could feel the ballpoint tip indent her skin. Slowly she retreated into the recess of her mind where she wouldn't have to think anymore. Where she wouldn't have to feel for at least the remainder of class. The voices of her classmates became distant echoes.

As soon as class ended, Kaleia made a zombie stroll to the girl's bathroom. She went to the stall at the very end, closed the door, and pulled out the razor she kept hidden in the seam of her book bag. The anxiety was more than she could handle.

Kaleia had let her father down when she told the details of their secret during his court trial. He had been the most important person in her life. People that knew about what happened, treated her differently. Khalil wasn't around to protect her from the stares and whispers. Her father was gone away to prison for a very long time. Because she videotaped Khalil trying to sleep with her, and then testified about what he had done, Kaleia may never see him again. It was her fault and she knew it. Guilt had control of her. Lifting the pleats of her skirt, Kaleia cut the skin below her turquoise cotton panties and let blood drip into the toilet bowl.

CHAPTER THREE

ME

Flashing shades of blue circles flowed from my screen saver. I watched the colors go from aqua to navy as I stared at my laptop.

Thoughts of the missing girl consumed me days after I saw that missing poster. I could admit I had been hesitant to look up Desiree's name on the Internet; not sure if the information I found on the great wide web would infuriate me, console me, or continue the unsettling that had plagued me. Even when I tried to focus on other things like the report I needed to e-mail my assistant first thing in the morning, or the new outfit Kaleia still had to pick out for her party, my mind drifted back to Desiree like willow before a storm.

"Being without knowledge can be just as damaging as not having the correct information," I mumbled to myself as I glided my finger over the pad to revive the Yahoo page. The little white numbers in the corner told me that it was almost nine in the evening. The cursor blinked in the search engine of my laptop as I stared at the screen and typed the name 'Desiree Carpenter.' I hit ENTER while holding my breath. A list of related subjects chopped up her name. There were other 'Desiree's' and plenty of 'Carpenters.' An award was given to Desiree Johnson in the Iron Man competition based in South

Korea. A download of 1970 songs was for Karen Carpenter. The Association of Carpenters and Electricians were giving free classes to union workers. But nothing merged for the 'Desiree Carpenter' I was searching for. I saw nothing that would give me an indication of what had happened to her. The second page was also full of the same type of inconsequential information.

I drummed my fingers against the keypad and wondered why I couldn't find the information I was searching for. I got creative and changed the browser topic. I removed Desiree's name and typed 'Missing Black Girls' and clicked on the year I was interested in. That particular search linked me to a page entitled, 'Lost But Not Forgotten,' and I was able to choose random captions.

Armetruis Chance of Florence, South Carolina, age 24 left home the morning of May 12th, 2007, dropped her daughter off at a babysitter, and hasn't been seen since. Her ex-boyfriend is a suspect in her disappearance, although no formal charges have been filed.

Elise Rodriquez, age 11, abducted by her drug addicted mother while in Cumberland County foster care custody. Last known whereabouts was a Department of Social Services parking lot.

Justice Sullivan, age 15, an endangered runaway, Minneapolis, Minnesota.

Carlin Thompson, age 3, taken from a Target Superstore in Phoenix, Arizona. The surveillance camera captured a woman with a bowed head leaving the front entrance while carrying the child.

Sojourner Hawkins, age 7 months, missing from a graduation celebration at her mother's best friend's home in Jacksonville, Florida.

On the side of the page were blogs about missing children and young women. There were also photos of children who had been found, runaways who had returned home, and bodies that were discovered and laid to rest. Memorials were also posted.

My heart deflated as I looked at all those brown faces missing across the nation, and I didn't want to look anymore. I snapped my laptop shut and inhaled deeply. Adding to my uncertainty, grief consumed me. I felt grief for all the parents who woke up this morning and didn't have their child.

The verse *'the Lord gave, and the Lord hath taken away; blessed be the name of the Lord'* came to mind from the book of Job in the Bible. A few weeks ago my pastor preached about Job and his faithfulness to God. Pastor Daniels explained to the congregation that Job lost all that he owned and all his children died. When that tragedy occurred, Job dropped to his knees and worshiped God despite his grief. I hoped that my faith would be that strong if something happened to Kaleia and Caleb, but that was a test I also hoped never to endure.

"Oh God, please keep your loving arms of protection around my children." Goose bumps appeared on my arms. I shivered, but couldn't shake away the feeling of uneasiness.

I rolled over and looked at the clock. I couldn't believe it read 2:47 A.M. Sleep hadn't come easily. I blamed my insomnia on the Internet search for information on Desiree. Caleb and Kaleia had gone to bed at nine last evening, and each hour after that, I'd gone into their bedrooms to check on them. It seemed that every sound disturbed me. Whether it was ice cubes in the freezer falling from the automatic ice-maker, the car with a loose muffler passing by, or the soft purr of a stray kitten outside my bedroom window; I couldn't relax and allow sleep to overtake me. My hearing was fine tuned like a cello in an orchestra. The rev of my neighbor, Mr. Orchenbuck's, diesel engine when he cranked his Buick Regal before he left for his third shift work schedule, along with the tree branches scratching my window pane, added with the hum of Kaleia's radio were things that normally wouldn't catch my attention. But when the hardwood floors creaked, I bolted from my bed and searched for the individual board that spoke. Again and again I did this. I was on the verge of becoming a paranoid schizophrenic.

At three A.M., I was tightly curled up in a lounger opposite Caleb's bed watching him breathe lightly in his slumber. The comfort of knowing that I had that opportunity to watch over my children when thousands of other parents were robbed of those precious moments filled me with joy and pain at the same time. I watched my son for a while. I reminisced about the uneventful stages of growth that I couldn't prevent, like when he chipped his baby tooth after falling from his tricycle at the tender age of three. I remembered the way my heart jolted when I saw blood ease from his mouth. It was that first rise of panic in my eyes and the shriek that uttered from my throat that made him cry. He'd had many other falls, bumps, and bruises in his twelve years. I could honestly say that Caleb was clumsier than his older sister. Often I had to remind myself that no matter how hard I tried, I couldn't protect either of them from all of life's traumas.

By four in the morning my eyes began to droop, and I decided to leave his room before he found me asleep in his chair. Caleb would freak out if he thought that I was treating him like he was a baby. He constantly reminded me that he was twelve years old.

I pulled myself up and heard the squeak of a ball as I stomped on it. I paused and looked over at Caleb who appeared unmoved by the noise.

I planned to head to the kitchen. Maybe a cup of chamomile would give me some much needed rest.

"Mom, are you okay?" Caleb inquired, catching me tiptoe out his doorway.

I guiltily pivoted on the balls of my feet and turned toward his voice. I could see the outline of Caleb's head below the Transformers plastered wall as I headed toward his bed. He turned on the coordinating Optimus Prime robot lamp of the nightstand to his left. He squinted at me as his eyes adjusted to the light.

"I'm all right. I just have a lot on my mind and wanted to check on you. A lot of crazy stuff goes on in this world and sometimes it gets to me," I said as I sat on the edge of his bed and patted his shoulder. I wondered if he realized I had been sitting in his study chair for the past hour watching him sleep.

"You don't have to worry about me, Mom. I'm almost old enough even to take care of you." His arm curved around mine as he tried to give comfort.

I listened to the sound of his voice; the bass that has recently developed. Puberty had begun. Caleb had already shown signs of other budding growth outside of the change in octave. His aim was off when he went to the bathroom. It was evident in the yellowish spots surrounding my toilet bowl first thing in the morning. New spots were there every morning when he was getting ready for school. That meant one thing when it came to an adolescent young man. His lower region was reacting to the increase in testosterone. I was too embarrassed to talk to him about his aim being off; didn't feel it was my place. I had no problem explaining the expectation I had for him as he grew into manhood, but *teaching* him how to be a man was beyond my capabilities. That was a man's job. Something Khalil should have been around to teach him. Responsibility I now pawned off on my own father.

"You are getting up there, but don't try to be grown too soon. You'll have plenty of time for that. Enjoy being a kid, and let me worry about the grown-up stuff." My eyes caught the picture of Caleb sitting atop his father's shoulders after a soccer game when Caleb had been five.

Pictures could tell a thousand stories, and some would be lies, manipulated. As I stared at the man I used to love intensely, I wondered how somebody could be vile and loving at the same time. Before his incarceration, he tried to make me think I was crazy. He had me questioning my own logic about his relationship with our daughter. He was even manipulative enough to convince a judge to give him custody of our children. Khalil was able to convince members of our church congregation that I was unstable. If Kaleia hadn't caught him on a web camera trying to molest her again, there was no telling what further damage he would have done.

I pondered on what Khalil knew about Desiree's disappearance.

"I miss Daddy," Caleb said. "I know that he hurt Kaleia, but I still miss him. Are you mad at me?"

The fact that my twelve-year-old son was torn between loving his father and worried that I'd be angry at him for doing so pulled at my heart strings. I hugged Caleb for assurance. "No, honey. Of course I'm not angry with you. There is nothing wrong with missing your father. From the letters he sends, we know that he misses you too."

Every month a letter to Caleb came from the correctional facility where Khalil resided. In the beginning they were only addressed to me. His first letters begged me to forgive him, to understand him, and to continue loving him. But after six months with no return response from me, Khalil's subject changed. That next letter came addressed to Kaleia and Caleb.

I sent him one back explaining why he was forbidden to have any contact with Kaleia, but he was more than welcome to write Caleb. Whether Khalil resided in our home or not, Caleb needed a relationship with his father. It was tough to allow him any access to either child, but I didn't want Caleb resenting me for denying him that relationship. Khalil obliged with the next correspondence addressed to his son. Caleb started sending art projects back to his father along with cards for Christmas, Father's Day, and Khalil's birthday.

"It seems like everything is harder without Daddy around. My soccer games aren't the same because he's not there. All the other kids' dads are always there. It's not fair that my daddy can't be there. I'm the only one without my dad," Caleb confessed, watching me look at their picture.

Caleb was right. It wasn't fair. It wasn't fair that he had to go through this mess. It wasn't fair that he was forced to grow up without his father. And it wasn't fair that I had to always try to make the best of a terrible situation. "Well that's not entirely true. What about Johnathan's dad? His parents are divorced, and I've only seen his father at a couple of the games. And because Lewis's father lives in Alaska, he can't come to the games either."

Caleb looked into my eyes. "But Mom, their daddies are not in prison."

I said nothing to his comment. Instead, I chewed the inside of my cheek. When Khalil initially went to prison, I thought both Kaleia and Caleb needed counseling to deal with the trauma. But I had prayed God would see the kids through all that had happened without therapy.

In the years since Khalil had been gone, I did my best to stop negative talk about him. I kept my conflicting opinions to myself when around the children. My sister made that a challenge. She rarely hid her disdain for any man, especially Khalil. She disliked him before we all learned his secret. The love Caleb had for his father stayed intact because I would have it no other way.

"I just wish he could come back home soon. Do you think maybe they can let him out early, like for good behavior or something?" Caleb asked.

Again I didn't comment. The last thing that I wanted was Khalil free. The criminal justice system had to keep him contained and restricted in his access to other little girls.

Instead of lying to my son, I changed the subject to my father, like offering one for the other would ease his frustration. "You know Paw-Paw wants you to go up north camping with him next week."

"Aw, Mom, I love Paw-Paw, but I'm with him all the time, and when we go fishing, he makes me clean out the fish guts. It's so nasty. Makes my clothes funky." I could feel Caleb scrunch up his nose. "There was a police officer at our school today finger printing us for the identification records, and he gave me his number. He said he knew you, and I can go play in the junior basketball tournament with him this weekend if I asked you. His name was Ruben."

Ruben? I hadn't spoken to my sister's ex-boyfriend since he came to my place on a domestic confrontation call. That night I had shot at Khalil for forcefully trying to take the kids from me during our separation. At that time, I couldn't prove he was doing anything to Kaleia and legally didn't have a leg to stand on. It was Khalil's word against mine; I had been willing to kill him before I allowed my children to go back into his care. I could have been arrested for my actions, but luckily, I wasn't.

I often wondered what Ruben was up to. Alicia never talked

about him even though they worked at the same police department. When I mentioned him, she'd cut me off and say her past relationships weren't up for discussion any more than mine were.

"Caleb, I think your Paw-Paw would be a little sad that you didn't want to go fishing, but we will see."

"Paw-Paw wouldn't be sad. It's only for one weekend, and Kaleia will be having fun with all her friends. I want to be around kids my own age too. Besides, the last time we went fishing he complained about his joints hurting the whole time. He should do things that old people do."

I cocked my head to the side. "And what exactly do old people do, Caleb?"

"You know, play chess and stuff."

My son had watched too much television and had bought into stereotypes. My father had never played chess a day in his life. His preference would have been to run around a court with Caleb, like he had with my brother, Otis Jr., when he was a boy. Dad's knees had given out long ago. But he enjoyed spending time with his grandson, and he tried his best to fill the void that Khalil had left behind.

I stated firmly, "We will see. I'll call Ruben tomorrow."

He yawned. "But Mom—"

I cut him off, checking the clock next to the bed. "Caleb, it is almost four in the morning on a school night. You go back to sleep, and we will get your weekend figured out after school, okay?"

He slouched down under his covers disappointedly. "Okay. But I still don't want to go fishing."

I chuckled as I closed Caleb's door behind me. Children would try to get the last word no matter what.

CHAPTER FOUR

KALEIA

The wound was still not healed five days later. An elongated cut at the junction above her thigh stung as Kaleia placed Neosporin on the gapping reddened flesh. She tried to push the skin closed with her fingers, but she had cut too deep. Stitches were probably required, but there was no way she could explain the gash to her mother.

Kaleia had conjured up an excuse for the wound when she felt blood trickle down her leg after she cut herself in the bathroom at school. While she saturated a wad of toilet tissue, she considered running to the school office and screaming that she had just been attacked outside in the back of the building. Dramatic with hysteria, she imagined telling Mr. Huff, the principal, that some man with a hooded jogging suit tried to snatch her book bag, and when she fought him off, he stabbed her in the leg. The story sounded real to her, and she was certain she could pull it off, except she would have to provide proof. She would have to show her thigh and the other scars from the previous razor cuts would be seen. All those multiple silver lines that ran the length of her thigh; those scars that had no explanation.

Carefully, she placed gauze on the open skin. Kaleia then pressed down with one hand while she used the other to slowly unravel the Ace elastic bandage around her upper thigh as she sat on a towel on her bedroom floor.

Somebody turned her doorknob and her head jerked up. Kaleia watched the knob move and remembered that she had locked the door when she came from her shower half an hour ago. Then came the knock. Kaleia was only half finished with the roll of bandage. She quickly tried to cover the wound.

"Yeah," she said pensively, hoping that her mother or brother would wait.

"Kaleia, open the door. I need to talk with you for a minute." It was Caleb.

Any other time he would wait until he caught her in the hallway, kitchen, or family room to ask for something. They had an understanding that if a bedroom door was closed, it meant one or the other didn't want to be bothered. It was a rule that hadn't been verbalized, but they had lived by it ever since the move to the condo. When the door was open, there was room for conversation, but neither sibling knocked on closed doors.

"I'm busy. What do you want?" she asked, still unraveling the Ace bandage.

"Just open the door," Caleb requested persistently.

"I'm getting dressed. I'll come down to your room in a few minutes."

"All right."

When the bandage was completely fastened, Kaleia pulled out a tiny lavender plastic case from the bottom of her first aid kit. She opened it and counted the number of razors she had left. There were four thin blades from a pack of shavers she bought at the dollar store.

"I won't be needing you soon," she told the container as she replaced the lid and placed it under a roll of sports tape. She stuffed the Neosporin, cotton balls, and gauze inside the first aid kit, then shoved it beneath the hollow area of her white Victorian dresser.

Kaleia went to her closet to pull out the outfit she and her mother had bought at a boutique the day before. It was a purple tunic dress with gray swirls down the front and black cinched leggings. The dress was beautiful, and purple was her favorite color. She held it against her body and looked at it. The material would hug her thin form and show her curves without being too revealing. Her mother would never approve of revealing clothing with skin showing. Kaleia had considered Tevin when she picked out the dress.

Gently placing the outfit on her bed, she smiled and went in search of her brother.

Caleb was hunched over the student desk in his bedroom, gluing a piece to a toy model car that was disassembled.

"How was the basketball tournament?" Kaleia sat on his bed.

"We lost. The final score was forty-five to seventy-seven. Our team just couldn't act like a team. One of the boys kept fouling everybody on the other side. And then my own team member got me in the chest with his elbow while trying to grab the ball. I wanted to clip him, but I was trying to play fair. It wasn't all that I thought it would be. I did like hanging with Ruben though. He made it fun even though we were losing."

Kaleia looked at the floor and noticed that Caleb's clothes were in a heap and his tennis shoes were thrown on top of them. "You know, Mom is going to kill you if you don't get your stuff up."

Caleb glanced back. "I'll get to it in a minute."

"What did you want? I have things to do." Kaleia wasn't interested in idle conversation and wanted to call Taija to find out what time she would be heading to the house. Taija had her driver's license, and Aunt Alicia had bought her a cute little Honda Accord at the car auction.

That got him to turn around. He grinned like he was about to get into something. "I want to come to your party and was wondering if you could talk Mom into letting me."

"Are you serious? Why would you want to come to my party anyway? You and I don't even be around each other like that. Plus there isn't going to be anybody you know at my party or that's your age."

"Don't make it sound like you're that much older than I am. It's only a little more than three years, and I could pass for sixteen."

Kaleia looked at his long legs and athletic build draped over that chair. He wouldn't look out of place with her age group. She just didn't want him there.

"Why don't you go skating with your own friends or hang out at the arcade?" she suggested.

"Now you know Mom isn't going to let me go anywhere without somebody she knows supervising. I asked to spend the night at Todd's house and she told me that she didn't know Todd's parents well enough, and when she called before, his father was rude. His father works third shift; that man was probably tired. But now I'm banned from spending the night at Todd's. I even asked if I could hang out with Ruben after the game, and she wouldn't let me do that either. It's like we can't go anywhere or do anything. I just want to have some fun for once without the rules."

They truly did live by stricter rules than most of Kaleia's friends. They were not allowed to snack in the middle of the night. Nor were they allowed to watch television after midnight. Twelve of the cable channels had parent control

blocks on them. No 'he said, she said.' Which also meant
no arguing over anything. No company after eight in the evening
unless it was Taija. Phone use was restricted after ten P.M. They
couldn't go out the house with a friend unless that friend had
a conversation with their mother. They had rules for their
rules. Kaleia had learned how to manage around those rules
so that she could stay sane.

Kaleia let out a breath. She wasn't trying to give in so easily.
"I thought you were going to spend the night with Paw-Paw
fishing or something."

"That's another problem. I tried to explain to Mom that
I'm too old to be hanging with our grandparents, but she's
not listening to me. I was surprised she let me go with Ruben.
I really don't want to be with Paw-Paw tonight after losing that
game. I need something to make me feel good."

Kaleia thought boys were too competitive about sports, and
she was hardly moved by his dilemma.

"Caleb, I don't know what to tell you, but I don't want you
at my sweet sixteen," she explained bluntly.

"Oh, it's like that?" His features scrunched together like he
was smelling sardines.

"Yes. You're going to have to sit with Paw-Paw in the cold,
musty waters talking about his good old days, and you're going
to act like you like it. And when you turn sixteen, I promise
you I won't come to your party either. Then we will be even."

Caleb frowned as he placed the glue on his desk. He pointed
at her. "Geez, Kaleia, be that way. But one day you're going
to need me."

"Well that day is not today." Kaleia left him with that. She
had a wonderful night to get ready for.

CHAPTER FIVE

ALICIA

The taste of cognac rolled around on Alicia's tongue before she swallowed her drink. The bitter sweetness slid down her throat like wonderful liquid flames. She took another sip and savored it before walking over to the second floor railing overlooking the hotel's banquet area. Music vibrated against the metal beams. The party had turned out beautifully. Alicia had been surprised to get such a nice discount for the party and overnight stay hotel rooms at the Hyatt. Her friend from college and the hotel restaurant manager, Trudy, had hooked Alicia up for less than two hundred dollars.

Her sister, Celia, was standing against the railing looking down at the teenage festivities.

"I remember just like yesterday when we were zipping our girls in those pink toddler snowmobile outfits. The ones with the white mittens attached. Whatever happened to those days? Now Taija and Kaleia are at the cusp of adulthood and signing up for college tours. Sixteen. I just can't believe it," Celia stated, astonished. "I feel so old. We are getting old."

Alicia chuckled at that revelation. "Speak for yourself. I don't feel any where near old. I'm still fine in my prime. Old is a state of mind. Personally, I am counting down the time until graduation. I know that Kaleia and Taija are only in their sophomore year of high school, but I can't wait to send Taija off to somebody's dorm room so I can have my house to myself. Maybe run around butt naked for the first week. Phillip would get a kick out of that. Maybe I'll let him chase me around the coffee table."

"Don't be vulgar." Celia frowned in disgust.

Alicia watched her sister's eyes roam to the stereo area where Phillip was deejaying.

"Ugh." Celia's shoulders shook.

"Stop hating," Alicia playfully warned. She wasn't the least bit concerned about Celia's opinion of her man. They had been seeing each other for three years, and Phillip was serving his purpose. There were only a few things that she needed a man for, and he excelled where it counted.

Phillip hit a button on the CD player, and the song selection changed from crunk filled noise to a slow tempo.

Alicia watched Taija take center stage with her boyfriend, Change, as they began a slow grind. Taija's thick hips matched his stride despite her being forty pounds larger than he. Size didn't seem to matter for either of them. Alicia remembered how excited Taija was when Change came by the house earlier in the week to take her shopping for the outfit she had on. Change was nineteen and acted mature for his age. Alicia was impressed that he had saved money from his job at a clothing store for a whole month to hook her daughter up. Alicia felt proud of herself for raising her daughter to expect a boy to bring something to the table in a relationship. She had stressed to Taija that if he didn't know how to step to the plate at a young age, then he also wouldn't have a clue in manhood. Alicia told her not to get stuck on that love emotion.

Celia saw how closely Taija and Change were dancing. To her it was intimate, maybe a little too intimate for teenagers. She scrunched her eyebrows and tilted her head to the side for a better view. "Do you think it's appropriate for them to be dancing like that?"

Alicia exhaled harshly. "Celia, dang. They are only kids having a good time. There's no harm being done. Last time I checked, bumping and grinding wasn't against the law."

"Don't get upset, Alicia. I'm just saying that two teenagers shouldn't—" The curly bang at Celia's brow couldn't conceal the disapproving glare.

Alicia held up her palm toward Celia's face. "Okay, you need to stop. You were just talking about the girls growing up. Let them do that. Stop judging everything."

"I don't have a problem with our girls growing into young ladies, Alicia. But there is such a thing as growing up too fast. They shouldn't have free reign to do whatever they feel like, even in our presence. I mean seriously, if Daddy saw us dancing like they are, we would have gotten pulled off the dance floor and taken home immediately. Daddy wasn't having it, so I don't know why you think we should."

Alicia's eyes roamed from her daughter having a good time on the dance floor with Change, to Kaleia who sat at a table with a boy. Kaleia looked bored out of her mind. It was her sweet sixteen party too. Alicia thought Kaleia should have been on the dance floor alongside Taija. Alicia would bet money that Kaleia had her guard up because her prudish momma was there. Celia didn't know how to relax and have fun. Even when they were growing up, Celia was uptight and afraid to have fun. She was always reluctant to take chances.

Alicia swallowed the corner of dark liquid left in her glass. The warm sensation that usually engulfed her after two drinks hadn't touched her like she expected, like she needed. If she were going to get through the night listening to Celia nitpick, another drink was necessary. Without a second thought she turned to head back to their hotel room.

"Where are you going now?" Celia asked.

Alicia held up her empty glass. "I need another dose of the good stuff."

Celia massaged her temples. "Can you please bring me an aspirin while you're down there? I have some in my purse."

"Sure." Alicia strutted down the hallway toward the elevators. When she opened the hotel door with her card key, her legs drew to the snack cooler like a quarter to a magnet. She pulled the bottle of Hennessey from the small refrigerator and grinned. *Joy in a pint bottle.*

It wasn't until she polished off her third glass that her buzz set in. The warm sensation covered her like a mink fur. After placing the bottle back in the cooler, Alicia searched for her sister's purse. She found the handbag in the mirrored closet and gave herself a once over in the mirror. Not one hair was out of place on her short pixie style. She got closer to the mirror to check her make-up, which was also flawless. Even the new brand of false eyelashes she had her hair stylist put on were seamed and perfectly aligned. They made her almond-shaped eyes look almost mystic.

Alicia pulled a bottle of Aleve from Celia's handbag and dropped the bag on the floor. Before shutting the closet door, she blew a kiss to the image in the mirror. "Go on with your sexy self." Alicia pocketed her card key, picked up the bottle of Aleve and left the room. The buzz of alcohol in her system had her feeling just right.

As she left the elevator and looked toward the entrance of the pool area, her mood began to shift downward. "Ain't this about a trip?" she hissed under her breath as she paused temporarily. Standing there, right inside the lobby with a light blue gift bag, was Taija's father, Eric. He stood formally dressed in a suit alongside a tall, tanned, white woman with bone straight blond hair in a black designer knee length dress.

Alicia listened to Eric talking to Celia as she approached.

"Yeah, there was a dinner party for mayoral candidate, Dave Bing, I had to attend. We tried to leave early, but you know how those things get. After the mockery that Kilpatrick made in my office, support for Bing is optimal. We have to get this city back on track, and Bing is just the man to do it," Eric explained.

As city manager, Eric had a stake in how local government was run. He had been a political science major when he and Alicia were a couple and often bored Alicia to tears with his aspirations. She didn't want to hear about them now either, but slowly walked toward them. She felt slightly tipsy and didn't want to appear drunk.

Celia stood against the door frame inside the lobby. "I was relieved when Kilpatrick resigned. Detroit already has a bad reputation. Hopefully, if elected, Dave Bing will do a better job than Kilpatrick. I can admit that outside of him being a basketball legend, I don't know a great deal about Bing."

"He played for the Pistons 1966 until '75, as well as the Boston Celtics and Washington Bullets, plus he's in the NBA Hall of Fame. That's how a lot of people remember him. He also has a remarkable reputation as a businessman. Made over forty million in the 80's and received an award for his expertise by Ronald Reagan. Bing had some serious accomplishments before he decided to run for office," Eric further explained proudly, a smile covering his pecan brown skin.

"You sound like you know Bing's career history better than he does. You sound like a groupie," Alicia commented, finally making her presence known. Her sarcasm was beyond blatant.

Eric grimaced like he had swallowed a pack of nails. He tugged at his gray stripped neck tie and cleared his throat. "Alicia."

Alicia looked into the green eyes of Eric's date. "Who invited you?"

Eric took the woman's hand into his own. "My daughter invited me, and before you get started, we don't need your permission to attend my daughter's sweet sixteen birthday party."

"Oh, is that right?" Alicia's head shook so hard that her hoop earrings slapped against the top of her neck. "Well, you must be confused about how things work. Taija can't invite you or your girlfriend without my okay. And last I checked, you had stopped sending child support payments, therefore your parental rights are null and void. Thought you knew." Alicia's glare ran from his date's black and silver stilettos up to her sun bronzed face.

Celia tried to intervene and keep her sister from making a scene. "Alicia, please don't—"

"Mind your business, Celia," Alicia retorted. She was not interested in mincing words.

Eric noticed a group of teenage girls walk toward them, then scramble back into the pool area. He lowered his voice to a whisper. "Why do you have to be so overly dramatic? I don't want to argue with you. That's the main reason we don't talk as it is. And you know good and well that Taija still gets money from me. She knows that whatever she wants, all she has to do is ask. You, on the other hand, are not relevant to my life."

The more Eric talked, the more Alicia's anger burned. He had no right. He had absolutely no right to talk to her that way or to be at the party she'd paid for. "Hmm . . . Okay." She tried to take his insult in stride, but it wasn't working.

Alicia had already dismissed Celia's input, but there she was again, jumping in and doing what Celia did best. Trying to make peace. "Everybody just calm down," Celia stated. "This is a special day for our girls. Let's not get any uglier. Eric, how about I take that gift bag to the table with her other presents."

Someone must have told Taija that her parents were in the lobby arguing, because she appeared with Change following closely behind. "Momma . . . Daddy, what's going on?"

As soon as Taija inquired about the commotion, Alicia lit into Taija. "When did you invite him, and what made you think I would be okay with that? You should have known how I would feel about him being here. And he had the nerve to show up three hours after it started. Real classy."

"I know you're not talking about class," Eric spat.

The woman with Eric had been quiet until that point. She tugged on his hand. "Eric, maybe it would be best if we left."

"Yeah, Eric, listen to Goldilocks. Maybe it would be best if you left." Alicia mimicked his date who had a British accent.

"No, I'm not letting her control things. It's always got to be Alicia's way or nothing at all. I'm tired of dealing with it." Eric turned to Taija. "Sweetheart, do you want me to leave?"

Taija looked like a deer in headlights. If she sided with her mother, she'd disappoint her father. If she sided with her father, there's no telling how Alicia would react. "Uh . . . uh . . . no. But, uh . . . uh," she stuttered.

Upset that Taija hadn't immediately taken a stand against her father, Alicia shoved the pill bottle she was holding in Celia's chest. Celia grabbed it before it fell to the ground.

Alicia threw up her hand. "You know what? Do whatever. I don't care. I really don't care." She stomped off in search of her liquid joy.

Alicia resurfaced an hour later. She grabbed a chair near the stereo system and placed it next to Phillip. She had emptied the bottle of Hennessy, but Eric's presence still put a damper on her intended high.

"What's wrong with you?" Phillip asked when she flopped in the chair, huffing and sighing.

"As if you don't know." She rolled her eyes. "I can't stand him. I want to take the heel of my boot and knock out all his teeth so he can stop cheesing like that."

"Oh, you're talking about Taija's dad. I thought you were mad at me." Phillip flipped through a collection of CDs, relieved.

"Look at him over there frontin' like he's dad of the year. And he has the nerve to have a white chick on his arm. The whole thing makes me want to vomit." Alicia made gagging noises like she was ready to hurl.

Eric stood at the opposite end of the room with one arm draped around Taija and the other around his girlfriend as they posed for a picture Change took.

"You need to let that hatred go. You make me think you still have other feelings for him. You act like you never got over him."

Alicia rolled her eyes yet again. She wasn't going to justify that with a comment. Eric had been her first true love. But that love died when she was pregnant with Taija and discovered the feelings were no longer mutual. Eric had secretly married someone else while she was in the hospital delivering their child. Then he showed up at the hospital baring gifts like nothing ever happened. He behaved like he didn't have a wife somewhere waiting for him to get back to her. He tried to explain his nuptials away as if the marriage was a business arrangement, but Alicia explained that she would be nobody's mistress. Eric dismissed her like she was a dried out hotdog bun . . . quick, fast, and in a hurry. She had never been so hurt or humiliated in her life. Alicia's illusion of love disappeared on Taija's day of birth. The thought that she'd be raising Taija as a single mother never crossed her mind. Alicia hated Eric for what he did and vowed to make his life hell every chance she got.

Alicia's head began to hurt like Celia's had earlier. Maybe headaches were contagious. "Phillip, turn the music off."

He leaned toward her as if he hadn't heard her correctly. "What?"

She pointed to the stereo. "Turn . . . it . . . off!"

Phillip looked at his watch. "For what? It's not even midnight yet."

Alicia reached over Phillip and pushed the OFF button. A crowd of confused people looked at the speakers on the wall, then over at the deejay table.

Alicia stood and sashayed to the buffet to fill a paper cup with sparkling juice, then made her way to the microphone on a raised platform. She hiked herself up on the platform and began a speech. "I would first like to thank all you young people that came out to celebrate Taija and Kaleia's birthday. I'm sure they are grateful for your friendship. As Taija's mom, I couldn't have a better daughter. I don't mind taking most of the credit for raising her by myself." Her eyes zeroed in on Eric. "But since Taija's father, or rather her donor, is present, why don't I go ahead and show him some love. Okay, I'm lying. I don't have any love for donors. I will say thank you for dissing me and your daughter on March 24th of 1993, the day Taija was born, so that you could live happily ever after with Trishette. Oh, my bad, that didn't quite work out with your wife, did it? And if I take things back even further, thank you for the three minutes of carnal love you gave that caused the creation of our beautiful daughter. I couldn't have done it without you. A toast to you." Alicia held up the glass and sipped as Eric's face appeared to drain of all its blood.

She didn't see the kids that began to snicker, nor had she seen her daughter's boyfriend ,Change, run from the room after Taija. Alicia only saw satisfaction for once again making Eric miserable just because she could.

CHAPTER SIX

KALEIA

"Psst. Kaleia, wake up."

Kaleia's eyes popped open when she felt a tug of her covers. It seemed like she had just drifted off to sleep moments ago. Her mind was in a fog.

Taija was standing at the foot of Kaleia's bed. She was zipping up her red parka jacket as she whispered, "I need you to cover for me if either of our mothers wake."

That request, plus Taija's outside wear got Kaleia's attention. Obviously Taija was ready to leave the suite they were in. They had done a lot for each other, but nothing that required sneaking anywhere in the middle of the night. Kaleia sat up and tried to clear her mind. She felt uneasy about the request as she looked at the outline of their hotel door.

Alicia had convinced Celia that the girls were mature enough to have a suite of their own. Celia relented, stating that she and Alicia must have an adjoining room that connected them to the girls. After the party ended, all the boys were promptly escorted from the hotel. Shortly thereafter, Celia came into the room while everybody was getting undressed and not-so-discreetly searched the bathroom. She then searched under both beds, finally stopping with the curtains. It was as if she were on a boy excavation hunt. All the while Celia talked about how she couldn't believe the girls were grown-up.

"Where are you going?" Kaleia asked. Looking around the room, she noticed the few girls under sleeping bags on the floor. Two more girls, sharing the other queen-sized bed, were lying still like mounds of rolling hills across from her.

Even in the dark Kaleia could see the frenzy on Taija's face as she grabbed her handbag and hoisted it on her shoulder. "I need to go meet Change. He was acting different toward me after my mom showed out.It was like he didn't want to be bothered with me anymore. We got into an argument. He said it was too much drama for him and that I needed to calm down. I called him an insensitive jerk, but I didn't mean it. I know he's mad. I have to fix it."

"I don't understand. What are you talking about? It couldn't be that bad. Why would you even think like that?"

Someone on the opposite bed shifted.Taija placed a finger to her mouth and they both became quiet while they waited for the body to still itself. Taija then used that same finger to signal toward the door.

"Follow me," Taija mouthed, moving toward the door.

Kaleia glanced down at her one piece footed pajamas with the zipper down the front. She looked like a mulberry Easter bunny rabbit minus the ears. "Where are we going?" she asked in a hushed tone as she got out of bed and followed her cousin.

It wasn't until they stood in the hallway that Taija answered. Her voice was still frenzied. "Change left without saying good-bye. He just left the party, and when I called he wouldn't answer the phone. I've been trying to reach him on his cell ever since. He only picked up an hour ago and said that he left because he had something to do. I know he was lying. He just didn't understand how embarrassed I was by my mother. I was beyond embarrassed. She just really took the cake tonight.

I mean, it's my birthday, and she had to go do something like that. Dogging out my dad in front of all my friends. Why do that? My daddy wasn't bothering her. Whenever she gets some alcohol in her, she starts acting crazy." Taija's chubby face was flustered.

Kaleia nodded her head. Her aunt did pick the wrong night to take things further than necessary. Everybody in the room was probably embarrassed for Taija. Aunt Alicia was usually fun to be around, because she did what she wanted to. She didn't take flack from anybody about her actions. When people called her aunt 'crazy,' Kaleia saw it as a term of endearment to show that Alicia was different. It meant that her random antics set her apart from other people. Kaleia respected that about her aunt. Alicia didn't live her life in a box, not like Kaleia's mother did.

They hardly ever did anything interesting in the Alexander home. Celia seemed to find great enjoyment just by going to church. Kaleia didn't get enthused about church like her mother did. There were just as many rules at church as at home. Rules, rules, and more rules. Celia didn't seem to know how to have fun without a rule attached to it. On the weekends that Kaleia stayed with her Aunt Alicia, they never went to church. Saturday night, Alicia, Taija, and Kaleia would stay up half the night cracking jokes or watching horror movies. Taija and Kaleia could talk on the phone without being monitored and do just about anything they wanted. Sunday mornings they would all sleep until late and sometimes Aunt Alicia's boyfriend, Phillip, would come over and take them out for breakfast. Aunt Alicia was fun to be around. Sometimes Kaleia found herself wishing that her aunt was her mother.

Celia would tell Kaleia to pray for the things that she wanted and that God answered prayers from a clean heart. She didn't know how clean her heart was supposed to be, but she prayed that she could switch parents with Taija. Kaleia prayed that she wouldn't have all the rules to follow or the scrutiny to live under. God had to see how miserable her life was. Kaleia believed, with her Aunt Alicia, she wouldn't have to keep secrets about herself; the kinds of secrets that made her question her existence.

"Aunt Alicia didn't mean to embarrass you. She was just drunk. Don't take it so hard. Those who know her understand that she was just being herself," Kaleia defended.

Taija bounced like she was on an invisible trampoline. She pointed to the door down the hall. "You don't get it because she's not your mother."

"Look, my mother has her issues too, you know." Kaleia paused anxious from Taija's rapid movement. "Do you have to go to the bathroom?"

"No, I'm upset. Very, very upset. Change could break up with me over this. He told me that he was on his way, and I want to be outside when he gets here. Are you going to be able to cover for me?"

"How long do you plan on being gone?"

"I don't know." She pulled a white hat out of her coat pocket and covered her head full of microbraids. Slowly she began to walk backward down the hall.

Kaleia held her hands up with shoulders scrunched. "What do you want me to say if my mom or yours wakes up?"

Taija pulled at the hat on her head. "Think of something. I got to go. I'll be back as soon as I can."

Kaleia stood with her mouth gaped open as she watched Taija get on the elevator.

A door opened three rooms down. Kaleia shifted her eyes in the opposite direction and watched a balding man in a T-shirt and boxer shorts limp down the hall toward her with an ice bucket. He walked as if one leg was shorter than the other. Kaleia did a half turn and pushed against her own room door. It was locked.

"No!" She hit her foot against the door in frustration.

Kaleia rubbed her hands down the fleece material covering her body as the man walked by. He released a gas bomb. The noise rippled through the hall. Kaleia covered her nose and mouth as the smell hit her. She almost wanted to cry as she lightly tapped at the door, hoping that one of her girlfriends would hear her.

After several minutes of tapping with no response and watching the man go back to his room, Kaleia decided to go down to the hotel front desk and get another key. She mumbled to herself the entire way down. She couldn't believe Taija had left like that. And for it to be because of a boy made Kaleia mad. It wasn't like Change and Taija had known each other that long. They had only been dating nine months. Kaleia had been with Taija when they first met at the skating rink. If he wanted to break up with Taija because she got a little upset tonight, then he wasn't worthy of Taija. Kaleia could never see herself giving a guy that kind of attention. No boy was worth rattling her nerves and getting worked up. Kaleia hoped that it was worth it to Taija, because it didn't look that way.

When Kaleia got to the front desk, there wasn't an attendant on duty. She bent over the counter looking for a button to push or a bell to ring. She was tired and just wanted to get back into her room.

A sigh of relief escaped Kaleia's lips when a lady wearing a starched white shirt and black slacks appeared behind the counter.

"May I help you?" the attendant asked with a smile.

"Excuse me, Heather." Kaleia recited the name she saw on

the green Holiday Express tag. "But I accidentally locked myself out of my room. Could you please give me another key? It's for room 421."

The fair skinned woman with a long brown ponytail looked at Kaleia in her pajamas and began clicking into the computer. "You said room 421?"

"Yes. Room 421." Kaleia leaned her elbows on the counter, watching the woman type.

The woman's eyebrows furrowed.

Kaleia tried to peek at the computer screen without success.

"May I have your name?" Heather asked.

"Um, it's Kaleia Alexander. I had my sweet sixteen birthday party here tonight. In the Olympic pool room."

"Hmm," Heather mumbled. "Is Celia Alexander your mother?"

"Yes, ma'am. That's my mom." Kaleia didn't realize she would have to answer a bunch of questions just to get back into her own room.

"I won't be able to give you a key. There is a notation on the account for your room." Heather picked up the phone.

"Notation." Kaleia's stomach flip-flopped. "What kind of notation? If you see my name, why can't I get a key?" She realized that she was being flippant. "I mean, I'm in my pajamas."

"Sorry, but we've been instructed to call Celia Alexander if there were any requests for card keys to that particular room."

Kaleia gasped. Her mother would be the one to have room restrictions. Since her father left, her every move was monitored. Last summer she went on a field trip to Mount St. Helens State Park in Seattle, Washington. The class was to explore the volcanic site. Kaleia was instructed to stay with Mrs. Arbor, the physics teacher, while all the other kids paired up. Celia suggested that an eye be kept on her daughter because she was fragile. Mrs. Arbor didn't let Kaleia move ten feet away from her. It was like being attached to a toddler's harness.

Celia also had mini wireless spy cameras placed throughout the house. One in a bookcase lodged between James Patterson's *Double Cross* and Jodi Picoult's *Change of Heart*. Another device peeked from the air vent above the refrigerator. Two teddy bears held the devices in the bedrooms. Kaleia's spy-cam lay against the mirror on her dresser, while Caleb's sat tilted on his student desk. Several times Caleb had placed his bear on the floor of his closet only to find it back on his desk that next day. There was even one for the outside so Celia would know who was near her home at all times. Kaleia should have expected that there would be silly restrictions at the hotel. Even at sixteen her mother refused to trust her. Celia might have called them grown-up earlier, but she definitely didn't act that way. Kaleia knew there was no avoiding the trouble she was about to be in. If she could get her hands on Taija at that moment, she would have strangled her. She mulled over in her head what she should say to save her own tail.

As Kaleia listened to Heather disclaim the reason for her call at nearly daybreak, all Kaleia thought was that she should have just kept knocking on the hotel room door earlier. She could have saved herself the trouble of looking like lost luggage waiting to be claimed.

Celia had tossed on a cashmere sweater and black slacks when she came around the corner. The parental irritation on her mother's face only made Kaleia want to choke Taija that much more. But at the same time she knew that she wouldn't rat her cousin out.

Kaleia didn't wait until her mother got to the counter before she started walking toward her. "Mom, I'm sorry that you were woken up. It was stupid for me to get myself locked out."

Her mother stopped her from talking with her hush wave as she trotted past her and spoke to the front desk worker. "Thanks, Heather, I'll take it from here."

The expression on Celia's face was horrifying as she left the front desk.

"I'm sorry that you were woken up over something this simple," Kaleia offered even though she knew that wouldn't be enough.

"What are you doing down here? How did you get locked out in the first place?" Celia asked almost accusingly.

As they both got back on the elevator, Kaleia inwardly balked at her mother's tone. In response, she lied as she watched her mother jab the lit button number four. "Taija wasn't feeling well when she woke up. She looked sickly and said she had been in the bathroom hunched over for the good part of an hour. Her stomach was cramping. She didn't know if she had eaten something that didn't agree with her or maybe her period was about to start. We stepped into the hallway to talk 'cause she wanted to go to a pharmacy by herself. I was worried because it's late and tried to convince her it was dangerous to be driving around Detroit in the middle of the night. I offered to go with her, but she told me no and that she would be fine. I even asked her to wake you or Aunt Alicia up. She didn't want to. I couldn't talk her out of going by herself. Then she was gone."

Celia's head swished back and forward like she was trying to shake off a bad joke. "You didn't think to wake us up after she left? Especially when you couldn't get into the room. I mean, come on, Kaleia. You didn't think we needed to know she was sick? Probably too sick to be driving. Period. Gosh, girl. There is far too much going on in this crazy world for Taija to be driving around in the middle of the night. Sick or not. What if something has happened to her? People snatch teenage girls every day. Every hour a child goes missing. Unbelievable. Absolutely unbelievable."

Kaleia felt her mother's disapproval shrink her insides. Technically she hadn't done anything wrong, but she was being made to feel guilty. Kaleia felt very small, like a midget on a basketball team. She was only trying to keep her cousin's secret, but it had bit her in the behind.

As she glanced at Kaleia's hurt face, Celia apologized, "I'm sorry for going off on you. You said you did try to stop her from going by herself. I don't mean to make this your fault. How long ago did she leave?"

"I'm not sure. It was around three thirty when she left. I don't know what time it is now."

Celia looked down at the wrist where she usually had a watch and wrapped her other hand around the bare skin. "We'll see what time it is when we get into the room. I believe it was almost four when I answered the phone call from the front desk. I don't remember seeing a pharmacy near here. At least not one open twenty-four hours. Maybe we just need to call Taija's cell phone and see where she's at."

Kaleia listened to her mother ramble nervously as they got off the elevator. She stayed a few steps behind her as they entered the room. Aunt Alicia's drunken, raspy snore filled the space. It sounded like tracker equipment in a cornfield.

"I'm gonna have to wake up Alicia. She's going to have a fit." Celia dropped the card key on the table. She pulled her cell phone off its charger.

"You have to wake up." She shook Alicia while punching digits.

Kaleia sat in a chair, her cut still throbbed. She pressed her hand on her upper thigh and wondered how Taija would collaborate a story she hadn't heard about.

Celia looked at her screen before placing the phone back to her ear. "She's not answering. Oh my goodness, she's not— Taija . . . I need you to call me right back as soon as you get this message, unless you are already in the hotel lobby. You need to call me immediately."

Aunt Alicia grunted and turned on her side as Kaleia's mother vigorously shook the bed.

"Kaleia, go through the adjoining door and make sure Taija hasn't made it back already," Celia ordered.

Doing as she was told, Kaleia went to the next room where the bed they were sharing was still empty. All the other girls still lay at rest. Kaleia gently picked up the hotel receiver and tried to reach Taija. She gritted her teeth as it automatically went to voice mail.

"Gurl, see you shouldn't have left. You got me in trouble. I tried to cover for you and told my mom that you went to a pharmacy because you weren't feeling well. You better stop somewhere and pick up some Tylenol or Pamprin or Pepto Bismol. I don't care if you buy out the whole pharmacy, but please make this disappearing act look legitimate. Okay bye," Kaleia whispered before sliding the phone back on the hook. She went back to report to her mother. "She's not back."

Celia was pacing as she rubbed her arms. "I can't get Alicia to wake up. Oh my goodness, Taija's still not answering. This is ridiculous. Where's the phone book? Kaleia, look in that drawer over there."

The Metro Detroit phone book was in the second drawer. Kaleia lifted it up. "Got it."

"Good." Celia stopped pacing. "Go through and look up

every Walgreens, CVS, or Rite-Aid pharmacy you can find. Let me think. Street names; um, check all down Washington Boulevard, then Michigan Avenue, uh, Woodward Avenue, Fort Street West. There has got to be a pharmacy nearby."

"CVS has a pharmacy on Michigan Avenue. It doesn't say whether it's open twenty-four hours or not."

"We're not going to worry about that right now. You go throw on some clothes. No, second thought, you stay here just in case she comes back, I'm going to need you to call me." Celia walked into the bathroom and came out with a glass of water. She went to the bed where Alicia lay and tipped the glass over.

Alicia woke up sputtering and gasping for air, "What in the world?" She thrashed about like a dying fish before she released a few explicit cuss words.

Celia appeared unmoved by the vulgarities. Kaleia remembered hearing her mother often say that she prayed God would deliver Aunt Alicia from her cursing and drinking.

"Alicia, your daughter is missing," Celia said calmly.

"Huh, no she's not. She's in the room next door." Alicia's bloodshot eyes blinked at Celia and Kaleia.

"We don't have time for your confusion. I need you to get up so we can go search for my niece." Celia spoke as if she were talking with a child having a tantrum. She threw a few articles of Alicia's clothes on the bed and told her to get dressed.

As Alicia stumbled from the bed, there was a knock at the door.

Kaleia rushed over hoping and praying that it was Taija. She threw her arms around her cousin when she saw her standing there with a Wal-mart bag in hand. "Oh God, I'm glad you made it back okay."

Taija seemed calmer than she had been when she left earlier. She must have made up with Change. "The pharmacy was closed, and I had to find another store. I got your message, Aunt Celia, and I'm sorry for not calling right back, but I couldn't get reception in Wal-Mart, and the message didn't show up until a few minutes ago. Please forgive me, but I don't feel well."

Relief settled over Kaleia as she listened to Taija lie so fluidly.

CHAPTER SEVEN

ME

At three years of age, Alicia saved my life. I almost died in a backyard pool. I always felt obligated to her for that.

In the 1970's, our mother, Patricia, had been part of a Mommies Free Group in which eight women took turns keeping the children of other mothers for one afternoon a week. On that particular day, Mrs. Jacobs and Mrs. Corredine were jointly watching Alicia and me along with nine other little people. Green safety tubes were placed around our waists before we were allowed in the water for Mrs. Jacobs's group. Alicia happened to be at Ms. Corredine's Play-Doh experiment table inside the house when my ponytail got caught in a drain entrapment. The force of the air suction pulled me under despite the safety tube. Ms. Jacobs didn't see me go under, but when it happened, Alicia had jumped up from her play area. She almost hyperventilated trying to tell people that something was wrong with her sister.

Four minutes was how long I went without oxygen. The average adult could only go without air for two minutes. My ponytail had to be cut with garden shears before my limp body could be released. Mr. Corredine performed CPR to resuscitate me. The emergency medical technicians that came that day said if I hadn't been discovered, in less than a minute, my life probably would have ended.

Once it was determined that minus half a head of long locks I would be fine, the adults asked how Alicia realized I was in trouble. Her explanation at that age was that she could feel it. An article in the local newspaper featured us and the power of telepathy. As I looked back I saw it as more a power of God. I believed God spoke to Alicia that day my life was saved. He used a toddler, my three-year-old twin, to intervene on my behalf. In adulthood, Alicia often acted like God didn't speak to her, but I thought the problem was that she was unwilling to hear Him anymore.

Growing up, Alicia found it to be her duty to protect me from bugs, bullies, and boys. Over the years there had been a few times when we intuitively sought each other out, shared a thought or a feeling. Yet none of those matched that phenomenon at the Corredine home. We just knew to be there for our identical twin. The bond stayed strong in our childhood, but the older we got, that bond changed. By the time we entered college the invisible glue between Alicia and me lost some of its adhesiveness as our personalities moved in separate directions.

When I looked at Alicia, physically I saw myself duplicated by DNA. Since we had become adults with children of our own, those outer characteristics summed up our similarities. We had radically different perceptions and parenting styles. From all that had occurred in my life, I was far from saying I had all the answers as a mother. For Alicia to be inebriated while her only child roamed Detroit streets had me concerned beyond the norm. Getting drunk was not the best answer to life's problems.

Whether she wanted to admit it or not, Alicia needed God just as much as I did. She needed deliverance from every pain that never healed. Alicia and I both had problems. Lord knows

I sought answers on a daily basis. I battled with so many emotions. Sometimes I feared for my children even though I knew God wasn't a Father of fear. I had to pray constantly just to keep it together. I believed God could work things out. Faith could feel so much better than alcohol. I had seen faith work like balm . . . felt it heal. If only Alicia would open her ears, like she had at three years old, and listen to Him speak healing into her life. I knew God wanted to be in her life just as much as He had been when we were small children. How could Alicia continue raising Taija through the tough teenage years if she weren't sober long enough to provide direction? What kind of example was Alicia setting for her daughter? As often as I tried to tell her that, she was still determined to drink herself unconscious. I was starting to see my older twin less as a fiery, unconventional protector and more as an irresponsible parent that needed a reality check.

Consideration of that ping-ponged through my mind like a tennis ball in a Venus-Serena match. The worry for my sister and my niece stayed while I sat in the office of Mr. Dwight Bennett at the Detroit Public Schools Board of Education inquiring about Desiree Carpenter. Mr. Bennett had just stepped back into the room after retrieving the file for her information.

The meeting transpired from me calling every school in the Metro Detroit area and becoming frustrated by the lackluster desire to help me. When I got enough of the runaround I spoke with Eric, Taija's father, who was sympathetic to my plight and happened to be friends with Mr. Bennett.

"So let me get this right, Mrs. Alexander. You want me to give you the last known address for the Carpenter family because you saw a poster of the missing child in a store window and, she is around the same age as your own daughter?" Mr. Bennett raised a thin eyebrow above silver wire glasses.

I couldn't very well say that I thought my husband had

something to do with her abduction. I had no proof, so I said the only thing that came to mind. "Yes, that's exactly what I want."

He sat back and flattened his olive green tie. "That's not a valid reason for us to share personal information. I can appreciate your empathizing with Ms. Carpenter's family, but our department has to consider the risk associated with giving out student addresses without that family's permission. I can see if someone on staff could try to contact someone in her family on your behalf. If you want to leave a number to be reached, that might be something we could do."

I raised my back from the cushioned chair and sat fully erect. "No disrespect, Mr. Bennett, but I have already had enough of the runaround with your staff. Desiree disappeared three years ago. I don't think it's in Desiree's best interest for me to waste anymore time."

I saw tension in his broad shoulders, a stiffness under the starched white dress shirt he wore.

"I'm not sure what happened when you spoke to my staff, but we are busy in this office. We have pressing issues that are being faced in this district. Only twenty-five percent of the children that enter elementary school in DPS are expected to graduate from high school. The media has hammered our already poor reputation." He picked up a pen and tapped it against the closed folder, visibly impassioned for his job. "Families are leaving the city in droves, and some parents just aren't taking the initiative to send their children to school at all. Our funding to run a district this large has dwindled to nearly impossible proportions. Plus, we had seven students who were shot on school property at a bus stop two weeks ago during a drive-by. Two of those students died and one is in critical condition. Granted, drive-bys happen in Detroit on a regular basis, but we are feeling the wrath because it occurred on school premises. Considering that, it is not a surprise that you haven't received the attention you seek." A melancholy stare from Mr. Bennett settled on me. He rested his elbow on his desk, pressed two fingers to his temple, and hooked his thumb under his chin.

I knew about crime in the area, and although I didn't live in Detroit, I saw the news story of the recent school drive-by. I loosened my posture and spoke gently, "I understand that you and your staff are busy here; probably even overwhelmed, but this is still an important matter to me. Please help me with this one thing, and I will be out of your hair."

He leaned forward, an inquisitive smile spread across his tapioca colored skin. "You can't expect me to believe that you don't have some kind of personal interest in Ms. Carpenter. Children go missing everyday. Teenagers run away on a regular basis. If you are indeed a bleeding heart, then you have your hands full."

I rubbed my finger across the bridge of my nose as I considered how much information I wanted to divulge to him. My guard went down. "Look, Mr. Bennett; I was married to a child molester. I'm not interested in discussing that, but I found a picture of Ms. Carpenter stowed away in my home. Do I think my husband knew her? Absolutely. Do I think he had something to do with her disappearance? Absolutely again. For my own peace of mind, I want to be proven wrong. The only way for me to do that is to get information about Desiree. I searched all local public records of runaways and missing teenagers for 2006. There is nothing there about her. I've checked the online registry for Missing and Exploited Children, and although there are files going back to 1984, there isn't a thing on Desiree Carpenter I can use. When I spoke to the people at the Missing and Exploited headquarters, I was told that the flyer was faxed to them, but there wasn't anything else in their files. Somebody created that poster of her. Somebody wanted her to be found. I have no control over my ex-husband's actions, but I need to know what happened to her."

"Don't you think that is a case for the police to solve?" he asked.

"I've been to the police, because her picture wasn't the only one I found. There were others. The police didn't help me out. At least not enough. Maybe because those pictures didn't have any other identification. Maybe they did look those girls up. I don't know. I wasn't contacted after I dropped off the envelope with the photos. I guess I will feel more comfortable going to them again when I have something to substantiate my concerns."

"Mrs. Alexander, I think you may be in over your head—"

I didn't want a lecture, I wanted help. "Mr. Bennett, do you pray?"

"Why, yeah. Of course. I'm Unitarian and practice religion. What does religion have to do with this?"

"I didn't ask you about your religious preference. In fact, I'm not even talking about standard religion. I'm talking about spiritual understanding. Prayer and spiritual understanding. Let me tell you what I pray for. When I get on my knees or sit in my car or find anytime to myself, I ask God to forgive me for my thoughts. I ask Him to remove the rage and resentment that keeps entering my heart because of what my husband did. I ask Him to forgive me of my judgment for that daycare worker who sodomized a two-year-old. I pray for that mother who took her three-month-old baby to the hospital thinking the child had an inflammatory virus only to find out that his stomach was full of semen and her husband had been the only other person watching him. I pray for the souls of those children drowned by their mother because she was a diagnosed schizophrenic and nobody considered that she may not be apt to handle her responsibility. I pray for the souls of the two brothers that were left to suffocate to death in a hot car during the middle of July because their mother didn't want a distraction while she got her hair done, or those seven from California who died at the hands of their father after he lost his job. But besides that, I also pray that God gives me the strength to keep raising my children, despite the mayhem and chaos I see in the news. Despite what I know they have personally seen." I shook my head as I absorbed the emotions rising to the surface. "Desiree became connected to me from the moment I saw her picture. I will not rest peacefully until I know what happened to her. Whatever that may be."

Mr. Bennett pursed his lips and nodded his hand as he slowly opened the file. "This goes against my better judgment, Mrs. Alexander, but I'll help you. The last known address for Desiree Carpenter is 5326 Sampson Street. She lived with her father, Joseph Carpenter. Her other contact was Hattie Duvall at 441- 5th Avenue. Looks like that was her grandmother."

I took the information from him after he wrote it down on a light green sticky pad along with two contact phone numbers.

"Ms. Alexander, nobody can know that you got this information from me. Are we clear?" Mr. Bennett's voice was stern.

"Completely," I said, standing up.

Finally progress. With the information I held, I was either walking out of a storm or into another one.

CHAPTER EIGHT

KHALIL

Clamor filled Security Level II of the Kinross Correctional Facility as inmates waited in line to make calls. Somebody shoved Stick, a short, beefy Filipino with a dragon tattoo on his forehead. Stick snapped at the three inmates standing near him. He was bipolar and refused to take his medicine. An argument ensued. Khalil plugged his left ear while listening for his attorney to pick up. He kept his back flush to the wall and watched two guards try to calm the noise. After being shanked in his first week on the inside, he knew to stay aware at all times. Word had spread before Khalil arrived at the prison facility that a pedophile would be the new resident. The reception wasn't friendly. A group of men called 'Conscience' cornered him in the laundry area. They cut him in the face as he loaded sheets into a dryer. Khalil fought all four men. He had to prove he wasn't a punk. It worked. They left him alone after that.

Raised skin where a sliver of metal lay embedded in his temple began to throb. He had refused to go to the infirmary for stitches or to get checked out after his prison fight. The pain reminded Khalil of how bad he wanted to be released from Kinross. He placed the phone on his other ear.

Harvey's assistant, Lila, answered on the second ring, "Hunt, Gamble, and Creed. How may I help you?"

"Lila, is Harvey there?"

The secretary instantly recognized Khalil's melancholic voice. She matched his blandness with cheerfulness. "Hello, Khalil; I hope all is well with you. Yes, Mr. Creed is in. I believe he is on another call. Would you like to hold for him?"

He looked at his watch. They were only allowed fifteen-minute increments per call. "Sure."

Airis, the guy directly behind watched Khalil with folded arms. At three hundred twenty pounds housed inside six feet five inches of solid mass, Airis's muscles strained against the orange prison jumpsuit. Incarcerated for manslaughter after snapping the neck of his wife's lover, the Dominican native could intimidate easily with his appearance. Khalil wasn't fazed by Airis. Khalil couldn't be intimidated.

He had already lost everything important to him. All that was meant to be had been snatched from him unnecessarily. His ex-wife, Celia, made sure of that. Before his trial, Khalil believed they would have an amicable relationship. Celia talked about prayer and forgiveness when he was arrested. That all changed as soon as he was handed a guilty verdict. Celia flipped the script. His daughter wasn't allowed to speak with him. He had letters and artwork from his son posted up on his cell walls, but that couldn't replace the relationship they would have had if Khalil weren't locked up. Celia was determined to make him pay for a misunderstanding. She thought she could make him suffer by taking away his rights as a father. He had absolutely no say regarding Caleb or Kaleia. Celia thought she had the upper hand because he was in prison, but Khalil refused to let her continue keeping him from his kids.

"Man, it don't look like you're talking. Some of us really have something to say. How long you plan on holding up the line?"

Airis took a step forward. The space shrunk between the two men. Airis stood several inches above Khalil and four inches too close for comfort. The tip of his boot skimmed the sole of Khalil's shoe.

Khalil tapped the screen of his cheap Timex watch. "We all get the same amount of time. I still have about seven minutes left."

Airis sucked his teeth, the vein in his thick neck pulsated.

They stared at each other for another minute before Khalil placed his arm above the phone bay and directed his attention elsewhere. Khalil watched the guards drag Stick down the hall, then counted the number of men standing behind Airis. At least nine men were snaked against the wall waiting to speak with someone on the outside.

Harvey finally came on the line. The nasal congested voice hacked, "Hey there, Khalil. Glad you were able to call, but things are in slow motion right now. I got this terrible cold that just doesn't seem to want to leave me. Been out of the office for a few days. I've already submitted the paperwork for your appeal process, but it takes time."

Harvey had been singing that same song for way too long, and Khalil didn't want any more excuses about time. "I thought you said I had a good chance due to my circumstances."

"You do have a good chance."

"And how about Celia, my ex-wife, having time to brainwash our daughter into saying I molested her as a custody tactic in our divorce? You know I'm innocent. What's taking so long to prove it?"

Harvey Creed had assured him at trial that he would have him freed in less than a year. That he would work day and night to get him out. A graduate from the Thomas Cooley law school, Harvey came highly recommended from one of Khalil's business partners.

"You have technically only been in prison for two years if you subtract your jail stay, Khalil. And then there is that video cam recording by your daughter. That was pretty damaging." Harvey sneezed and coughed. He sounded like he was about to cough up both his lungs. "You have to realize that Michigan's overall commitment rate for sex offenders is much higher than the national average. As far as the state is concerned, sex offenders present a serious threat to public safety. Even though it's a known fact that sex offenders rarely end up back in prison for re-offending victims, there is a stigma from all the high profile cases in media. The headlines skew public opinion. Megan Kanka, Jessica Lunsford, Sarah Lunde . . . they were all molested and killed by repeat sex offenders. Khalil, you have to recognize what I am working against. Sex offenders are vilified and ostracized; especially if you are a *child* sex offender. You know how it is."

Khalil could feel tension stiffening his back. "Stop calling me a sex offender! I'm not a sex offender, and I told you that the video cam was misleading. My intentions for my daughter were misconstrued. Don't put me in that sex offender category."

"I understand that, Khalil, but I'm not the one that placed you in that category. Society placed you there, and we have to work from that angle."

"No. We need to stick to the original story and get some progress. We need to prove that my emotionally impaired ex-wife snatched our children from the home in the middle of the night and disappeared for days. Those days, she used to brainwash our daughter into believing I touched her inappropriately. Then that very same woman tried to kill me. So I am somehow not understanding how the appeal process is not working to my benefit. That is unless you can't handle the job and maybe I need to seek another attorney that cares about my best interest." The calmness in Khalil's voice sounded like dry ice burning through snow.

Harvey sneezed, and then blew his nose into a tissue. "Hold your horses, Khalil. I'm on your side and working my fingers numb to get you out of that place. I'm sicker than a dog, but I'm here working for you. Looking out for you. You can't allow yourself to get riled up over the process. Everything has a process. Don't lose focus on our ultimate goal to have you released."

"Man, your time is up," Airis interrupted.

Khalil rubbed the bump on his temple as he glanced at Airis. "Harvey, I got to go, but this conversation is far from over."

Khalil pressed the receiver to end the call and dropped the mouthpiece without waiting for another response from his attorney. Whether Harvey knew it or not, there was a back up plan that didn't include his attorney, and Khalil had his own 'process' currently in motion.

CHAPTER NINE

KALEIA

Sweat beads glistened her forehead and saturated the top of her lip. Kaleia could taste salt from the moisture as she licked her chapped flesh. Heart palpations thumped erratically in her chest. The bed felt like it was floating around the room. Focused on a gold bumblebee she had won during a spelling bee in the fifth grade, Kaleia tried to stop the room from spinning. The bumblebee multiplied in front of her eyes. It became one, two, three, four blurry visions.

A moan rose from deep within as she kicked covers to the bottom of the bed. Her alarm clock fell to the floor as she reached for a cup of Gatorade left by her mother earlier.

Kaleia's head swarmed with heaviness as her fingers wrapped around the aqua plastic cup. Her drink was lukewarm going down her throat. She couldn't keep her eyes open. It was as if they were fastened down with weighted ten-pound dumbbells.

A cool hand pressed against her damp forehead.

"Kaleia, you are burning up!" Celia's voice exclaimed. "We need to get you to a hospital."

The only response Kaleia gave was another moan as the bed rocked like a ship in the ocean. The merry-go-round from the summer festival . . . that's what it felt like. No . . . faster, maybe the Flying Dragon was a better fit.

"Mom, I can't move." Tears slid down her already damp face. She tried to swing her feet over the side of her bed. "The room won't stop spinning."

Kaleia could hear herself speaking, but didn't know if the voice was just in her head. Her tongue felt thick and pasty.

Celia pushed her up and shoved one arm into the sleeve of a coat.

Kaleia tried to shrug the material from her skin. "Mom, it's too hot."

"Girl, it is forty degrees out. Whether you believe it or not, you are going to need this coat on."

Like a rag doll, Kaleia let her mother put her other arm through a coat sleeve, zip the material up to her neck and place tennis shoes on her feet.

She heard Celia leave the room and come back seconds later with another voice. A male voice asked her to hold onto him as her body slowly lifted from her bed. Caleb. Kaleia's legs wobbled like Jell-O cubes pulled from an ice tray. Pain shot down one thigh. She wrapped her arm around her brother's waist and placed her face on his shoulder as he supported her weight.

"I told you one day you would need me," he quirked as he slowly walked her from her bedroom.

"This . . . don't . . . count," came her labored replied. Kaleia's eyes remained closed through each room as she was guided to the car by her brother. The brisk air felt like balm from the moment they got outside. "You want to lie down in the backseat?" Celia asked her as she heard the car door open.

"Uh, huh." Kaleia crawled onto the cold leather seat and drifted off to sleep. In the dream she was with her father on a snowmobile.

Her insulated body sealed snug between his legs as he navigated terrain down a rolling hill through a brush of birch trees.

"Dad, I'm scared," she shrieked as the mobile hit a bump and rose from the ground, gliding through the sky only to smash against the snow seconds later.

"I got you, little lady. Nothing is going to happen to you when you're with me," he assured her with his comforting voice as he turned the wheel. A fawn perched its ears as they breezed by. "You see that little village in the distance?"Khalil asked.

Kaleia watched the specks of light glisten against the white snow. It was a magical sight. "Yes, it's beautiful."

Her father slowed the snowmobile and pointed toward the square houses. "Beneath those houses is a lake. It's called the Big Manistique. You can't see the water because of the thick layer of ice, but when I was little my dad would take me water rafting during the summer months. We could see rock bass, bullheads, perch, and a bunch of other fish flowing downstream as we rode."

"Why have you never brought Caleb and me here in the summertime to raft?" she asked, pressing her head back against his blue parka jacket.

"You know your mother; she's afraid that you will fall off the raft. One day maybe I'll sneak and bring you here."

He revved the snowmobile back up and they headed toward an enormous peak. Just before they raced down, Kaleia felt them plummet. Everything turned to a sea of blackness.

She screamed, feeling alone, "Daddy, Daddy, where are you? Please don't leave me. Come back. Daddy . . . Daddy . . . Daddy." Her voice became hoarse with desperation.

"Kaleia. Come on, honey. Let's get you out of this car." Her mother pressed a concerned hand to her cheek.

"Where am I?" Kaleia asked, disoriented as light filtered through her cloudy vision.

"We're at the hospital," Celia said. "Caleb, bring that wheelchair around here so we can get her inside."

The sound of metal clattering against concrete came around the car as Kaleia tried to pull herself up. Other sounds followed as her hearing became acute. The wheeze of busy traffic, a dog barking, the sirens from an ambulance approaching; noise clamored Kaleia from all directions.

Caleb locked the wheelchair in front of the car door and Kaleia tumbled into it. She rested her feet on the metal brackets as a wave of nausea washed over her. She focused on the cold air and swallowed repeatedly as Celia rolled her into the building.

Her eyes fluttered open as Caleb situated the wheelchair next to a row of connected hospital chairs. He sat down by her and slouched in the seat while her mother talked to a nurse standing below a registration sign.

"You look terrible." Caleb squinted at her like she was a science project. "Maybe you have H1N1, that flu that's killing people. I heard that it's a pig's disease from Asia. That's what you get for eating pork fried rice. I told you about eating pork from foreign countries. I heard they had to shut down a school in Livingston because the disease was spreading, and a little girl died from it. You may get on my nerves sometimes, but I don't want you to die."

If he had any kind of intelligence, Caleb would know that the disease came from Mexico, but Kaleia wasn't in the condition to argue with him.

"Shut up," Kaleia hissed.

"Oh, wait don't breathe on me." Caleb covered his nose with his University of Michigan blue and yellow sweatshirt. His voice was muffled when he spoke. "I don't want to catch what you have. Somebody has to carry on the family name."

If Kaleia had the energy, she would have licked her hand and slapped him straight across the forehead. She would have taken great pleasure at watching him squeal like a trapped seal as he tried to wipe her tainted saliva from his skin. But her body wouldn't allow her to move one finger, let alone a whole limb. Her heart felt like it was running track in her chest, and heat rose inside her like she was about to internally combust.

Celia came from the nurses' station and leaned down by the wheelchair as she rested both her hands on Kaleia's cheeks. "Oh, honey, you're burning up. Fortunately, it's not that busy in here. They said it won't take long to get you in a room. There are three people ahead of us."

Kaleia's head felt too heavy to nod in understanding.

"Caleb, move down one chair." Celia instructed Caleb before patting the thigh of Kaleia's sore leg not realizing the pain blazing through it. She sat down in the chair previously occupied by Caleb and glanced at her brother.

Celia did a double take when she noticed that Caleb's head was nearly covered by his shirt. "Caleb, what is wrong with you?"

"Mom, there are too many germs in this place," he responded, peeking out from the collar of his shirt.

Kaleia knew her mother wouldn't say anything else to him. She knew her mother's pattern like the back of her hand as she watched her open her purse and pull out her cell phone.

"Tyrese is calling me," Celia said, referring to her boyfriend. "I'll be right back. I'm going to talk to him and let him know what's going on."

She came back a few minutes later and stared at her seat, then her phone. All her thoughts seem to be scattered. "I forgot that I need to call Justice and tell her that I won't be able to deliver the donations to the Clothes Closet or drop off the chicken dinners to Heartland assisted living home today for the seniors ministry. Maybe she can do it for me. Ms. Gatsby will not take it well if we don't bring her that plate. I can just hear her complaining about lazy young folks." A smile covered Celia's face as she got lost in her own thought. Her eyes turned to Kaleia. "I'll wait until we get you situated. I wasn't supposed to be there until later this afternoon. I hate hospitals. I guess everybody hates hospitals. Well, I'm sure they will get you fixed up and we will be out of here in no time."

"Mom, I need to throw up," Kaleia groaned as another wave of heated nausea overtook her. She could feel it slowly rising like the temperature on a cooking thermometer.

Celia placed her phone back in her purse and twirled her own hair into a bun, oblivious to Kaleia's words.

"Mom, I'm gonna throw up," Kaleia repeated, dry heaving as a lump swelled in her throat. She could taste the bile coming as her head continued to swarm.

"Oh. Oh." After a mad dash back to the nursing station, Celia came running with a bedpan.

Her mother placed the bedpan under Kaleia's chin as she released the contents of her stomach. Tiny chucks of pasta from the chicken noodle soup she had hours before stuck to her mouth palate.

"Gross," Caleb balked, turning his head away from them. His shirt was still hiked up to his nose.

"Alexander? Kaleia Alexander?" a nurse called out.

Celia handed the nurse the bedpan. Caleb opted to remain in the germ infested lobby and watch ESPN Sports Center on a wall television. As Kaleia and her mother went through the patient area of the emergency room, the bedpan was dumped into a red hazardous waste receptacle.

A cuff went around Kaleia's arm, accompanied with a thermometer to her mouth as a nurse named Sandy checked her vitals. Kaleia was incapable of stopping her mother as she stripped the coat, pajama top, jogging pants and tennis shoes from her body. Kaleia was also incoherent when Celia noticed the ace bandage wrapped around her thigh.

"What happened to your leg?" Celia inquired, closing the ties of Kaleia's gray flowered hospital gown.

"I . . . I . . . I—" Kaleia couldn't focus enough to lie. Instead she lay prone on top of the covers of her inclined bed as she listened to the beep of a machine somewhere in the room. Kaleia didn't argue when Sandy unwrapped the Ace bandage covering her wound. She didn't flinch as the gauze pad, stuck to her thigh, was gently tugged free. Dead skin pulled away with the pad from the red pus filled area on her leg.

"Looks like you have quite the infection." Sandy used a hydrogen peroxide solution bottle to irrigate the wound.

Kaleia winced from the sting shooting through her leg, but she kept her eyes leveled toward the ceiling. The pain wouldn't allow her to panic. Her regret gave chase to delirium. She let the nurse, the physician, and her mother see her scars in all their glory.

While they discussed starting an IV and admitting her, Kaleia passed out.

CHAPTER TEN

ME

"Septic shock," Dr. Stilewell explained. "It is blood poisoning from a severe bacterial infection. The symptoms are usually an elevated heart rate, abnormal body temperatures, hallucinations, and possibly dehydration. If untreated, the infection would have been life threatening. Fortunately, you got your daughter here before any infection spread to her organs. We are running intravenous antibiotics through her system to cleanse the bacterium. We will put her on a low dose steroid to improve the outcome. Usually that takes five to seven days for effectiveness. We have also stitched her wound closed to prevent any further trauma to the area."

I pressed my arms into my chest as I listened to the medical diagnosis of my daughter. Kaleia had been transported to the Intensive Care Unit on the third floor. I was forced to sit outside her room with Caleb for an hour while the staff at Sinai-Grace hospital worked on Kaleia.

Dr. Stilewell looked at me with a worried expression. "But to be honest, it's not the infection that concerns me. Your daughter has multiple healed cuts along a diameter on both her legs. There are thirty-four cuts to be exact. It appears she is a self-mutilator."

I gawked at Dr. Stilewell and instantly assumed he didn't

know what he was talking about. Kaleia would never do bodily harm to herself. That didn't even sound like the intelligent, vibrant, and well adjusted young lady I was raising. Not the child I saw everyday that had a low tolerance for pain. Not that little girl who required a Band-Aid for paper cuts. Kaleia cried each time she went to the orthodontist for an adjustment before her braces were removed. He couldn't be talking about my child.

Dr. Stilewell nodded to a woman who had been standing with him. "This is Caroline Dias. She's a medical social worker who has been assigned to give you and your daughter some resources. When a patient is admitted with emotional or psychological issues, Caroline's job is to help the family adjust. I'm going to leave you two together while I complete my rounds." Dr. Stilewell pocketed a pen and walked away with Kaleia's medical chart under his arm.

I had thought the woman was his nurse and looked at her name badge, which clearly stated Caroline's position at the hospital. Shock and humiliation coursed through my veins. If it wasn't one extreme, it was another. Regardless of how he had put things, it felt like condemnation. The poor dysfunctional Alexander family with our array of socially unacceptable issues. I didn't want my daughter to be labeled as 'troubled.' I couldn't stand the notion that we'd be treated with delicate gloves for the duration of Kaleia's hospital stay.

Ms. Dias took a step closer to me and pulled several colorful brochures from a manila envelope. "Ms. Alexander, you shouldn't be ashamed about your daughter participating in self-mutilation. She's not the first child known to be a cutter. Many parents have to confront this very same thing. Between fourteen percent and thirty-nine percent of teenage girls are involved in some form of self-mutilation. An estimated one to two million people in the United States intentionally and repeatedly engaged in self-injury as a coping strategy. There was also a study at Cornell University that discovered about seventeen percent of college freshmen surveyed admitted to knowing someone that was a cutter. In fact, there is a ratio of three to two for female cutters versus male. Young girls have a lot to stress about. Cutters are usually seeking an escape from their feelings of adolescent anxiety or depression associated with the challenges of growing up. I have pamphlets in this packet that address the statistics to ease your mind."

Textbook statistics? What was Ms. Dias talking about? All those ratios and percentages made it sound like I was an incompetent parent. If we were in an Algebra or Chemistry class, the conversation would have been appropriate. Had those numbers been a part of the marketing goal for our new security launch at work, I would have felt some appreciation. But we were talking about my sixteen-year-old daughter that was lying in an ICU room. For lack of better terminology, the percentages didn't equate.

I felt my defenses skyrocket. "Lord, help me." I silently prayed to myself so that I would remain calm. Before Ms. Dias could say another word, I stated, "I'm sure you are very qualified to do your job, but am I required to talk to you? Do I need to sign paperwork stating that I've been informed my daughter likes to harm herself? Whatever is necessary for this conversation to be over with, I would like to do that."

The four pamphlets she held toward me were suddenly pressed to her chest. "Mrs. Alexander, I don't think you understand how important it is to get your daughter some psychological help. Self injury isn't necessarily recognized as mental illness affiliated, but it's a dangerous coping mechanism as you can see."

As I glanced toward Caleb, I saw Tyrese heading down the

hall toward me. Worry lines covered his forehead. I didn't want him to know about the "new" development. Me and my family drama.

"I can see clearly. I'm not in denial. Kaleia will get the psychological help she needs. Thank you for your assistance, Ms. Dias, but no thank you." I jaunted away from her and her packet. My attitude could have been seen as disrespectful or uncouth, but I had enough on my plate to shatter like glass.

Tyrese held his arms up to embrace me as the distance between us closed. But my eyes traveled to Caleb leaning against the wall behind him.

Tyrese dropped his arms back to his sides. "I drove as fast as I could. How's Kaleia?"

After the admittance process, I had made three calls. The first one was to Tyrese. I had spoken to him when we got to the hospital, and I promised him that I would keep him informed. My parents were on a five-day Caribbean cruise, so I knew I couldn't reach them for another two days. Alicia hadn't answered her phone, and Justice had picked up my scheduled duty with the church and was out delivering dinners to the nursing home. One of my best friends, Monique, was out of town visiting her in-laws. Usually when something was going on, Monique would have been the main person to pray me through. It was unfortunate that she was unavailable, because Lord knows I needed somebody to help me deal with this situation.

If I were still close to some other members at my church, I would have called them, but since Khalil and I separated, I just didn't feel comfortable telling people my business. There were just as many people in the church that gossiped about my problems as there were outside the congregation. Some of the comments and accusations I heard were extremely painful. Plus, Pastor Daniels tried to stay neutral when I told him what Khalil had done. Khalil denied doing wrong, and our pastor didn't know who to believe. I respected my spiritual father, but the experience still hurt, and the church gossip was ridiculous. It was like being betrayed by close family members. I had a hard time getting past the hurt. I prayed that in time I would trust and confide completely again.

I closed my eyes and inhaled deeply as I spoke to Tyrese. "Kaleia has a severe bacterial infection. Her doctor thinks she went into septic shock. It is potentially life threatening. She's been unconscious for the past two hours. Her vitals are all over the place. Her blood pressure is too low and her temperature is too high. The nurse just started her IV to flush out her system, so I couldn't tell you whether it's helping or not. I just—" I couldn't finish as emotions overwhelmed me.

Tyrese enveloped me in his arms, "It's going to be okay. Kaleia will be just fine."

I shook my head. I wanted to believe him. From the gut of me, I desperately wanted that to be true. But something deep in me knew my storm with Kaleia was far from over. If she awoke without permanent damage, we would have to deal with her self injury. And just like my new discovery, I didn't think I was equipped to handle more bad news. If ever there was a time I needed divine intervention, then the time was right in the moment.

"Do they know what caused the infection?" Tyrese asked. "Was it like that contagious skin virus called Mrsa? I believe I heard on the news that quite a few kids were getting the skin virus. It was spreading like wildfire. Could she have gotten it from another student at school? Schools are breeding grounds for infections. You send your kid off to school and you never know what germs they are going to come in contact with."

"It wasn't from school," I said. "Kaleia had a cut on her leg that became infected. The wound wasn't properly cared for, and I didn't know anything about it, otherwise we wouldn't be here right now."

As Tyrese, Caleb, and I went into Kaleia's room and sat near her bed, I had to exhale again. There were tubes and cords hanging from every corner of her hospital bed. The IV line dripped on her left side. An oxygen mask connection dangled from the right side. A catheter hung underneath a blanket covering her legs.

Her leg. I thought about how Kaleia had a slight limp two weeks ago. During her birthday party, her walk seemed a little off, but when I mentioned it to Alicia that night, she thought I was seeing things. But then again Alicia was drunk out of her mind. *How could I have relied on her opinion?* And last week I saw a big wad of tissue in the bathroom wastebasket with blood on it, but I assumed Kaleia's menstrual cycle had started. The doctor said the infection could have been in her system for weeks. If I had really paid attention I could have questioned Kaleia about that limp. *Why wasn't I paying her more attention?*

"Caleb, did you notice her limping?" I asked my son who was completely engrossed in his game.

He sat perched against the windowsill. He didn't look up from his game. "Mom, I really don't pay attention to Kaleia like that."

A disconnection somewhere along the lines had developed between Kaleia and Caleb. I couldn't blame sibling rivalry because they hardly ever argued. It was less obvious. When they were at home, each of them retreated to their own rooms unless it was meal time. I could no longer get them to do anything together. We no longer went bowling or skating because they had friends to do those things with. I was told that those were activities they preferred doing with their friends, like I was a plastic water bottle that needed recycling. Hanging out with Mom wasn't a cool thing to do. Typical teenage stuff, or so I thought . . . until now. Now my daughter, who I thought was typical, was cutting herself. Maybe this disconnect that I'd been shrugging off as normal wasn't normal at all. *What else was going on in my home that I was missing?*

A nurse wheeled a tray into Kaleia's room. Caleb moved from his position and examined the contents under the tray cover. "What in the world is that?" he scoffed, jiggling Kaleia's platter.

The smell of beef gravy mingled with the already present antiseptic air. I felt my stomach rumble, but I ignored it.

Caleb placed the lid back on the platter. "I'm hungry, but I'm not that hungry."

"You haven't eaten," I realized and was stunned by my recollection. Aside from the chicken spinach wrap during lunch that he refused to eat because he didn't think a vegetable manufactured inside of dough was edible, he had not been offered anything.

Tyrese offered a solution as he stood nearest to the door. "Hey, Caleb, how about we get out of this hospital for a little bit and go find some real food? Maybe go down to Maestro's and get a sub sandwich and some fries."

My son licked his lips. "Oh yeah, I could kill a deluxe steak and cheese with that special sauce right about now."

I pulled my wallet from my purse and fished through it for bills. I found a five dollar bill, four ones and a pocket full of change. "I don't have a lot of cash on me. Do you think ten dollars will be enough?"

The urge to beat myself up because of yet another oversight warred within me. From my daughter being molested to Kaleia permanently scarring her body to my son's hunger, I was missing a variety of important issues. *What's wrong with my vision, my focus, my intuitiveness?* I felt guilt piled onto more guilt, topped off with more guilt.

My hands shook as I pulled change out to count. Several pennies and a dime fell to the floor.

Tyrese put his hand over mine, "Celia, keep your money. You don't have to pay for anything. Just relax. We'll be back shortly."

I couldn't see myself relaxing as long as my daughter lay in front of me unconscious. What mother could? Yet I nodded my head in compliance as I hoped that things would get better. After Tyrese and Caleb left the room, I had a moment with God. "Lord, I'm trying to find a way to deal with this. I don't understand why things keep happening to my family. I truly believe in you. I believe in you with everything that is in me, but somehow you got to make me understand all of this. All I'm asking is 'Why?'"

I waited for a calm to come over me. I waited for His arms to hug me. I wanted God to assure me that everything was going to be all right. I felt lost in a foreign land, isolated by my circumstances, like somehow the connection to God I had was no longer as strong as it had been before. It was as if I did something wrong to bring chaos onto myself and those I loved. But I shouldn't have allowed myself to think like that. God was a sovereign God that wouldn't allow my family to suffer without good reason. I had to trust in Him, even if I didn't trust the situation. I had to keep trusting in God, because it was the only option that made sense.

CHAPTER ELEVEN

ALICIA

At approximately 0330 hours we, Morales and Stevenson, were detailed to 341 Jackson Street on a report of homicide. We were dressed in full uniform of the day.

Alicia read slowly through the report as she checked for grammatical errors. The paperwork in a criminal case had to be pristine like a pair of sheets in a five star hotel. Cases had been overturned for sloppy work. It was the detective's job to write the report, but as far as Alicia was concerned, the male officers weren't skilled enough to catch all the errors. She knew this because there were many times that she had caught something they hadn't.

Her cell vibrated on the second mouse pad where she kept her phone. Her brother, Otis Jr., was calling from Australia.

"Good day, Mate. Are you having a tally of a time in Sydney?" She picked with him every time they spoke, which was only a few times a year. He hadn't lived in the United States for so long that he really did sound like a native Aussie.

Otis Jr. sighed. "Not with worrying about Kaleia. I couldn't reach Celia. I assume she is probably at the hospital."

"Of course she is. She has been posted at the hospital like she moved in when they admitted Kaleia. The good news is they are releasing her today. Celia told me last night that they ran more tests, and the bacteria was cleared out her system. She was alert and eating Jell-O. It was touch and go for a minute. I was scared out of my mind." Alicia's niece had been in the ICU at the hospital for five days with some kind of virus. Everybody in the family was praying for her speedy recovery including Alicia, and she wasn't a praying woman.

Otis Jr. explained, "That was why I was calling this morning. I wanted to find out if I needed to go ahead and book that flight there."

"You could have booked a flight anyways. We haven't seen you or Midori since Christmas three years ago. You act like you have a problem entering the United States."

Otis Jr., the eldest brother, moved out of the country after taking a job with a digital imaging company in Singapore. He received the job opportunity straight out of college twenty-one years ago. Five years later, he branched off into his own software editing firm and hadn't looked back. Midori became his wife two years after that, and they relocated to Australia where he opened another software firm. Otis Jr. only visited once every few years. Alicia knew he had strong opinions about the United States government, and she found his passion on the issue to be humorous.

Otis Jr. scoffed. "Don't get me started about the disastrous political choices the United States has made to impact the international economy. I'm fortunate that the fluctuations in the stock market haven't affected my firm. We have seen an increase in sales because of our aggressive use of the free trade agreement, but others in my field have crumbled. Businesses are suffering across the world with this stupid war they got going on, and if you heard what people over here and in Japan were saying about the ignorance of Americans, you would be dismayed. I can guarantee you that the United States won't be winning any international popularity contests."

"At least we have a black president now," Alicia chimed, proud of the handsome new Commander in Chief.

"What you have is a black clean-up man that they will use as the fall guy if international affairs don't straighten up and the economy doesn't bounce back."

"Don't rain your negativity on my Obama," she joked. "How's Midori doing, and when are you going to add to the family? We need a little Isaye or Akihiro running around."

Otis Jr. exhaled a soft sigh of frustration. "Now you know kids are not in my plans. I don't know why you like to play so much. If I need a kid, I'll fly your daughter to Australia. That way I can send her back when I've had enough."

"By all means, send for Taija. I'm sure she would love the Great Outback. In fact, why *haven't* you sent for her? What's the hold up? You have the money."

"I'm busy bouncing between here and Japan. I don't have the time. I'll send for her someday."

Alicia had been hearing that same thing for years. "Yeah, right. Promises, promises."

"Little sister, you are too much. I've got to go. I have a conference call taking place in ten minutes. Tell Celia to call me when you speak to her." Otis Jr. disconnected the call before Alicia could respond.

As Alicia placed her headphones on and cranked up the music playing from her computer, Detective Carlos Morales shoved a handcuffed man through the clerk's area, toward the booking area. Alicia thought she recognized the arrestee. He had blood shot eyes, a patchy beard, and wrinkled lips. He wore a brown ripped T-shirt with baggy blue jeans. The arrestee's mouth was moving as Detective Morales practically dragged him across the floor. Alicia lowered the volume on the song playing from the Live365 Internet radio station.

"Man, I keep telling you that I didn't have anything to do with that," affirmed the cuffed man as he and Detective Morales passed Alicia's desk. His Tims slid on the floor when he tried to use his full body weight to stop and be heard. Detective Morales outweighed him by at least seventy pounds and ignored the rant of the suspect as they disappeared behind the glass doors.

Where have I seen him? Alicia asked herself.

She tried to recollect whether she had seen him in a store or at the car wash. *Is he a former classmate?* They looked to be about the same age. But for some reason, she couldn't put her finger on it.

Her coworker, Sheila, noticed Alicia staring at the glass long after the man had disappeared behind closed doors. "He's the man from the news last week. Remember the case about that woman who was beaten in her home on the west side? She was strangled with a pillowcase. Her nude body was found lying in the living room doorway. There was a lot of press coverage about her. Evidently, she was the Angel's Hope director." Sheila smiled with an ugly overbite against thick lips and copper skin. Sheila wasn't considered pretty, but she had an outgoing personality. She stayed on top of current events, which seemed to endear her to people.

Alicia had heard about the Angel's Hope non-profit organization that provided counseling and housing assistance for drug addicts. Flyers had been posted in the police department lobby. The murder of their director was news to her. Alicia didn't remember seeing the suspect on television. That wasn't where she knew his face from.

Sheila continued like they were discussing a daytime soap opera. "Yeah, he claimed that he found her body when he went to cut the grass. You should have seen his dramatics about how terrible the world is and how he would offer his assistance to bring the murder victim justice. He even talked about being a deacon at his church and how God was going to bring her justice."

Alicia pursed her lips. "Umph. People kill me using church as their gimmick when they know they are shady as all get out.I can't stand preachy church-goers. As if mentioning God's name makes them better than everybody else. That's why I gave up my membership. It is like being a part of a snobby country club where you have to act a certain way to fit in."

Although Alicia grew up in church, attending service was an unnecessary pasttime. She didn't need those kinds of four walls. She would rather spend time in the county jail than in a religious house. On special occasions she attended church with Celia or her parents. But that was the extent of her tolerance for church and those associated with it.

Sheila looked offended. "Well, I am not like that. You should stop generalizing people that go to church. It is a shame what happened to that lady. Nowadays, you can't let anybody into your home. It's like everybody is out to do some evil deeds. You have to watch your back when you go to your car or your own garage. Evil lurks everywhere. Working here heightens the awareness. I wouldn't begin to know how ramped crazy people are if I didn't work in a homicide department. This place, with all the violent murders, will make you jaded about life.I have to stay prayed up just to come in here."

Alicia nodded her head in understanding before putting the ear pieces from her headset back in. Just as she hit the PLAY button on her Internet radio, Phillip came through the door with his sister, Larika, in tow. Alicia dropped her headphone back onto the desk.

A black fedora barely covered the tangled brown weave on Larika's head. Alicia and Larika hadn't gotten along since she accused Alicia of hitting on her man at a backyard barbecue at Larika's house. Alicia remembered that Larika called her a dirty name while they sat at a picnic table. Alicia, at the time, didn't know what had possessed Larika to put her in the same category as a female dog, but impulse made her try to slap the taste out of that mouth before the last syllable left Larika's lips. She didn't learn until later that Larika's man had accused Alicia of pressing up against him. Truth be told, Alicia happened to be walking out of Larika's matchbox sized kitchen at the same time he was coming in. Larika's man couldn't even catch Alicia's eye to pass the ribs, let alone get pressed up against on purpose. Alicia was offended at Larika's nerve that day. Neither Alicia nor Larika had a kind word for each other since the barbecue.

Alicia thought Phillip had some nerve bringing that hussy to her job. Then it dawned on Alicia. Her man . . . that's where Alicia recognized the cuffed brother from. He was Larika's man.

"We need to talk to somebody about Jaquan being arrested. The police just picked him up, but I know they have the wrong person." Tears ran down Larika's light brown face as her chest heaved. "How they gonna just come in my house and take my man out of bed? We were 'sleep. That's not legal. They were not invited into my home."

Phillip found a chair and pushed it toward Alicia's desk. He gestured for Larika to sit down.

Even though Alicia couldn't officially document the complaint, she listened intently while Larika described how her two-year-old opened the door for the police and they trampled through her house without her permission.

Alicia knew that Larika didn't watch any of her four kids and let them run wild through the house while she spent half her day in bed when Jaquan was around. Phillip was always complaining about how his sister didn't need any more kids. He was upset that she was pregnant again. Larika should've counted herself grateful that they didn't take her kids away for neglect when they grabbed Jaquan.

"If they don't release him, I will be on the news tonight telling the world about how the Detroit PD violated our rights. The police are always plotting to do our people wrong. They don't care if Jaquan is innocent or not. They just want somebody to blame for that woman's death. All he did was cut her grass a couple times a month. Why would he need to kill her? She didn't have any money for him to steal, and Jaquan wasn't a thief either, so they can't say that about him."

Phillip asked Alicia in a pleading voice, "Can't you do something or talk to somebody about this?"

Alicia didn't want to do either. Jaquan's arrest wasn't her issue, and she wouldn't make it her issue either. "I can't help with this situation. If Jaquan was Mirandized, then you will probably have a hard time suing the police department. And if you want to take the story to a news station, then go right ahead. But Jaquan was already on the news last week and you see where that got him. If you try to do the same thing, it will only make him look worse. The public doesn't like criminals professing innocence on the news for murder charges when there is evidence to the contrary. They must have new information about the case; otherwise, the police could've arrested him last week. You are better off going home and trying to get some bail money together. And you might want to find Jaquan an attorney. Other than that, I don't know what to tell you," explained Alicia dryly.

"Oh Lord. They can't take my man away. How are we supposed to survive without him? He pays all the bills. I can't pay for that house without him, and we got a baby on the way." As she blubbered, a line of clear snot ran from Larika's nose down toward her lips.

Alicia pushed a Kleenex box toward Larika. She looked over at Sheila and they both shook their heads. She couldn't think of a kind way to get them out of her area. As she searched her brain for something not offensive to say, Ruben walked through the office doors with a report in hand. He walked past Alicia's desk and over to Sheila.

That didn't pass Phillip as he noticed the uniformed officer near them. He didn't know that Ruben used to be Alicia's man. Phillip sat on the edge of her desk as he stroked her arm and pointed at Ruben with the other. "Baby, you think you can have one of your officer friends listen to what Larika has to say. I told her you were cool and could run interference."

Alicia refused to look Ruben's way as he asked Sheila to look over his report. Instead, she stared at Phillip's black lips as he tried to charm her. He must have thought she had magical powers or fairy fix-it dust. What made him think she would want to help in the first place after his sister had disrespected her? Alicia didn't easily forget being called a female dog. She almost said that out loud, but Larika looked a hot emotional mess and Alicia couldn't bring herself to do it.

Alicia stood from her desk to escort Phillip and Larika out since they weren't leaving. She pulled Phillip from her desk and said calmly, "Rub some pennies together and get a lawyer. That is your best bet."

Larika went into hysterics when she got up from the chair. "You see, Phillip. I knew she wouldn't help us." Her eyes scolded Alicia. "Tramp. I know you want my man. You're probably happy he's in here so you can be closer to him." Larika turned her angry glare back to her brother. "Phillip, you need to open your eyes and see her for the tramp she is. She's trying to play us for fools just like the rest of Detroit PD. I don't need your help." Larika's pregnant belly vibrated as her voice got louder.

Alicia couldn't respond like she normally would for two reasons. Slapping a pregnant woman just wouldn't be right, and Alicia was on duty. She needed her job and refused to get herself arrested or fired. She had no choice but to stand there and seethe while Larika staged the verbal assault.

Ruben stepped in. "Ma'am, I'll have to ask you to leave if you can't compose yourself."

Larika snatched several more tissues from the Kleenex box on Alicia's desk before wobbling toward the door. She didn't speak another word.

Phillip held his hands up in a surrendering motion and looked at Alicia. "I'll call you later."

"Don't bother." Alicia was done with him and his dysfunctional sister. Phillip always catered to his mother and sister, even when they were wrong. She sat back down at her desk and tried to let the funk of Larika's attitude leave her.

"Wh—I'm going to call you later," Phillip repeated before leaving.

"Are you all right, Mija?" Ruben asked Alicia, sitting in the chair formerly occupied by Larika. He had given her that nickname a few years ago, and it still touched a warm place inside Alicia when he used it. As she glanced at Ruben's tanned Puerto Rican skin, she wondered how she got mixed up with Phillip. Even though she had regrets about breaking up with Ruben, she didn't believe in reuniting after the relationship was over. But a part of her wanted to be back with him. A part of her wanted what she would never allow herself to ask for.

CHAPTER TWELVE

ME

"Denial is a powerful coping mechanism," Dr. Malawi, Kaleia's former psychiatrist, affirmed from her office chair as I explained the recent hospitalization of my daughter.

I had never expected that our paths would cross again. After ending several months of sessions more than three years ago, I devoted my energy to building security for my children and a stronger relationship with Kaleia. My office hours at SecureTech dropped a third, and travel out of state, in half. I thought all she needed was more of my attention.

"When something traumatic occurs, most people go through a stage of denial. Divorce, death, and rape are examples of experiences that may be followed by post traumatic stress syndrome. It's like a mental cushion or blockage. I've seen rape victims completely block out their assailant's face and sometimes even the entire incident as a defensive cue. That is why hypnosis is so popular in my practice. We have to gently probe for that information without causing further emotional damage. Twelve step programs also center recovery around dealing with denial. As long as a person can avoid acknowledging an issue, they are incapable of conquering or getting to the root of the problem."

"I've worked myself numb trying to protect my home and

my children. That is my job, to protect Caleb and Kaleia. I plan each day with that goal in mind. Sometimes I function on an hour or two of sleep because I'm up thinking about what I can do better for their security. Yet, somehow I feel I have failed miserably."

"Mrs. Alexander, you aren't superhuman. There is only so much that is in your control. It is possible that you've suffered post traumatic stress syndrome right along with Kaleia. Insomnia is one result of hypervigilance. If you have increased anxiety that causes you to stay exhausted, and you spend the bulk of your time trying to detect threats to your family, then I strongly urge you to consider counseling for yourself as well as Kaleia."

"I think I'm doing just fine considering the circumstances." I watched Dr. Malawi write vigorously on the notepad. I leaned my head forward, but I couldn't tell what she had written on the paper. I felt it was in reference to me, but I didn't want the session to become about me.

"If you are really devoted to helping your daughter, don't go into denial. That would defeat the purpose," Dr. Malawi stated bluntly as she glanced up from the notepad.

I clasped and unclasped my hands in my lap, then changed the focus. "I just believed we could go back to normal with Khalil behind bars. You know, out of sight, out of mind. Kaleia looked fine, but then again, Khalil looked fine too, and we see how that turned out.

"Kaleia quit the swim team that year. Right after the trial, she quit the team. After four all state championships, she decided that swimming no longer interested her. That was probably when she started cutting herself. It had to be, otherwise I would have noticed the scars before now."

"We don't know that. Kaleia is the only one that probably does know."

A sickness eroded my stomach as I thought about Kaleia's swollen, infected leg. "Why would my child mutilate herself like that?"

As I saw Dr. Malawi's mouth open to respond, I interjected, "Please don't give me some psychological mumbo jumbo or the technical terminology from your DSM-IV. Actually, I'm just thinking out loud in frustration."

Maybe there was an affliction passed down from Khalil to Kaleia. Perhaps like a genetic mental illness such as bipolar disorder that couldn't be detected from just looking at a person. Could it be similar to a crippling physical impairment like that disease the talk show host, Montel Williams, battled? One in which the nervous system slowly, overtime became compromised until a person was barely able to function. The possibility was there whether I liked it or not.

After Khalil went to prison, I searched for his family. I needed to know what kinds of people raised him. During our marriage I knew next to nothing about his relatives. He only spoke of his father, who had passed away of black lung disease when Khalil was eleven years old. I knew that by the time he was a teenager, his paternal aunt had custody of him. The aunt, Ernestine Alexander, had never married and moved to Florida when Khalil became an adult. I found Ms. Alexander's current information through a genealogy network, which cataloged family lineage.

I had hoped to discover a better understanding of what made Khalil tick. Ms. Alexander told me over the phone that she had lost touch with Khalil's mother, Janice, shortly after he moved in. According to Ms. Alexander, Janice didn't have a maternal instinct, and after the father died, she treated Khalil more like her man instead of her son. Ms. Alexander explained that she was happy to raise Khalil when her brother died, because she felt there was something just not right about Janice and her nephew's relationship. She asked me about Khalil and how he was doing. He hadn't stayed in touch with her. I told her about him being in prison for molesting our daughter. After speaking with Ms. Alexander, I wanted to track down Janice Alexander, but it appeared that she remarried in 1982 and no further information was available. I wondered if Janice Alexander was a pedophile too.

A cherry wood framed plaque engraved with gold letters of Dr. Malawi's doctoral degree in psychiatry from Penn State hung on the wall facing me as I sat in the leather wing back chair.

"Dr. Malawi, do you believe in generational curses?" I asked.

She set her eyeglasses atop her gray streaked shoulder length coiffure. "How do you mean?"

"A generational curse. As in, when bondage or a judgment falls upon one individual or the next line of family members because of the sins of their parent, grandparent or even through a legacy long gone. My pastor preached on it. He said that it can come in the form of drug addiction, sexual sin, idolatry or abusiveness to name the most common. He talked about how many of his uncles and cousins were alcoholics. That the generational curse started with his great-grandfather who ran a juke joint and sold moonshine by the barrel. Pastor Daniels told us that he never allowed alcohol in any form to touch his lips because he didn't want the curse to attach itself to him or his children. That breaking the cycle required constant prayer and spiritual cleansing. I used to worry about my niece, Taija, falling into the same pattern as my sister, who doesn't try to battle her alcoholism, but now that I look inside my own home, it's my own children I have to be concerned with due to the generational curse that Khalil has brought upon us."

Dr. Malawi tapped her index finger against her chin. "I don't believe in generational curses. Alcoholism can come from a genetic disposition and associated with depression. A lot of issues are culturally relevant. The things you mentioned, the drug addiction, sexual sin, and abusiveness all are increased by watching a parent or other family member participate in those activities. Children mimic what they see or experience. I see it as a social problem as opposed to a generational curse."

I wondered if both Dr. Malawi and Pastor Daniels were right. Either perspective required me to break a cycle. It forced me to acknowledge that Kaleia's wounds had cut deeper than the gashes on her legs.

"Kaleia was hallucinating on the day she was hospitalized. I was driving and she was laid across the backseat barely able to move. Out of nowhere she began to mumble incoherently. I thought she was having a conversation in a dream, but later, her physician explained that hallucinations were a symptom of septic shock. But anyway," I rubbed the soft buttery leather arms of my chair, "Kaleia kept calling his name."

"Her father?" Dr. Malawi asked.

Regret and disgust always emerged when I thought of him. I bit my lip hating that Khalil could make me feel anything. "Daddy. She called out for her daddy to please come back. She sounded so anguished . . . tortured. I can't believe that she wants him back."

Dr. Malawi's cell phone vibrated next to her computer. She quickly shut it off. "Hallucinations come from a deep cognitive state. You can't assume that she's awaiting the return of her father. And even if she does feel that way, you can't fault her for missing a man she has loved her entire life."

As if Khalil deserved that affection. Malevolence surfaced

in me, and I didn't feel like fighting it. I countered Dr. Malawi's comment. "What's there to love? He molested her. He took away a piece of her that can never be returned or replaced. Khalil stole her innocence like a common thug . . . thief . . . burglar. But worse."

"You're still angry at him," Dr. Malawi assessed.

"Of course I'm still angry. Three years have vanished." I held that number of fingers up. "And my family is still in disarray. My daughter is hacking herself like we're in some freak horror movie. For God's sake, I have a right to be angry."

I tried to compress my emotion and gain my self-control back. "He is the center of all that has gone wrong in my family. He is the reason she is messed up. Dr. Malawi, I want many things for my daughter. I want to see her walk that stage at graduation next year without a limp as a reminder of bad decisions. I want to send her off, a thousand miles from me to Stanford University, which is her top pick, and know that she will survive just fine on her own. I want her to lean on God, even when I'm not there for her to lean on me. I want her to get through this better, stronger, and wiser, where she doesn't feel a razor can solve her problems. I want that for her, and I realize that I can't help her on my own. In order for my wants to come to existence, her needs have to be met. Those needs that I may not understand."

"I'll do everything in my power to help, Kaleia."

In that moment we built an unspoken alliance, and I was dependent on things working out, so that the healing process for my family could begin. The cycle had to be broken.

CHAPTER THIRTEEN

KHALIL

Locating a released sex offender was far from difficult. Khalil delighted in that knowledge as he pressed the down arrow on his Lotus phone. He clicked on the page with his cursor and expanded the map that appeared on his screen. He studied the page on the little rectangular phone screen like a scientist studying a specimen. One that demanded a lot of attention and one in which he had visited many times before.

His phone was one of the luxuries he was able to keep a secret despite incarceration. It wasn't that he was allowed use; all cell phones by inmates were considered to be contraband and explicitly prohibited. His phone was snuck into the facility and had to stay hidden in the cove of a loose wall brick. Khalil never actually placed an outside call. Instead, the luxury was used for unlimited Internet access and text messages. Things that could be easily erased.

A variety of sites catered to one purpose, the registration of sex offender information. Some required an e-mail address to access details, while others expected a disclaimer acknowledgement be check marked before further information could be provided. Khalil had been to almost all of those sites as he expanded his research.

When it came to reported sex offenders, Michigan, the state

for which he was incarcerated, held third place in the nation with thirty-eight thousand. The only others with a higher number were Texas and California. Khalil knew that his name wasn't on that list because he was still locked up. But sooner or later it would be. Even if his appeal was granted, his full name would still appear on lists across the nation upon his release. According to some of his research, Khalil had learned that prior to release from a prison, jail, or a mental hospital, all sex offenders were notified in writing their duty to register. All sex offenders were notified and required to report their living arrangements every ninety days. He, too, would have to report on a quarterly basis. Like sex offenders were children that needed constant supervision or like cattle that were branded by their state of residence, his life was forever altered.

Instead of being wrought dry with the defamation his imprisonment caused, Khalil chose to use it to his benefit. If he were to be classified as a criminal, he might as well use his status to his benefit.

He used it to make money. His main goal was to earn enough to get through his appeal process and have a nice cushion to survive since his chances for employment were blown to heck with his conviction. The business he started shortly before being arrested, YoungLuv.net, required constant communication with his contact on the outside and constant monitoring. While the state was monitoring him, he was molding his business. He managed the unique services because of his constant hours alone in his cell with nothing but his thoughts and memories of freedom to keep him focused. Unlike some who had become accustomed to Kinross Correctional being their home, Khalil refused that comfortability. Incarceration incensed his desire to be free again. His confinement further fueled his brainchild.

The inception of YoungLuv merged the ideas of social networking sites. It was his version of eHarmony meets Myspace. A site where young females could earn money uploading their pictures and participating in conversations with men attracted to unblemished, supple adolescent skin and blossoming minds. Indulged men that were forbidden to touch.

Khalil enlisted the help of an old friend to maintain the Web site for him. Simon Di Franco had been a valuable friend since childhood and business acquaintance since right before Khalil's imprisonment. A former pimp from Flint, Simon, at the peak of his game, had many prostitutes before getting shot in the back by another pimp for allegedly stealing some of his girls. The bullet paralyzed him from the waist down. Simon was not only a good friend, but efficient, detail oriented, and smarter than average despite his seedy lifestyle. After Khalil's incarceration, Simon was more than enthused to help Khalil continue his business. Khalil knew that Simon could be unscrupulous and liked money just as much as he did. Khalil also knew that Simon was the only person he could trust to keep the business a secret from the general public.

The marketing plan revolved around the target of girls in lower income urban populations. *Earn Extra Cash* flyers were initially posted all over middle and high schools in the most debilitated areas of Detroit under the premise of being a paid-to-chat room. Word spread amongst young girls interested in making easy money. Men had to pay a monthly rate for access. The pictures of the males were either fake photos of younger looking men or shown as "photo not provided." Within the three years of operation, Khalil had girls uploading pictures and live chatting all over impoverished areas throughout the Midwest. The girls were paid for the number of hits to their profile. It relied on the likelihood that a community which refused to snitch on drug dealers doing drive-bys would also keep his site private, active, and profitable. Poor people turned a blind eye when their kids were making money. Especially easy money.

Khalil clicked the search menu below the face of a bulldog, which happened to be his favorite sex offender registry. Family Watchdog was by far the most advanced sex offender search that Khalil could find to service his purpose. The site map provided proximity of beaches, parks and schools to the addresses of registered sex offenders. Designed to give families a bevy of resources and alerts for safety, the site also provided color coded squares linked to the work and home address of sex offenders. Blue was for sexual battery, yellow for rape, red for offenses against children, and green for other offenses.

Using names picked from sex offender sites, Khalil had his contact person send the potential client a packet filled with flyers on felony re-entry programs, pamphlets about jobs search with a criminal background, and a postcard for a support group chat room. Ten minutes after an individual entered the chat room a pop up box appeared with two young dancing girls in bikinis. The length of time it took for that sex offender to click the box closed determined whether they were invited into Khalil's dating network for teenagers called YoungLuv.net. The longer they stayed intrigued by the gyrating images, the more likely an e-mail with an access pass code would be sent for the pedophile to enjoy.

Khalil laid in his bed with his covers shielding the light from his phone and read the name attached to the red square. The face of a well-groomed Caucasian male with blue eyes, a pin straight nose, and sandy blond hair appeared on the screen.

Johnathan Thomas Swain, Home address: 4213 Perkins Street, Work address: GPI distributors, 606 Boyd Ave. Jack-

sonville, Florida. *Date of birth: May 21, 1957, age 52. Other aliases: Johnnie Thomas, Joe Swain and J.T. Swain. Conviction for child pornography. No tattoos or markings noted.*

"Mr. Swain, I think you will be quite pleased to hear from my acquaintance," Khalil said to the screen as he memorized the information and logged off the Internet. He pulled Simon's name from his contact list and clicked into his text box.

Khalil: I've found another potential client for the second phase of our business venture. His name is Johnathan Swain at 4213 Perkins Street in Jacksonville, Florida.

Simon: Occupation?

Khalil: He works for GPI Distributors in that same area. It doesn't say what he does. Find that out and learn how much he made this year before you approach him. He's clean cut and looks like he would be a great asset to the new marketing team.

Simon: Good. Florida could provide us with some interesting revenue potential since operations are going so well in the Midwest. Florida is a test market that could determine the usability of Phase II. Would you like me to use his local county information or the I-Search database for this one?

Khalil: Use the I-Search database. He's had several aliases. The local information isn't going to provide us with what we need. Once you get the basics, don't send him a letter like we did with Brad and Andrew. Instead, fly down there and have a personal meeting. We must proceed with caution as we add more people to our team.

Simon: Of course. Also we had a little complication this past week. One of our members was arrested in Gary, Indiana for solicitation of a minor. His name is Harper Judson from Concord, New Hampshire. Evidently, he flew to Gary to meet one of the girls from our Web site. Of course, we don't know which girl that was because they are leaving her name private due to her age. The kid's father was there and got into a fist fight at the mall with this Harper person before the police came and picked him up. I got the information through a local newsfeed.

Khalil: Crap. What's that, like the second arrest this month?

Simon: Yes, the other arrest was in Chicago. We haven't had a problem in all this time and now there are two in one month. Some of our members are careless despite our suggestions.

Khalil: Some people can be extremely stupid. Was our site mentioned?

Simon: Not that I know of in this case, and I don't think the Gary, Indiana police force is interested in our site for one case, but we can never be too careful. Harper Judson's pass code has been immediately revoked.

Khalil: Good. We need to revise the No-Fault clause in the online contract as well. These members need to understand that we won't be held responsible for their impulsiveness or stupidity. If they end up back in prison, it's their own fault.

Simon: Don't worry, I'm on top of it. Since our e-mails and search engine links for the site come from various college campuses, there is nothing out there to trace YoungLuv.net to either of us. And all the money continues to go to the offshore account in the Caymen Islands. I'm pretty confident that we are safe. But if you are concerned, we can postpone Phase II until we are sure that our system's information hasn't been breached.

Khalil: That won't be necessary. As I said earlier, we will proceed with caution. It's all a matter of staying on our game. We will talk further soon.

With that, Khalil closed his cell phone and placed it back behind the brick wall.

CHAPTER FOURTEEN

KALEIA

Blueberry pancakes with turkey sausage and a cup of apple juice were already placed at the table when Kaleia sat down. Every morning since she had been released from the hospital a week ago, a home-cooked breakfast was fixed for her and Caleb. The selection changed every day. French toast and turkey bacon on Monday, a spinach and mushroom omelet on Tuesday, biscuits with apple butter on Wednesday, a bowl of oatmeal with raisins on Thursday. And now, the last day of the school week, perfectly round blueberry pancakes were the meal of choice.

Kaleia watched her mother scrape pieces of dried batter from the skillet. Until last week, they were used to eating Pop-Tarts and cereal on the go. Home cooked meals hadn't been a part of the routine since their father cooked breakfast. Celia's efforts to make Kaleia feel comfortable at home were only making her feel more alienated. She never knew quite what to say to her. There was an awkwardness that lingered in the air, but nobody wanted to take ownership of it. Instead, they played like things were the same as usual. They played like Kaleia hadn't been close to death only a short time ago. Caleb had his Nintendo DS at the table as he swirled a little pen on the screen. It was as if the game was surgically joined to him.

Kaleia thought at least he had a diversion from their 'let us pretend' routine.

Kaleia and Caleb both waited for Celia to join them before they touched their food. Hands linked around the table as Caleb prayed over their meal. That was another thing that changed according to the day. They each took turns praying at mealtime. Even when her mother tried to switch things up, it all still stayed pretty much the same.

Celia cut into her sausage and said, "Did you know that Stanford University has a freshman scholarship program where you can get not only your tuition and room and board paid, but they also give you an eleven hundred and fifty dollar book allowance and a laptop? I don't doubt that we can get your four-year degree covered if we apply for enough scholarships. Considering how much books cost, that would be a blessing to have those covered as well. It's called the presidential scholarship and is based on academic achievements. That would be wonderful if we could get you that. I know we've applied for a few other scholarships, but we need to sit down together and go over other applications this weekend."

Kaleia forked a pancake triangle as she nodded. "We can do that, Mom."

What other choice did she have? It wasn't like her mother would be letting her out of her sight anytime soon. Especially not after what happened. Kaleia noticed that if she were in the bathroom for more than half an hour, Celia would stop in front of the door. Kaleia was sure she was placing her ear to the door as if she would be able to hear Kaleia searching for a new place on her anatomy to cut with a razor. She had the embarrassing task of allowing her mother to help redress the wound on her leg after Kaleia's nightly shower. It wasn't that hard for her to wrap the bandage on her own, but Celia insisted on helping.

"My coworker, Stephanie, said that her son received over a hundred thousand dollars in scholarships. He's going to the University of Oxford in England. I would expect that he is going to need all that funding. It's expensive enough with out-of-state cost; I can't imagine having to pay that amount of tuition. We wouldn't be able to afford Stanford without some scholarships. Are you still thinking about doing a study abroad program?" Celia was smiling, but joy didn't show in her eyes.

That was a topic of conversation Kaleia was interested in. Reminded her that one day she would be able to get far away and do something she loved. "Yeah, I've narrowed it down to Egypt. I want to do an archaeological study of the pyramids. I also hope to see the tomb of Nefertari. That would be the best. What's left of her body is on display in the Egyptian Museum of Turin. They only allow limited access, but I'm looking forward to being able to see it during my studies," Kaleia said with a hint of excitement.

Caleb had several questions. "Mom, I know that we are supposed to have a goal for our life when we leave high school, but how do you know that you want to spend the rest of your life doing something at eighteen years old? I don't think I will have that figured out by then. What if Kaleia got all the way to her senior year of college and changed her major? What then? My friend, Joseph's, brother changed majors five times before he quit school and joined the Marines." His plate was clean except for a few syrup drips, while both Kaleia and Celia picked over their food.

Celia chewed on a turkey sausage link. "I'm not sure about Joseph's brother, but I don't expect either of you to have your lives figured out once you leave high school. That's why it's good to take classes that interest you, like Kaleia with archaeology. Just enjoy learning. If you love something so much that you could do that forever, then great, but it takes different people, different lengths of time. When I first started college I thought I wanted to be a molecular biologist. But after taking a marketing class as an elective, I discovered that I liked that field more."

"I don't think I will change my mind. I'm sure I want to spend my life traveling the world and doing excavations," Kaleia responded.

Caleb placed his gaming system in his book bag. "Girl, you are weird. Who wants to spend their time studying dead stuff? And Mom, just so you know, I'm going to a historically black college like Johnson C. Smith or Howard. Not Stanford or some other snotty elite university. We got to keep hope alive." Caleb threw his fist in the air. "Power to my people."

"Whatever, Caleb. You can stop with all the ode to your blackness. Keep your power to the people. Breakfast is not a civil rights movement." Kaleia rolled her eyes.

"It is when I'm sitting next to you."

"Both of you chill out," Celia interjected. "Hey, do you two want to go bowling with me this weekend? I know you would rather go with your friends, but how about you entertain the old lady for just one evening of family fun."

"Do we have to?" Kaleia and Caleb spoke in unison.

"I'm not going to make this an option. We're going to go bowling on Saturday. And if you keep complaining, I'll make it our plans for every weekend. How do you like those apples?" Celia stood from the table and began gathering their plates.

"Those are sour apples. But I don't mind killing you two in a game. Meet you at the car." Caleb hoisted his bag onto his back and headed out the kitchen door.

Kaleia drank her apple juice and went to get her coat from the hall closet. She hated bowling just as much as she hated pretending things were normal. At least cutting gave her relief from the routine and rules she lived under.

Tevin had been calling a lot lately. He even came to the house when he found out Kaleia had been in the hospital. Thinking of games, if she played her cards right, he could give her the next distraction.

As Kaleia pulled on her coat and grabbed her stuff, she smiled to herself. There was more than one way to deal with an unbearable routine. With that thought, she got into the front seat of the car so she could make it to school.

Kaleia was called out of class early. She was called down to the office right in the middle of her fifth hour class while they were looking at the nucleus of skin cells under a microscope. She was instructed to take her coat and book bag with her. When she got to the office, her mother was talking with Kaleia's guidance counselor, Mr. Dunn. Kaleia's stomach dropped. She hoped Celia wasn't telling her secret. Kaleia quickly glanced at the clipboard sitting on the front counter. Next to her name it read, 'appointment' as the reason for early pick up.

She caught the tail-end of the conversation between Celia and Mr. Dunn. "I can definitely help you with the various scholarship applications, and if you need a letter of recommendation for Kaleia," Mr. Dunn said, "I would be more than pleased to provide one. In fact, I think I will begin drafting one now as opposed to waiting until senior year. There is a chance that I may be taking a position at Catholic Central in Novi."

"That will be quite the change from working here. I can bet more than a few students will miss you. We have somewhere to get to, but I will be in contact to discuss those other scholarship applications."

Celia didn't say another word as Kaleia followed her from the main office of the St. Mary's building. Kaleia wondered why her mother didn't mention an appointment that morning over breakfast. She could only assume it was to Sinai-Grace to have her physician check the area where the stitches had been removed.

The sun beamed down on her head as they walked to the car. Kaleia took off her winter hat and stuffed it into her coat pocket. It had been freezing when they were dropped off at school, but now the weather was moderately warm. May in Michigan could bring such strange weather.

A neon green flyer was under the windshield wiper as they got to the car. Her mother plucked it from beneath the blade. "There is a basketball game here tonight. I forgot that your school has games on Friday. Basketball season. You usually go to these. Did you want to go tonight?"

Kaleia thought about Tevon playing. She hadn't gotten the chance to see him during school hours and the game would be the best chance she had. "Sure. I would love to go." That would give her a chance to be with her friends. She would have to text her best friend, Megan, and see if she could ride with her and Lucy.

"I'll see what Taija is doing tonight, and I'll take both of you to the game. I have never been to a St. Mary's basketball game. I'll sit several rows back so you can enjoy yourself with your friends."

"Great, Mom. That will be great." Kaleia forced a smile even though she was completely disappointed on the inside. She felt like she was in a witness protection program. Constantly watched. Constantly protected.

"How was school today?" Celia asked as they headed down W. 10 Mile Road.

"We were given our PSAT scores. I haven't opened the envelope yet, because I knew you would want to see them too. I figured I would let you do the honors. I'm kind of scared to look," Kaleia confessed, pulling the envelope from a side pocket in her book bag.

As they turned on Evergreen Road in Southfield, Kaleia realized that they were driving in the opposite direction of Sinai-Grace.

"Where are we going?" Kaleia inquired when they passed a T.G.I. Friday's restaurant.

"To see Dr. Malawi." Celia's eyes stayed on the road.

"As in Dr. Malawi, the psychiatrist?" Kaleia knew that was who she meant, but she didn't want to believe they were going to therapy again. She couldn't believe she was being forced to endure more sessions to explore her feelings. Kaleia already knew how she felt. She didn't need anybody dissecting and analyzing her brain.

"Yes. I should have never stopped your therapy. It was poor judgment on my part. The hospital scare clarified things for me. This time around I'm not going to feel bad about you needing somebody to talk to besides me. Obviously there is some stuff going on in your head that I can't begin to relate to. And you may think this is a bad idea, but you don't have a choice. The more you fight this, the longer you will be in therapy," Celia explained with authority.

Another routine to follow. Kaleia planned to do the same thing she did last time. She would exercise her right to not speak and spend those hours staring at Dr. Malawi until time was up and eventually Celia would let her be.

CHAPTER FIFTEEN

ME

It took a little over a month of me holding on to Desiree's poster before I got up the courage to go see her father. I had to remind myself that God meant for me to see her poster. God meant for me to follow through on my findings. I knew that to be true despite distractions . . . despite fear. My spirit wouldn't rest about that missing girl regardless of all that had occurred with my own daughter. Maybe it wouldn't rest because of what had happened with my own daughter. The pictures in my home were a sign. It wasn't coincidence. It was divine intervention.

Nondescript brown brick enclosed all the quaint ranch style homes on Sampson Street. The only features to separate one house from another in the neighborhood were the types of cars in the driveways. A white Ford Taurus was in the particular driveway I pulled up to at eleven that morning. All the curtains were drawn closed.I couldn't see movement inside. There was a note on Desiree's information card that said Mr. Carpenter worked second shift. Maybe he was asleep. Two little girls played hop, skip, and jump at a home, two doors down.

How do I ask this man about his missing child?

A crick aggravated my neck muscle as I sat across from the

house with the full intent to casually talk with Mr. Carpenter. I held the printout of the missing poster in my lap. I wanted to know about Desiree, but then I didn't. The more I learned, the more responsible I felt. A nervous twitch rolled up and down my spine like an elliptical machine.

Taking a deep breath, I pulled the keys from my ignition, opened my car door, and pressed one heel to the pavement only to quickly pull that leg back and slam the door again. I wondered what kind of man he was. What was his temperament like? Did he blow up easily, or was he mild mannered? No matter what kind of personality he had, I didn't think I was ready to bring back Mr. Carpenter's grief. Pain and loss that he had probably learned to cope with after all the time that had passed. I felt like what I was about to do was just as bad as ripping open a scabbed wound similar to the ugly gash my daughter had on her leg. I wondered how I would feel if a stranger knocked on my door and requested details about my child's disappearance. I probably would slam the door in their face like it was some sick joke. I expected him to be upset with my inquiry based on a hunch. I placed myself in his shoes and didn't like the outcome.

The sheer fear of his response kept me in my vehicle. I couldn't bring myself to knock on his door; at least not by myself. My hands shook as I placed the key back in the ignition. If I were going to approach that man, I wouldn't be doing it alone.

Two hours later I was back at the address with Ruben to accompany me. Tyrese was in Houston on a business trip, and although I could have waited until he got back, the anticipation wouldn't let me. My father thought I should leave well enough alone and had no intention of showing up at Mr. Carpenter's with me. The only other man I trusted besides

Tyrese and my father was Ruben. Since taking Caleb to the basketball tournament more than a month ago, he had made himself available as my son's mentor. I had a hard time taking him up on his offer because my sister treated him badly when they broke up, but Ruben was a decent man, and Caleb clicked well with him. I was fortunate that it was his day off. He didn't seem bothered that I had called for my benefit instead of Caleb's. I had to admit I felt safer with an official authority figure by my side.

Before Ruben stepped out of the passenger side of my Jag he asked, "Are you sure about this?"

I felt uncertain, yet determined as I closed the driver's side door. I smoothed out the wrinkles on the flyer as the doorbell rang.

Ruben rang the door a third time. "He may not be here."

It hadn't dawned on me that maybe the owner of the car wasn't home or that he had more than one vehicle.

I crammed the flyer of Desiree under my armpit and fished through my purse for a little task notebook that was kept there for quick jotting. As I wrote my name and phone number on the lined paper, the door cracked open.

A weary eyed man peeked out at us in a plain white shirt and plaid pants. He squinted at us. "Can I help you?"

Ruben pulled his badge out and held it up in his palm.

"We're here about your daughter," I declared.

The door opened wider and something happened that I didn't expect. Instead of pain and grief, right there in the depth of his eyes was hope. The look of a father who, after three years, still hadn't given up believing in the safe return of his child.

"Have you seen her recently? Is that why you're here? Has she been in contact with you?"

My heart went out to him as I pocketed the paper with my contact information. I felt like maybe my quest was a bad idea. But that inner voice in me wouldn't let it go. Couldn't let it go. There was a chance that Khalil knew where Desiree was. And if that were true, then maybe I could help get her back home.

As we entered his small box like living room, I became speechless. I didn't want to deflate the hope of Mr. Carpenter. "Umm . . ." I looked to Ruben, but he knew less than I did about Desiree.

"We haven't seen Desiree, but there has been some information given to us that may lead to her whereabouts," Ruben said.

"I was sleeping. I work second shift, but sometimes I don't get to sleep until three or four in the morning. Please sit down." Mr. Carpenter gestured to a pink paisley sofa.

I looked around the room. Everything had a feminine touch, from the sway curtains to the silk flower vases. I wondered if Desiree's mother was around and somehow her name didn't make it on the contact sheet given to Celia by the Board of Education. On the glass coffee table there was a five by seven picture of Desiree, Mr. Carpenter, and a woman that Celia assumed was Desiree's mother. The two females looked almost identical with their ebony complexions, wavy hair, and petite figures. Signature statues of gold winged horses at Atlantis water resort were in the backdrop. They had been on a trip to the Bahamas. Celia had made a family trip to the same location.

"Mr. Carpenter, is your wife around?" I asked pointing to the picture.

He blinked as if he were confused by the question.

"My wife, Iris, is dead," he said.

"Oh." I wanted to shove my foot down my throat. "I apologize. I had no idea. Please forgive me. You have my deepest sympathy."

He walked over, picked up the photo, and swept his fingers across the glass. A small smile twitched at his lips as he appeared to reminisce about a happier time.

"No, it's okay. Iris has been gone for four years now. Breast cancer. Desiree didn't take her mother's death well. They were extremely close." He placed the picture back on the end table, and then sat down on the love seat. "Tell me the reason for your visit."

I pulled out the flyer and pressed out the crease across her face. I reached into my purse and also took out another photo of Desiree. The one that was stored away. I showed Mr. Carpenter the poster first. "I saw this poster at a store on Evergreen in Southfield. I recognized her face because I had a picture of her in my house. This picture." I handed him the photo of his child in a hot pink two-piece bathing suit posed provocatively against a wall.

His look of bafflement tightened the knot forming in my stomach. "I don't even know how to say this without just coming right out. I was married to a . . . umm . . . child molester. He had pictures of a lot of little girls. Well what I would consider little girls. I don't know what the pictures were used for. I almost don't want to imagine, but hers were amongst the group. Does the name Khalil Alexander ring a bell?"

I could tell from his expression that I had said too much too quickly.

"No. The name doesn't sound familiar, and you have got to back up. You're saying that your husband, a pedophile, had my daughter's picture. Why would he . . . how would he? And if you knew this, why didn't you come forward before now."

"I didn't know anything about her. As I said a few minutes ago, I saw this missing poster in a store window about a month ago. I would not have been able to live with myself if I knew anything and didn't report it. What I've told you is the same thing I've told the police." I gestured toward Ruben, but knew that was misleading.

Mr. Carpenter rubbed his mocha skin. I couldn't tell if he were disgusted or angry with me. I was sure he couldn't trump my disgust at marrying a child lover.

"Why don't you ask your husband how he knows my daughter? Wait a minute; does he work at Kettering High School?"

"No, he doesn't work at her school. He doesn't work anywhere. He's in prison on child molestation charges. He was locked up around the same time of your daughter's disappearance. And he is no longer my husband."

"Yet you are here because you think he had something to do with her being gone." He stated it as more fact than question.

"In my gut, I do. And I don't want to bring you grief or frustration from my feelings. I just want answers as I'm sure you do."

"What do you need to know?"

I sighed in relief because Mr. Carpenter was being accommodating when he didn't have to be. "I can't find anything on her disappearance. What exactly happened on that day?"

"It was a Thursday. That morning I was outside checking the tread on my tires. It looked low, and I planned to go get some new ones. Winter was coming, and I didn't want to be slipping and sliding all over the road when the snow fell. I only saw Desiree for about two minutes. She came out and told me that she had band practice after school and that she would catch a ride home with her friend, Shayla's, mom. Then she went running down the street to her bus. I could see her get on the bus from where I was standing. That was also the last time I saw her. I work second shift at Cannon Manufacturing. We were on ten-hour shifts then. I normally call home on my lunch hour, which is around eight in the evening. I would check to see if she got her homework finished and make sure any company she might have had was going home. Sometimes Shayla came to our house, and sometime Desiree went to hers. They did that pretty regularly. I meant to call back again on my break, but one of the calipers broke in the machine and we had parts backing up the line." He stopped talking as his face went blank.

"Mr. Carpenter?" I asked after a couple minutes when he didn't say anything else.

His eyelids fluttered like a bird with broken wings. "Where was I? Oh, the line . . . I didn't take a break that night. I didn't get worried until I made it home. She wasn't in bed, and Desiree knew that she wasn't allowed to spend the night anywhere without my permission. I called Trish, Shayla's mom, at around one thirty that night. She told me that my child wasn't there, that Shayla told her Desiree didn't show up at band practice. I was on the phone with Trish and Shayla for about an hour trying to figure out where Desiree could have gone. I called her grandmother's house in the hopes that maybe she took the city bus over there for some reason. My mother-in-law didn't drive because she has glaucoma. She hadn't seen Desiree since the weekend. Nobody knew where she was. I had the police come to my house before dawn. I was told that I couldn't file a report until she had been missing for twenty-four hours. I learned later that was a lie. They could have put out an Amber Alert immediately. The first twenty-four hours were the most important, but she was presumed to be a runaway."

I could see anger, regret, and frustration all merge together on his face.

"Mr. Carpenter, they didn't follow protocol. Even if she were a runaway, an Amber Alert could have been signaled. Which officers came to your house that night? Do you remember their names?" Ruben pulled his Blackberry phone from his leather clip holder.

"One. Only one officer came that night. His name was McAngus. Officer McAngus."

Ruben typed something into his phone, then put it back in the leather holder. "When I get to work I'm going to have a talk with McAngus and see about getting a copy of the official report. That is, if you don't mind, Mr. Carpenter?"

"I don't mind at all. I'm glad somebody's actually paying attention. I went to the newspapers, but they wouldn't take the story. A coworker of mine printed up the posters of Desiree for me. A few people from the neighborhood distributed the posters. I tried every avenue I could to get people to help me find my daughter. Three years is a long time to wait for your child to come home. And now you bring new information. I need to know what your husband, I mean ex-husband, was doing with a picture of my daughter."

I wanted the same answer and realized that Mr. Carpenter and I were in the same boat of non-cognizance. "Khalil was a youth minister at our church. Did your daughter ever attend the youth revivals at Greatness in Faith?"

"No. Not unless she went with her grandmother or Trish. I can find out for you."

And like a pen on a crossword puzzle, I tried to connect the dots. I was aggravated that things weren't lining up. Either Khalil took pictures of all those girls or somebody gave them to him. The only way I was going to find out what I needed to know was by going straight to the source. Visiting Khalil hadn't been high on my agenda. Now I would have to make it a priority.

CHAPTER SIXTEEN

ALICIA

DELETE

Alicia hit the button eight more times as she erased his voice mails.

Phillip was no longer a convenience for Alicia. Their relationship had gotten messier than the baby oil she'd sloshed on her elbows, knees, and foot soles that morning. She didn't need his family drama in her life. If he hadn't been serving it right, things wouldn't have lasted as long as they did. He lived in the hood and was beneath her standards. The only connection between the two of them was pure unadulterated sex. She had no other need for him in her life. A few wants, but sex was the only need. Phillip was also good at fixing the plumbing in her house. Now she would have to find somebody else to take care of her wants and needs.

Alicia really did care about Phillip. It wasn't as if she didn't have a heart. There weren't a lot of men who could handle her brash attitude or love for the booze like Phillip could. She just didn't care enough about him to deal with his family's level of extra. His loving wasn't worth that. Every time Alicia thought about how Phillip let his ghetto sister come in her place of business and curse her out, she wanted to kick him in his throat in exchange for beating down Larika's pregnant behind.

Delete . . . delete . . . delete . . . and delete for all four text messages too.

He should have gotten a clue yesterday when Alicia dropped a laundry bag of his dirty clothes on his mother's porch without saying two words to Ms. Johnson while she watched. She couldn't stand his mom anyway. Ms. Johnson was needy and always called Phillip for petty stuff and at crazy hours when he was at Alicia's house. One time she'd called and requested that he pick up some pickled pig's feet at eleven thirty at night. Ms. Johnson knew doggone well that Phillip was at Alicia's performing his maintenance job. His mom did that crap out of spite because Alicia was getting too much of his time and attention. His mom needed a man. Alicia was certain that if Ms. Johnson was getting served up right, she wouldn't be bothering them. It didn't matter anymore though. Alicia didn't want to talk to him, text him, or even e-mail him. She wanted all communication with Phillip and his people to cease.

"Aunt Alicia, my mom isn't going to let me wear this outside the house," Kaleia said as she pulled at the material of a lavender backless halter top.

The clothing store where Change worked was having a clearance sale, and he had offered to let Taija use his discount card for an additional twenty-five percent off anything they wanted to buy. With the weather warming up, Alicia needed to get Taija summer clothes and also wanted to spend some time with Kaleia now that she was out of the hospital.

Alicia routed her finger. "Turn around and let me look at those jeans. Don't worry about your momma."

Kaleia stepped around in a circle at the three–view mirror. The denim low rider jeans hugged her rear end tightly.

"Girl, to be so petite, you have a lot of butt. You've got a Beyoncé booty. Don't be afraid to show off your cute figure. Let them boys see what they can't have," Alicia chimed with admiration for the child she watched grow into a beautiful young lady.

"We wear uniforms to school. I don't own that many pairs of jeans. I've seen some of the girls wear these type of jeans at the games, but I never thought I would. Are you sure my mom's going to be okay with this outfit?"

"You can keep what we buy here at my house. That way, your momma won't even know you own it. When you and Taija go out, you can come over to my house to get dressed and spend the night. Celia won't know a thing." A little rebellion didn't hurt anybody. Alicia didn't mean to be deceitful, but Celia was so strict that she was going to wreck Kaleia's teenage life.

Kaleia smiled at the idea. "Thanks, Aunt Alicia. That would be great. I'm going to go try on something else."

As Kaleia disappeared, Taija tiptoed from the fitting room in Baby Phat apparel from head to toe. From the diagonal placket polo shirt, pair of cargo pedal pushers, and black shoes with gold spiked heels, she looked like she was auditioning for a Kimmora Simmons runway show. Except the child couldn't walk in the shoes she was wearing, let alone strike a pose. Taija's arms were spread out like she was an Olympic gymnast on a balance beam. She had a difficult time standing upright.

"Taija, that outfit is hot. I love it. If you weren't plus size, I would definitely raid your closet for that. But those shoes have got to go. Your legs are too big for a heel that high. You will fall and break your neck. Unh, unh for you."

Taija's face turned sour. "But Mom, they are *Uma Studs*. They look great with this outfit."

"Unh, unh. You can't walk in them. I'm not wasting my money on those shoes, even with a discount. What about those gold wedge sandals?" Alicia asked, pointing to a ledge adorned with multi-colored heels. "Those are hot too."

"I like these though," Taija whined as her foot tilted out and then back to the floor.

"Well, then have your boyfriend buy them. And when you break your neck, because you can barely stand in them now, tell him to pay for your leg or neck cast too. There are way too many cute shoes in here for us to be arguing about one. And you know I won't argue with you. I'll just walk out this store and leave your whining tail here. Don't act like I haven't done it before," Alicia warned.

Taija sighed hard as she tiptoed back to the fitting room.

That was the main reason Alicia stopped having kids after Taija. She knew she couldn't handle more than one child. She didn't have tolerance for mouthiness or attitude other than her own. Taija wasn't as bad as some of the kids Alicia had seen in the mall. Some of them had no home training whatsoever. If Taija ever thought she could be disrespectful like other teenagers, she would find her clothing shipped to a homeless shelter quicker than she could say, "Baby Phat." Alicia didn't have a problem getting rid of things or people that worked her nerves.

The girls continued trying on clothes for the better part of two hours while Alicia gave suggestions on what worked with their body types and what didn't. She felt like a teen fashion guru.

Change was behind the cash register when they were done picking out what they liked and went to checkout. "Hello, Ms. Evans, how are you?" He scanned the first item.

"I'm fine. We appreciate you letting us use your discount card. You are saving me all kinds of money."

He smiled at Taija. "It's okay. I don't mind doing anything for my girl."

Taija and Change made goo-goo eyes at one another. Alicia remembered being that way in the tenth grade with her first boyfriend, Lewis Walker. Alicia and Lewis stayed together four months. It took that long for him to start getting on her nerves with his sloppy kisses. Taija's first serious relationship lasted twice as long as Alicia's had. Alicia thought they should enjoy that feeling while it lasted. Eventually it would go away.

As Change folded items and put them in a shopping bag, Taija set the pair of Uma Studs on his counter.

"Change, can you buy these for me? I really want them." Taija's lips pouted

"How much are they?" he asked.

Taija looked at the price tag. "Seventy-five. But they were on a half off shoe rack, and with your discount, they are barely nothing."

He smiled as he scanned. "Don't worry about it. You can have them. I don't mind paying for them."

Taija's grin almost touched her earlobes. "Are you sure?"

"I told you, I would buy you anything I could afford to. I got you."

The lovebird looks they were giving each other almost made Alicia want to vomit.

As Alicia pulled the five bags off the counter, she kept a blank face and replied, "I hope you got her hospital bill too, because I will be calling you when she busts her tail in those shoes."

Change laughed as Alicia handed each girl two bags and she kept one.

When Alicia made it home later that evening, none other than the recently dissed and dismissed, Phillip, was sitting on her doorsteps. He had a pint of brandy between his legs. Alicia hadn't paid any attention to her mobile phone once she deleted his messages at the mall. After shopping, Alicia had taken the girls to get pedicures at the salon that did her hair. The girls debated over what they wanted to eat before they decided on the Villa Pizzeria, which wasn't too far from Alicia's house. She was going to get a to-go order, but Kaleia and Taija were complaining about how hungry they were, so they ate at the restaurant.

He held up his cell phone screen. It glowed neon blue in the dark of the night. "You broke up with me by text."

She stepped right over him and unlocked her door. "Girls, go hang up your clothes, I'll be inside in a minute."

"Okay," they said in unison.

"Hello, Mr. Phillip. Excuse me," Kaleia said, folding the bags on her arm and stepping over him to get in the door.

Taija didn't speak to him as she made her way into the house.

"If you got the text, why are you here?" Alicia replied coldly as she closed her front door after Taija and Kaleia entered.

As Phillip stood up, some of his drink spilled on his already dingy shirt. "That's foul, Lish. My family is going through changes now and you want to break up with me?" He said it like he couldn't bring himself to believe it.

"Phillip, people go through changes everyday. They also get over them." She leaned against her door frame and crossed her arms.

"But we've been together a long time."

"Yes, we have been, and it's way past time for us to be over."

"But why?" He stumbled backward with his cell phone in one hand and the bottle of E & J in the other.

"Dang. I thought you read the text." She was annoyed with his presence. Alicia snatched his phone out of his hand. "Here's what it says: 'I don't want to see you or your trifling sister ever again. Don't call me. Don't text me. Don't show up at my job or my house. Move the heck on and don't look back, because I promise you I won't. By the way, I left your funky boxers at your momma's house. Let her wash your clothes since you're so close.' Period."

Alicia tapped his phone screen. "I don't see how my words could be any clearer. In fact, I assure you it don't get any clearer than that. I *texted* you this morning because I didn't want to *see* you here. I repeat . . . don't call, don't text, don't come by. It's not that hard to understand."

The text was short and to the point. She wasn't going to waste keystrokes on a long drawn out Dear John letter about how she was sorry it had to end. That would have been a lie she didn't feel was necessary. Alicia wasn't that type of female. She believed in cutting to the chase. They were both grown up and should have been able to handle a break-up.

"Lish, look." He stumbled again. "I understand that you're mad at Larika, but you don't have to take it out on me. We were cool up until the day before yesterday. I shouldn't have let her come up there. I didn't know she was going to act like that. Her man was taken out the house in handcuffs in front of all the kids. You got to understand that she's pregnant and emotional. Man, we were trying to get Jaquan out that jail. He ain't killed nobody."

Alicia was so sick of Phillip's stupidity that she was close to taking that bottle from him and busting him upside his head. She decided to share a little knowledge about Jaquan. "How do you know Jaquan didn't kill that girl? You don't know, because you weren't there. Have you seen his rap sheet? I have. Larceny in nineteen ninety-one. Larceny again in ninety-three.

Jaquan was caught driving with a suspended license in ninety-four, ninety-five, and ninety-six. He was arrested for disorderly conduct in ninety-nine. Not to mention his assault charges in two thousand. His rap sheet is longer than the route from my house to Canada. I don't see how you assumed I wanted anything to do with Jaquan or his criminal activities."

Phillip defended. "That was the past. Jaquan hasn't committed a crime in over eight years. He is innocent. He takes care of my sister. Even though all those ain't his kids, he still holds it down. Yeah, he had troubles back in the day, but that's my homeboy. His past doesn't make him a murderer. Heck, I live in the hood, I know a murderer when I see one. I went to school with some dangerous cats that went to prison for knocking off whole families. Jaquan ain't that type of guy. He just was in the wrong place at the wrong time, trying to be a good Sa—Sa—Samaritan."

"Jaquan is not my problem. Larika is not my problem, and you are no longer my problem. Take your Erk and Jerk out of my yard. Quit disturbing the peace." Alicia shooed him away.

"Man, I ain't no dang fly. You . . . you can't be dissing me like that. I care about you, girl." Phillip lifted the bottle to his mouth and took a long swig. "Maybe my sister was right about you. She said you were a coldhearted snake and you . . . you . . . you're a witch. I ain't gonna call you out your name like she did. I ain't never disrespected you. She might have been right after all. You are evil. You got evil in your blood."

Alicia folded her arms back and pursed her lips. He looked like a complete fool. She hoped that wasn't how people saw her when she was drinking. "Phillip, my girls are here. Stop making a scene. I need you to leave before one of my neighbors sees you with that open bottle of liquor and you end up being cell mates with Jaquan. I don't want to see you anymore. Deal with it." Alicia went into her house, shut the door, and watched Phillip from a sliver in her curtains.

He stood and stared at her front door for five or six minutes before he dumped the remaining contents of the bottle on her grass and staggered to his car.

"Good riddance to a bad decision," she said to herself as she watched him drive off in his Buick Lesabre.

CHAPTER SEVENTEEN

ME

I listened to the rhythm of Tyrese's heartbeat and found the synchronized thumps to be soothing. Our arms and legs intertwined like coiled springs adjacent to the alcove of his sofa. The movie, *Taken*, was playing on the flat screen above his fireplace. I watched Liam Neeson chase a man across a highway, then that same man fell to his death.

"I can't keep doing this with you," Tyrese whispered against the top of my head. "Celia, I need you to understand that I can't keep doing this," he repeated again hesitantly.

My breath caught in my throat before I slowly exhaled. I placed my chin on his chest and looked up into his eyes. I gnawed on the flesh of my bottom lip. I knew what the 'this' was. He wanted me to love him freely, without reservation. Tyrese had been such a patient man that at some point things were bound to change. I didn't bother to act ignorant. He deserved more than that.

"Oh, Tyrese." Even though I wanted to say something to make it right. I was stumped for words.

"Every time I say 'I love you,' you cringe." His voice was throaty with emotion.

I involuntarily tensed.

"See." He touched my face with his hand and stroked my

cheek with his thumb. "I know you aren't doing it on purpose, but how am I supposed to keep taking that kind of reaction?"

I rolled off Tyrese and sat on the chair as I absorbed his words.

He slid up the couch to rest his back against the armrest. We looked at each other, and I could feel what he felt; could tell through those charcoal gray eyes that everything about him was irrevocably genuine.

From the beginning of our relationship, Tyrese gave me patience and understanding. When we initially met, I was still going through my divorce and numb over all that had occurred in the preceding months before our encounter. For several months after, I had accepted dates from Tyrese only to cancel a day in advance, sometimes even the hour before our scheduled meeting. One minute I was excited about going out with him, and in the next moment, I was calling to say I wasn't ready to date. I see-sawed like playground equipment. I was indecisive, unsure, and just plain scared of where another relationship could lead me. I wondered how dating would affect my children. Kaleia and Caleb had been through so much with Khalil that I couldn't endure placing them at risk for anymore harm.

Tyrese didn't falter during my inconsistent phase. He also didn't press me for anything or pass me by for a woman with less baggage. Instead, he gave me space to pull my head together and offered his ear when my guilt and anxiety overwhelmed me. He was everything that I could have prayed for, yet I still had reservations.

He patted the couch cushion next to him. "Celia, could you come back and sit next to me? Please?" he requested.

I slid back over next to him and tucked one leg underneath

my bottom while I waited for him to finish what he was trying to say. I picked up his remote and pressed mute. "I'm listening."

He reached forward with a cloud of emotions and tucked a long loose strand of hair behind my ear. "Sometimes you seem so scared, and I'm not sure if it's me you are afraid of. I feel like despite the fact that I am not near capable of doing the things your ex did, you are holding me responsible for his actions. No matter what I do, you keep me at arm's length." Frustration flicked in his beautiful eyes.

I said defensively, "That's not true, Tyrese. Maybe in the beginning that was true, but not now." I held up my hand and waved it around the room. "I wouldn't spend time at your home on a regular basis if I didn't feel a connection to you. I wouldn't lie with you or confide in you. There would be no communication on any significant level if I believed you were like Khalil. Maybe you think I'm somehow subconsciously harboring a grudge against you because of the sins of my ex-husband, but I can assure you that that is not the case."

Tyrese took my flaying hand, the one I didn't realize was still moving, and placed it in his. "I'm starting to wonder how strong this connection is between us and if it can continue to stand at the pace we are going."

A light bulb went off in my head, shined like a sunrise over clear water.

"So this is about sex." I recalled our trip to the Art Museum in Milwaukee, Wisconsin two months ago. His first anniversary gift to me. The romantic carriage ride on a bridge overlooking Lake Michigan before we enjoyed an exquisite dinner at the highly praised five star restaurant, Bacchus. I came so very close to becoming intimate with Tyrese at County Claire, the Irish Bed and Breakfast at which we spent that weekend.

Close, but not too close as my morals kicked into gear. I realized that I wasn't ready for what came with making love to him.

He winced at me. "No, it's not about sex." There was a pregnant pause before he spoke again. "Or at least not *only* about sex. It's . . . us . . . and your kids. It's about how stagnant our relationship is."

My eyes fell down to the crinkles in my khaki pants at my bent knee. "I understand." But I didn't want to.

"I don't think you do." His hand squeezed mine gently with affection like the conversation wasn't going where I knew it was.

"For Kaleia's party, I offered to take Caleb off your hands. Because he's your son, I wanted to spend some time with him. But you had all these reasons why it couldn't happen. You have only allowed me to be alone with either of your children one time, and that was when Kaleia was in the hospital. We barely spend any time between the four of us."

I pulled my eyes back up to his and furrowed my eyebrows. "Tyrese, Caleb already had plans on the day of Kaleia's birthday. He wanted to attend the basketball tournament. And you knew when we started dating that I didn't want my children to be a part of the equation. You're dating *me* not them."

I could see the frustration etched in his mocha skin, the hurt beneath thick dark eyelashes.

Tyrese's voice was thick. "I've been in your life for over two years. We've officially been dating for a year. I'm emotionally invested in you. I . . . love . . . you."

I closed my eyes and exhaled. For every time I heard those words, I still couldn't find a way to absorb them.

He was absolutely correct. The walls were up, and it seemed that even an earthquake wasn't strong enough to knock them down.

The ramifications of love nearly catapulted me the first time. By allowing an emotion to tear down the safely constructed haven of concrete I used to center me, that meant I was placing my vulnerability under his control. After numerous years of trusting a disturbed Khalil, I was uncertain that my mind was keen enough to distinguish the emotions between us from the reality of our relationship.

"I care greatly for you, Tyrese. I'm sorry I can't give you more than that. I'm sorry that the wall hasn't come completely down." I pulled my fingers from beneath his warmth. "I've been through a great deal. I wish I could change past events so that I don't feel how I feel but . . ." I shook my head and shrugged my shoulders. "I can't."

He looked up at the ceiling as he rubbed the thin mustache above his lip, his index and middle fingers separated around the curve of his mouth only to join at the top again. Lines crinkled his forehead. He was clearly conflicted by my inability to give myself freely.

"Speaking of walls going up." He gave a pained smile. "A few weeks ago we signed a deal with Scoggins Construction for the renovation of a property in Houston to build a night club adjoining the Odyssey Hotel. The hotel was having some financial difficulties associated with poor real estate ventures from a former CEO, and we had the prime opportunity to get the location we desired at a steal. Evidently some other company, Crape Incorporated, offered them five percent above the original asking price two days before we solidified our negotiations. Now Odyssey is having second thoughts. They are seeing green. Greed is what got them in the red. I think they are confused about their colors. Crape isn't as established in the business as we are, and I need to go out there to remind Odyssey about the bottom line. We can bring them a much more lucrative long term profit than Crape can."

"Aren't you concerned that maybe they will pull out? I mean, if they are known to make poor business decisions, do you even want to take a chance on investing in their property?" I asked, taking a sip from the glass of cranberry spritzer I left sitting on his marble top coffee table.

"Odyssey may have made a few bad choices, but they are far from irresponsible. Joel and I wouldn't place our money with them if we thought they were. Crape has approached them before. I don't think they really want to mess with them. I think Odyssey is using the offer from Crape as leverage to get more money out of us. Real estate can be a nasty business, but I wouldn't be in the game if I didn't know how to play."

With the creation of upscale nightclubs in Miami, Manhattan, San Diego, Las Vegas, and the Detroit location in the last three years, Tyrese had the professional savvy to keep his businesses afloat. Despite the recession and decline in property value throughout Southeast Michigan, somehow his night club, The Set, still drew a crowd.

Tyrese explained, "I'm more concerned with assuring that all the code regulations are met. Renovation of the building shouldn't take but a few months, and I need a liquor license issued. I need other things in place. Instead of hiring staff in that area, we've decided to relocate our people from here for the completion of the project. With us now only operating The Set on the weekends, some employees' hours have been significantly cut. It will give them the chance to gain a livable income again. Plus, I think a few of our staff are looking forward to that southern weather. I know Drake has already packed up his things and is going down to Houston to find an apartment. He will be our night surveillance manager."

Drake had been the bouncer for The Set since its ascension and the change in position was a definite move up. I met Drake on the night they had a live jazz set with, Kem, the national recording artist and native of Detroit. The house was packed to the hilt with people. I had a VIP ticket. Drake was instructed to keep an eye out for me and make sure I was comfortable because Tyrese had to handle several problems throughout the night.

"I'm debating whether I will relocate also. Maybe make Houston my home again."

I was stunned. "Oh." Houston had been where Tyrese was born and raised, but I never suspected that he wanted to go back. He had become such an important person in my life. I didn't want distance to divide us. My hands shook as I placed the spritzer back on the table.

He watched my posture and seemed relieved at how his possibly leaving would affect me. "The decision isn't permanent yet. I've been debating with myself, but I'm seriously considering it. There really isn't a need for two managers here in Detroit."

"I thought business was still going well here in Detroit."

"The business is doing fine, but there are better opportunities for expansion elsewhere. Houston has a solid job market and a great deal of wealth. I can do some amazing things down there."

"It sounds to me like you've already made your decision," I said, dejected.

"Yes and no. I'm taking our relationship into consideration. I don't want to leave without you." He paused again and hunched his shoulders. "Or maybe we can try the long distance thing and see where that takes us."

"A long distance relationship." I repeated that option to myself. "Tyrese, this has taken me by surprise. That's a lot of pressure. I . . . I can't keep you from your pursuits."

"Celia, you wouldn't be. I just need to know if we have a chance for something long term. If you can see a future with me. I need to know if I can purchase a jackhammer and tear down that wall around your heart." He smiled.

I smiled too. I couldn't see not having his sense of humor around to lighten my days. "I can't make a decision like that on the spot. I don't want to see you leave, but a long distance relationship is hard to maintain."

"It doesn't have to be hard. It's what we make it." Tyrese was obviously determined to do whatever it took to make the relationship work.

"Well." I sighed.

"Well." He wanted an answer.

For all that was placed on the table, and I didn't include my spritzer, I had a lot to think about.

CHAPTER EIGHTEEN

KALEIA

She had heard about that kind of high. The euphoric rush that would numb her limbs and free her mind of any bad thought or insecurity. That unexplainable feeling that promised to wipe all her troubles away if only for a few minutes or hours. Kaleia had heard from several classmates. Drugs did that for them. Pills, shrooms, laced marijuana, and Xanax bars were all popular at Montgomery Christian. The pills were the easiest to pass around. Those prescribed muscle relaxers like Hydrocodone that miraculously disappeared from their parents' bathroom cabinet or Adderall, which was really their little brother's ADHD medicine meant to keep the kid from bouncing off the walls and focused in the classroom. Pills were pedaled throughout the school quicker than Girl Scout cookies at a PTA meeting. The other drugs required a little more effort to find. Those took euphoria to a whole other level. Nobody talked about them during class. Instead, certain people whispered about it during lunch or games. It was like being part of a secret society, and Kaleia was eager to join.

Kaleia thought about that as she waited by Tevin's car for him to get dressed after the basketball game. Kaleia knew her mother wouldn't let her hang out with Tevin if she had come. She had begged Celia to let her attend the game with

Taija, and Celia agreed to it. Her aunt had dropped her and Taija off. Taija had called Aunt Alicia during the game to tell her that Change would bring them home. She then left with Change during second quarter and told Kaleia to call or text her when she was ready to head back to the house. Determined to spend some time with Tevin alone, Kaleia ditched her other friends as soon as the game was over.

She pulled at the bottom of her halter top, trying to cover her exposed midriff. Bumps rose on her arms. The night air was chilly, and she hadn't brought a jacket with her.

"Nobody can touch us. We're blazing a trail. Number one . . . number one. We're number one." A car full of cheerleaders rolled by screaming at the top of their lungs.

Students were all over the parking lot shouting in victory. Montgomery had been on a winning streak since starting the season and had just won a game against Catholic Central, which would put them close to winning the state championship.

She looked around the parking lot at the pandemonium as some kids from Catholic Central made a commotion. Kaleia heard so much noise that she couldn't tell if a fight was about to break out. She craned her neck over the top of Tevin's hood, trying to see the action.

A pair of arms circled around her bare midriff. "You look so good tonight. I almost fumbled the ball when I saw you in the stands."

Kaleia tried to turn around in Tevin's arms, but he held her fast.

He whispered against her ear. "Stay like this for a minute. Wow. I would have never known you had all this cushion back here. The school uniform does you no justice, and even when we were at your birthday party, I didn't see all of this."

Kaleia felt him cup her behind, and she wanted to push his hand away. She knew that would be a bad idea, so instead, she let his hand linger until she became anxious. Trembling she said, "I am freezing. Can we please get in the car?"

As soon as his hand dropped, Kaleia stepped back like she was waiting for him to open the door.

Tevin took his keys out of his jacket pocket, pressed the keyless entry button, and pulled the jacket off. He draped it over her shoulders and walked around to his side. Kaleia opened her own door and slid inside his black Lexus.

"There's an after game party at Coach's house. Did you want to go with me? Or rather, can you go? Your mom seems pretty strict. If you have a ten o'clock curfew or something, I can drop you off at home before I go."

"I'm staying at my aunt's house, and she won't mind what time I come in," Kaleia responded confidently. For the first time ever, she felt totally free to do whatever she wanted to. No restrictions and no rules.

"You mean the aunt from your birthday party?"

Kaleia nodded as they headed out of the parking lot and down W. 10 Mile Road.

"Your aunt is so crazy. She was tipsy that night. Me and my boys talked about that night for a week straight."

Although she was embarrassed that her Aunt Alicia acted like that in front of her classmates, she hadn't expected her aunt to be a topic of conversation for her friends once the night was over.

"I bet she is entertaining all the time. I bet you could get away with murder around her. I would love to hang out at her house with you one day. For her and your mom to be identical twins, they don't act nothing alike." Tevin turned on N. Campbell Road.

"My mom was sheltered or something. We can't relate to one another. She's scared to let me breathe on my own. When I get around my Aunt Alicia, I know I'm going to have a good time because she is really cool and down to earth. She's more like a big sister instead of an aunt. I kind of wish she was my mom," Kaleia admitted for the first time to anyone. She hadn't even told Taija how she felt.

"Are you hungry, because I'm starving?" He turned his wheel as they headed toward Burger King in Madison Heights.

"Not really, but I would love a vanilla shake." As Kaleia looked at Tevin, she thought he had the potential to possibly become a nice boyfriend.

At the party, after leaving Burger King, Kaleia stayed near Tevin like they were an official couple. Because it was at the coach's house, there wasn't any alcohol served or other things that Kaleia expected at a house party. Music played in a huge game room, and a bunch of kids were dancing, shooting pool, or chilling in a lounge area.

"Why do you do it?" Kaleia asked as they sat squeezed together on a chaise off to themselves.

"Huh?" Tevin said as he tried to hear her over Lil Wayne playing on the loud speakers.

"Why do you sell?" Kaleia repeated her question.

"What are you, the F.B.I.?" Tevin's hands started roaming all over her back and legs. "Are you wearing a wire and trying to get me caught up?"

Kaleia couldn't tell if he were joking or serious. She stopped his hands on her thighs. "Of course not. I'm too young for the Federal Bureau of Investigations. I asked because I'm curious. You seem so sweet. I wouldn't expect a drug dealer to act like you." She whispered the words drug dealer like nobody would know what they were talking about. That was if anybody caught their conversation.

"I'm not a drug dealer. I am a businessman. Drugs just happen to be a hot selling item." Tevin watched the dance floor.

Placing her head on his shoulders, she asked, "What kinds of drugs are hot?"

She could feel tension as he shifted in his seat. Kaleia didn't want to push things too far with him and needed to make sure things stayed comfortable between them.

"Tevin, I feel kind of naïve, like there is a world full of stuff going on that I don't know about. I don't want to be naïve anymore. If you don't want to talk about it, I understand." She played the innocent role to the hilt.

All the tension left his body as he relaxed again. "I'm not used to girls I date asking stuff like that; not unless they trying to be my customer."

He hit the nail right on the head, but Kaleia wasn't going to let on why she wanted to be with him. Her hope had been to get him to show her some of the drugs he had, then maybe she could sneak a little something from his stash. His reaction let her know automatically that she would have to find a different angle with him.

"Really? Well, that's just tacky." She laughed and pulled her long hair to one shoulder. "I've never done drugs, so I won't be trying to get you for your product. Like I said, I was curious."

Growing quiet they lay back and listened to the music. Tevin bobbed his head while Kaleia kept her head on his shoulder.

He said, "I sell two things. Xanax bars and marijuana laced with Oxycontin. It used to be crystal meth, but this college girl I sold to had a bad trip and tried to bungee jump off the patio of her dorm apartment without the bungee cord. She lived on the third floor and would have killed herself if her flower bushes hadn't broken the fall. I heard about that and had to stop. Crystal meth will mess you up."

Without looking up, Kaleia smiled on the inside. He was trusting her a little bit. "Oh. Wow."

She kept all her other questions to herself. He was the type of person that required her patience. In time she would get what she wanted. In just a matter of time, it would all work out.

CHAPTER NINETEEN

ME

The funny thing about expectations were even when you couldn't predict the outcome, there was still hope. As the gates to Kinross Correctional Facility slid open, I thought about that and all of those milestones between Khalil and me that had brought us to this point. Such as our wedding day, when I strolled down the aisle in a beautiful lace princess gown with spaghetti straps. The dress was the only thing from our special occasion that Khalil hadn't helped me pick out. He had been an important part of the approval process in everything from the four tier cake with white chocolate butter cream frosting to the embroidered napkin holders and the trinkets for the guest gift bags. On the way to make vows to my husband that day, I had contemplated all the years of planning things we had ahead as a team. When our children were born I expected Khalil to be the kind of father who coached his son's soccer team and drove his daughter to ballet class, while we switched days for school field trips. I expected him to help coordinate family vacations and juggle work schedules. I expected our marriage to last. And even when our world crumbled, I expected closure with the finalization of the divorce proceedings. I expected peace of mind when they sentenced Khalil for seven to twelve years. I expected a multitude of things.Some of those expectations occurred, but the most important ones didn't.

Stepping into the building, I smelled sawdust in the dry air. An officer held his hand out for my purse. I handed it to him and watched the contents fall on a table. My wallet . . . car keys . . . Peppermint Patty . . . M•A•C lip gloss . . . Mr. Chicken wet wipes . . . Desiree's pictures. As I walked through a metal detector the machine beeped.

"Ma'am, I'm going to need you to step back through," another officer requested. I turned around and did as I was instructed.

That officer used a hand-held device to scan me from my head to my feet.

Beep . . . beep . . . beep . . . beep, beep, beep, beep.

The noise intensified at my black leather pumps.I took the shoes off to show I had nothing to hide and I definitely wasn't trying to take in anything illegal. I again went through the metal detector and picked up my purse, which the officer had nicely resealed.

I walked to a desk that read 'Visitor Registration' and requested to see Khalil Alexander. My name as Mrs. Alexander was quickly located on a list so that I could enter the waiting area, where the room was full of mostly women and several children. They appeared to be from four months old up to fourteen or fifteen years of age. I thought about Kaleia and Caleb, whom I hoped would never pass through a pair of prison doors. I was certain that Khalil left my name on his visitor list because he believed that I would eventually bring his children to see him. The likelihood of that happening was zero. My stomach tensed with a knot of nerves.I wished I had brought my roll of Tums, but was sure they would have confiscated them as paraphernalia when they checked my purse.

As he approached my table, Khalil looked the same, yet different from the last time I'd seen him. Maybe it appeared that way because my feelings were different. At a glance, he was still handsome, his face clean shaved. The goatee he wore for years was gone. He had packed on a little weight, ten or fifteen pounds.

Khalil pulled out a chair and sat across from me.

"Celia," he stated with a blank face.

"Khalil," I replied, praying inwardly that I would get through the meeting without my nerves being shot.

"You are just about the last person on my visitor list I expected to see. Not that many people come to see me here anyways."

I nodded. Besides my mother, who I knew visited him several times a year and refused to believe he was guilty, nobody wanted to see him while he was in prison.

"Pastor Daniels comes to see me sometimes, which I am appreciative of. He told me that I was still part of his flock even from in here, and that he had to check on his sheep no matter where they were. He convinced me to join the prison ministry," Khalil exclaimed.

I knew the heart of our pastor. I realized that he wasn't the type of man who easily judged anybody, no matter how disgusting or trifling their deeds. He preached often about the man beyond the flesh and kingdom mindedness and about how flawed we all were.

"How have you been? How are the kids?" he eagerly asked.

It dawned on me that Khalil thought I was there to socialize. He thought that I wanted to see him. As if time had closed a gap and forgiveness had faded the pain. He gave me more credit than I deserved.

I didn't want to participate in the pleasantries, but in order to get information, I had to give some. "I'm fine. The kids are fine. Caleb is very tall now. He is just as tall as you are. It's like he sprung up overnight. I don't have any pictures of him on me now, but I'll have him send you updated photos. He was just in a basketball tournament."

Khalil smiled. "He's probably really good at basketball now. I wish I could see him in person. How about Kaleia? What is she involved in?"

My stomach lurched. *Self-mutilation because of what you did* is the first thing that popped in my head. I swallowed my tongue almost literally. I couldn't come off as nasty and realized that I had to control my emotions.

"She is doing well." That was all I offered. That was all I could provide for him, four words more than I wanted to say.

"Thank you for allowing Caleb to correspond with me. I look forward to the times I hear from him. He sent me his soccer jersey from last year. He told me that he didn't want to play anymore since I wasn't able to coach him. I've missed being there.I miss all of you and all the things we used to do together." When he said that, it sounded incredibly sincere, but I knew better than to fall into a conversation about what used to be.

"I've been trying to convince Caleb to stay in soccer, but his heart just isn't in it. I figured if he's no longer enjoying soccer, than there is no point in forcing him to play. He's involved in so many other extracurricular activities; I decided to leave well enough alone."

"I'm glad you're handling things without me. It looks like you're able to let some of what happened go. I want us to be able to get along. You shouldn't feel alone in raising our children. I want to participate in the kids' lives as much as I can from inside here."

What kind of parenting assistance did he think he could offer me from inside a prison cell block? It was his parenting skills that got him locked up in the first place. It made me wonder what kind of parenting skills his mother passed on to him. I wanted to cut his conversation off and ask about how he was raised before his aunt got him. I wanted to find out if pedophilia was in his genes. I wondered if I needed to have some obscure child molester genetic tests done on Kaleia, or Caleb, for that matter.

The more he talked, the more the animosity inside me grew. It was like having somebody purposely drive an eighteen wheeler through my living room, then come by to ask if they could help clean up the mess afterward. There were only so many times a person could insult me and get away with it. There was a limit to what my emotions could handle.

Before I allowed Khalil to roll deeper into his delusion of a happy ending with his family, I decided it was time to get to the true reason for my visit. "I have to be honest. I didn't come here about them or us, Khalil. I need help with some information, and I hope you can be of assistance."

"What kind of information?"

I opened my purse and pulled out the folded 'missing' poster. "There is a young lady missing. She has been gone for several years now, but I think that you may know her. And I'm hoping that you can tell me what you know so that she can possibly get back home."

He watched me unfold the poster and set it in front of him. He stared at the picture, then back at me. I couldn't tell what was on his mind. If he were a card player, his game face would have me beat. But I knew enough about Khalil to expect the unexpected and to hope for whatever I got.

Khalil looked me dead in the eyes and said, "I don't know this kid."

"Are you sure about that?"

"Positive. I've never seen her before."

"Well, that's awfully strange that you would say that because," I pulled out the other picture of Desiree; the one in which she wore the skimpy bikini. "I found this picture at our old house. It was in a metal box with a bunch of other pictures. There were photos that nobody else in the house would need to hide. Looked like little girls to me, unless my eyes deceived me, but I don't think so. And yeah, you could put it off on Caleb, but he wasn't thinking about girls back then, let alone interested in collecting their pictures." I waited for him to come up with another lie.

He rubbed the back of his neck as he looked at the pictures side by side. "They were Stan's photos for a modeling business he was trying to start. You know he was always trying a new venture. As his friend he asked me what I thought of the poses, because he knew I dabbled in photography. He wanted me to give constructive criticism. I meant to get those pictures back to him, but I had forgotten about them when we started having our problems."

"If I call Stan, will he remember this business venture he was trying out?" I asked with a hint of cynicism in my voice.

"I don't know.Stan changed businesses like some people changed underwear. I would guess so. I assume that he would, but I really wouldn't know. He desperately wanted to get out of landscaping, because he said there wasn't enough money in the job. Last I heard he had moved to Nevada and was running a heating and cooling business. What does this missing girl and these photos have to do with me?" Khalil pushed both pictures back my way.

He was playing my intelligence. He was playing it hard, and I was trying to keep my game face just like him. But Desiree deserved to be acknowledged. "Khalil, that girl disappeared in

October of 2006, a month before you went to jail. I mean, that is more than a little suspicious considering what you are in prison for."

It wasn't a coincidence that Desiree's picture was in his hidden box. It wasn't a coincidence that he just happened to like little girls. It wasn't a coincidence that everything led back to Khalil. It was divine intervention. Time and time again, I kept receiving heavenly confirmation. God was using me to help find Desiree, and I wouldn't rest until His will was done.

"You're on a witch hunt." Khalil scowled. "What did you want me to say, that I kidnapped this kid? Or better yet that . . . that I murdered her and buried the body in the backyard? Are you trying to figure out how you can get me more time in this dump? That is what your visit is about, isn't it? You thought you could waltz up in here and pull some half-tailed confession from me. Here I'm thinking that we can finally leave the past in the past. You are crazy. You were crazy then and you are still crazy."

The gloves were off, and I was ready to come out swinging. "There is nothing wrong with my sanity. I am far from crazy. I'm not the one having love sessions with thirteen-year-olds or hiding pictures inside plant pots. You have some nerve to call me crazy. And further more, I didn't come here to have you confess anything. I think you are too diabolical for that. I hoped for civility. I hoped you could shed some light about Desiree, because I want this girl's father to be able to sleep at night without wondering what happened to his child."

He slanted his eyes at me, "Desiree? Listen to you saying her name like you personally know her. You sure that you aren't the reason she's missing? Now that wouldn't be a stretch of the imagination seeing how you tried to kill me."

I hissed, "If I really wanted to kill you, trust and believe that you would be dead."

"I don't know anything. "A smug glare crossed his face as he stood up. "I don't know about a box, I don't know about any pictures, and I don't know about this kid. Whatever witch hunt you think you're on, won't get you any information to contradict that."

I couldn't hold back my disdain any longer. If he thought I was the same naïve woman he married, he had another thing coming. "You are still a liar and a manipulator, Khalil. You lied about Kaleia and didn't get away with it, just like you are lying now. But if you had anything to do with this girl missing, I mean anything at all, I'm going to find out, and when I do find out, the law will make you pay."

"The law? Celia, you don't have a clue about the law." He didn't say what that meant as he walked away from me.

I looked up at the ceiling, regretting that I couldn't keep it together without stooping to his level. I hadn't accomplished what I set out to do. I wasn't an inch closer to finding out what happened to Desiree. "I'm so sorry, Lord. Please forgive me." That man had taken me out of my element.

CHAPTER TWENTY

KHALIL

Khalil was seething when he got back to his cell. His ex-wife's unforgiveness made him sick with anger.

Celia knew nothing, and he couldn't believe she had the audacity to almost blatantly accuse him of doing harm to that girl. Khalil had banked on his ex-wife still having some feelings for him. She used to trust him, and he used to glory in the delightful way her eyes followed him when he was in a room. There had been a rare love . . . a passionate union throughout the fifteen years of marriage. But now she wanted to act like he was such a horrible person. Now she behaved as if he were lower than a Lake Michigan bottom feeder.

"How did it go, man? You seemed pretty excited to see your ex-wife. Are you two going to reconcile or what?" Stick piped from the top bunk as their cell doors clanked shut.

After three weeks of solitary confinement for fighting, in which he was only allowed outside his cell for two hours a day, Stick was allowed back to his cell. His mood swings kept getting him in trouble. Right before they locked him down, he tried to strangle another inmate with some dental floss he had found. Nobody ever knew when something in Stick's brain would click and make him violent. If he got another offense on his record, they would be sending him to a super maximum security facility. They forced him to take a prescription of Risperal for his bipolar disorder. Since being returned to the general population, Stick was as mellow as a sundried cucumber.

Khalil gritted his teeth. "Not likely.She's giving me a hard time and wants to hold the past against me. I can't change anything that happened back when we were together, and I refuse to keep being badgered about it. She made some unnecessary accusations. Seeing her just confirmed that I need to move on with my life. I'm going to stay focused on getting out of this place, and somehow I'll find a way to see my kids without her say-so."

Stick's voice flowed from the top bunk. "Never trust a woman. Women are nothing but trouble. They don't know what they want and play too many games. Women are the reason most of us are in here in the first place. All my charges come from me trying to take care of my woman. When I robbed that Check-n-Go, it was to pay our bills, because I didn't have a job. Did she see it that way? Heck, no. She thought I was being violent because I had to knock the cashier over the head with the butt of the gun for him to open the register. She visited me for the first year, rode up here with my homeboy from Saginaw. They stopped coming, and I didn't know why. Then I find out they moved in together. I didn't know who I wanted to kill first . . . her or him. They are lucky I have four more years in this joint. When I get out, I'm paying them both a special visit."

Khalil plopped on his mattress and placed his hands behind his head. He wondered how Celia ran across the pictures he had in that locked box. Who would have thought to search for anything at the bottom of a plant base? It wasn't like she watered or replanted any of the large palm trees they had in the hallways. They paid a maid service to take care of the plants once a week when they came to clean the house.

It shouldn't have surprised Khalil that Celia would snoop around their house in some mock investigation while he was locked up. He had caught her snooping one other time after she moved out of their home when they separated. Celia claimed then that she was searching for a uniform for their son, but he knew better. She hadn't been in the house since she'd seen their daughter in bed with him, plus his computer login had been tampered with.

When Celia placed those pictures in front of him, Khalil had been more than a little shocked, although he made certain not to reveal his dread.

Desiree had been one of the first.

It was when YoungLuv.net was in its infancy stage. Khalil had been personally interviewing young girls for the site when he first started the business. He had wanted to make sure the girls understood the business opportunity before they took it.

As he laid there waiting for the dusk to change the sky and security to do a bed check, he reminisced about the warm fall afternoon they'd meet.

Red, orange, and green leaves sprayed the ground of the park near her home. He checked his watch at 6:09 P.M. She was late. Punctuality mattered. The meeting was scheduled for exactly six o'clock through e-mail. Khalil stood from the picnic table ready to leave when he noticed a girl running toward him from an open area to the left.

She dashed through the fence next to a baseball diamond and screamed, "Please wait." He watched her lug a black case under her arm and a book bag on her back. "I'm sorry for being late. I had practice, and my band teacher wanted to talk with me".

He stared at her as she rambled out of breath.

"You are Mr. Cook, right?" she asked, uncertain if he were the interviewer she signed up to meet.

Khalil had used an assumed name. It was safer that way.

"I am, and your name is Desiree?" He responded with a warm smile as he sat back down at the picnic table.

Her head bobbed up, then down as wavy jet black hair grazed her shoulders. She seemed flustered as she placed a black case behind her and sat next to him.

"What do you play?" he inquired, taking in how beautiful and flawless her deep brown skin appeared. She looked innocent, yet exotic. It was a perfect combination for his pursuits.

"Clarinet. I'm first chair as of today." She seemed shy.

"Congratulations. Now let's get down to business. I have somewhere else to be in less than an hour." The teens at church were putting together a play, and as one of the youth ministers, he had helped plan things.

"Have you ever had a job before, Desiree?"

"No, not yet. When I was eleven I did help my mom with a paper route she had though. I collected the money every Saturday. I helped out the whole time she had a route."

"Okay. Did your mom get a new job?"

"No, she became sick and couldn't work anymore." She looked sad for a moment as she watched a group of small children playing on a jungle gym. "But I liked that job. I got to meet all the people in the neighborhood and make a little money. My mom shared her profit with me."

"Pretty nice mom you have."

"Yeah." He watched that cloud of sadness cover her face again. Khalil assumed that her mother was a single parent and probably having a hard time maintaining the bills without a job.

"Well, I would like to help you make some extra cash if you're interested."

"Yeah, the flyer said it was, um, Internet fun for cash. I could make money without leaving my home."

"Do you have Internet access on a home computer?"

"Yes."

"Good. Have you ever used a chat line like MySpace to talk with friends?"

"All the time when my friend, Shayla, comes over. She knows people everywhere, even in Boston, New York, and California. She met all of them online."

Khalil slowly smiled, thinking that maybe he could recruit Desiree's friend too. "That would be your job, to talk to people all over the country. The only difference is you would get paid for the conversation. The more you chat, the better your chance of making a lot of money."

Khalil explained that the conversations would be with different men who were shy like her and just needed somebody to talk to.

She seemed to ponder the option in her head. "You want me to talk with strange old men?"

"Not strange or old. More along the lines of men like me. You don't think I'm old, do you?" He smiled again. He didn't want to scare her with the unusual business deal.

"No, you're not really old," she responded hesitantly.

"See, that's what I mean. And it would be safe, harmless fun because you will never see them in person, and you can say whatever you want online. Do you think that is something you can do?"

"It sounds easy enough." She pulled her book bag from her back and began to dig inside. When she pulled out a notebook and pen, Khalil placed a hand upon her leg. "You don't need that. I'll send you an e-mail with the information in the next couple of days."

"Oh, okay." Desiree pushed the items back inside the book bag, zipped it up, and hoisted the strap on her shoulder.

"I have to go, but it was very nice to meet you, Desiree." Khalil held his hand out.

She took it and squeezed before quickly letting go. "You too, Mr. Cook." *She paused.* "Um . . . what if I have questions? How can I contact you?"

"Everything will be done through e-mail from here on out."

Seeming to understand, Desiree picked up her instrument case. Khalil walked right, and she went left.

Desiree turned out to be one of his best recruits for the short time she worked for YoungLuv.net. Pulling himself from thoughts of her, Khalil laid in bed until he heard Stick breathing heavy in slumber. He slid out of the lower bunk to get his cell phone from behind the wall. Stick didn't know Khalil had the commodity. The Filipino was an all right guy, but his mood swings and unpredictability could cause trouble for both of them. Khalil couldn't afford to have his phone confiscated.

He got back in bed, pulled the covers up like he always did to shield the light, and he typed one sentence.

Khalil: Celia came for a visit.

CHAPTER TWENTY-ONE

ME

"It seems to me like you don't want to forgive him. It's like you would rather stay angry at him and it won't matter if he's changed or not." My friend, Monique, dipped a piece of fried squash into a circle of ranch salad dressing on her plate. "But I must tell you from the outside looking in, it does seem like you have a vendetta against Khalil. He may not be that far off in thinking that you are on a witch hunt."

Monique, Justice, and I had just left Tuesday evening Bible Study and were sharing food at Myra's restaurant around the corner from the church. The trio of us hadn't spent time together since Kaleia was in the hospital and I had called Justice to help deliver dinners to the nursing home. Despite the distractions in my life I tried to keep them informed about all the recent events. I had told them about my visit to the prison three days ago and how I had let my emotions get the best of me. I wasn't proud of how things turned out at the prison and was mostly ashamed of myself because I was not able to control my temper. I did Desiree an injustice by not keeping the conversation positive. I should have kept my insults in my head. It wasn't like I was provoked by him; but on the other hand, everything Khalil had done in the past aggravated me in the present.

"Celia, I wouldn't go as far as saying that you are on a witch hunt, but you are definitely angry. You should see the look on your face when Khalil's name is mentioned." Justice seemingly had agreed with Monique as she pointed at my clinched jaw. "See, that look."

I couldn't help my involuntary body reactions to Khalil's name no more than I could stop breathing. Some things came naturally. Some things I was still praying on.

"I don't want to be this way. Do you think I want to spend my nights up worrying about my kids and all the damage he has done to them? Or being fearful that he caused a child to disappear? I would rather be able to sleep comfortably without a concern for my children or anybody else's kids. And now, on top of everything else going on in my head, I have to worry about Kaleia cutting on herself."

Justice and Monique had been the only people, outside of Dr. Malawi, who I could share that information with. I knew that kind of news would devastate my parents, and they wouldn't know what to do with the situation. There had been a wedge between my mother and me since the accusation of child molestation first came out. She would go to her grave believing Khalil was innocent no matter what kind of proof was thrown in her face. I also refused to tell Alicia because she had enough of her own personal coping problems and couldn't help fix Kaleia's issue.

Justice wiped her hand on a napkin before sipping from a glass of raspberry tea. "You have Kaleia in therapy. That is just about the best thing that you can do for her. I know it hurts to see your child doing crazy things to hurt herself, but it's not your fault. You didn't make her cut herself. That would be the equivalent of your child being hit by a car while crossing a busy street and you blame yourself because you didn't drive them to school that day. You can't predict an accident, and you can't control what your children do. With our four kids, Richard and I have a heck of a time keeping tabs on when they hurt themselves. Johnathan and RJ are hyper little boys that like crashing into each other and play wrestling just about everyday for some strange reason. And I can't count the number of times Shelby fell head first on the floor when she learned how to get out of her walker. Luckily she is older, and I don't have to worry about that now. But you don't stop wondering or worrying about what your kids will get into or won't do the right way. You just have to take it in stride, Celia."

Just like Dr. Malawi, Justice was trying to act like I wasn't responsible for Kaleia's mistakes when I believed otherwise.

I chewed on my food and swallowed before saying, "That is different. I wouldn't be this frazzled if it were about an accident. Kaleia didn't accidentally cut her leg thirty-four times. She purposely cut herself thirty-four times. And she could have died when that last cut got infected. It's like she has a sickness, and instead of getting her treated, I decided to avoid the problem. I might not have made her do it, but if I hadn't taken her out of therapy in the first place, she might not have this need to cut herself. Then we wouldn't be having this discussion. In fact, if Khalil had never put his hands on Kaleia, we wouldn't be talking about this now. That is my point. That's why I'm angry."

Monique dipped a cracker in a bowl of chili she had ordered. She pointed her cracker at me. "The problem isn't your being angry. We all get angry. The Bible says in Ephesians, *Be ye angry, and sin not. Let all bitterness, and wrath and anger, and clamour, and evil speaking, be put away from you, with malice.* Your problem is that you are letting anger consume you. Even worse, your anger is coupled with unforgiveness.

And you know what Pastor Daniels says about unforgiveness. He says that the Holy Spirit will die when overtaken by the toxicity of unforgiveness. Poison will corrupt and destroy the spirit. You can't let your flesh control you. You have got to find a way, deep within yourself, to let this thing with Khalil go."

I knew Monique was talking to me in love, but I couldn't do what she was requesting. Not yet. "I thought I had forgiven him, but when he started talking . . . um, um, um . . . I can't explain it. I just felt disgust and rage. It was like everything just happened yesterday. I almost wanted to shoot him again. The Lord knows it's not right, but that is what I felt." I wished God would work something on the inside of me to clean the slate. Maybe I needed to pray harder for my heart to heal from the damage of my ex-husband's sins.

"Quite honestly, I can't tell you how to feel. If I were in your shoes, and Richard had molested Shelby, I probably wouldn't have a good perspective. Five, ten, fifteen years from now, I might have still struggled with that kind of issue. Neither Monique nor I want to make light of what you feel. We only hope that you don't spend all your time trying to fix a past that is long gone," explained Justice.

Monique added, "Celia, you know I've always been in your corner, but I completely agree with Justice. And no offense to that girl's family, but she has been missing for several years now. She either ran away and doesn't want to be found, or she's no longer with us and her body is buried God knows where. Maybe you should let that go too and focus on something positive. You are putting a lot of pressure on yourself and weighing yourself down with responsibility that is not necessarily meant to be yours."

They didn't understand why it was so important to me that

Desiree be found. My gut wouldn't let it go. My heart couldn't forget about her. Even if she weren't alive, she was still out there, and she still deserved to be brought home.

I passionately explained, adamant that my search was not in vain, "If that were my daughter, if that were Kaleia, I would want somebody to find her. Bad or good, I would still want to know. Neither of you saw the hope in Mr. Carpenter's eyes. He wanted somebody to care about his daughter besides him. And there is no way that I could show up at that man's house, tell him that I would help him try to find his only child, then turn right around and say never mind. Like Desiree is some kind of inconvenience. All personal feelings aside, I'm telling you that Khalil knows something. He remembers Desiree. I could tell by his body language, and I don't think he would have gotten that defensive if he didn't know anything about her. He still has some secrets. I am certain of that with every fiber of my being."

Justice shook her head. "Regardless of what he may or may not know, you can't say it's not personal, and you can't place your feelings aside. Just be careful."

She made it sound like I was on a dangerous mission. As if I were volunteering for service in Iraq. My biggest concern was disappointment for me and Mr. Carpenter.

"I'll be careful; I promise. I'm not going to do anything that will put me in harm's way," I assured her.

As the waitress came around to collect our plates, she placed the bill on the table. Monique glanced at the bill. "I'll take care of this one, ladies. On a different note, Jason took a new position at his job. He will be a Technical Consultant for financial services. He got a serious bump up in salary." Monique's eyes glistened with joy.

"Tell Jason I said congratulations!" I couldn't have been

happier for the newlyweds. They had finally tied the knot six months ago, after a two and a half year engagement.

"Same here. Tell Jason we're proud of his accomplishment," Justice replied.

"I will, and that's not the best part of the news. You know I've been thinking about going back to school in order to finish my degree in Health Science. I only have a year left for the program, but as you both know, I took that job in medical billing and kinda got myself stuck paying for those student loans. I've already told that story, probably one too many times. Anyway, Jason said it would be okay if I stopped working so I can get my classes done. Talk about a relief. I can't wait to give my two weeks notice. That job is boring me to death. I hate all the paperwork. When I become a dietitian, I won't have to deal with that much paperwork."

"How are you going to handle that, Ms. Independence, having to ask your husband for money?" Justice asked as the three of us stood to leave.

"I don't think it will be all that bad. Jason isn't controlling. If I need anything, he will make sure I have it. I'm just excited about being able to get my degree. It doesn't make any sense to be paying loans on something I don't have. Plus, those loans will be deferred while I finish my education, so that's one less payment we will have to budget every month."

"See how things fall into place? I remember when you thought Jason wasn't going to actually go through with the wedding."

"I still didn't think we needed to be engaged that long, but it's all water under the bridge. I am happily married now." Monique almost glided through the exit sign like she had skates on as we headed to our cars.

We weren't able to park next to each other in the back of the restaurant. The parking lot had been full when we first arrived.

As Justice got into her car, I pulled the car keys from my purse. "Have a good night. I'll call you tomorrow."

"Okay, talk to you soon. You too, Monique," Justice shouted to Monique who was already headed toward her vehicle a row over.

I went toward where I thought I'd parked, but there was a black Ford minivan in the space. I hit the button on my key ring, expecting to hear the familiar chirp from my Jaguar somewhere else in the parking lot. But the sound didn't come. I began walking up and down all the rows trying to remember where I'd parked. I looked at the row of cars, where mine should have been, or where I thought it should have been. A blue Toyota Camry, gray Chevy Impala, burgundy Honda Accord, and white Lincoln Navigator were all in the row as I retraced my steps.

Monique saw me pacing through the lot, rolled down her window, and stopped two rows from me. "What are you doing?"

"I can't find my car. I know I parked it right over there." I was perplexed as I circled around trying to spot the Jaguar's silver hood emblem.

Monique looked as confused as I did. "Hit your panic button to set off your alarm."

I did that, but again, no sound.

"Where is my car?" I mumbled to myself. Anxiety washed over me. I jogged over to the row in which Monique's Jeep Cherokee was idling.

"Still nothing?" she asked

"My car is not here." I pressed the panic button repeatedly.

"Maybe somebody towed it?"

I didn't try to hide my anxiety. "That can't be. My car wasn't in a tow area. It was in the middle of a row. That row over there, and it's not there anymore." I pointed toward the minivan feeling more exacerbated by the minute.

"Celia, calm down."

I pulled my cell phone from my purse to call the police, and there was a text from an unfamiliar number. I would have ignored it, but the words on the screen jolted me. Fear rose up over that anxiety I had.

"Oh my God . . . oh my God . . . oh my God." My entire body shook as I stared at the screen.

Monique got out of her car, "What's going on?"

"It says, 'TWO THINGS ARE MISSING OR SO IT SEEMS. WONDER IF YOU'RE GOING TO BE NEXT?' Oh my God."

And though my fingers were shaking, I dialed 911. When the operator asked me what my emergency was, the dam burst and tears spilled from my eyes. "Somebody stole my car."

By the time I had finished explaining that my car was stolen as a warning, I filed the report, checked on my kids who were at my parents' house, and got Ruben to follow Monique's car to the condo, my nerves were truly destroyed. The police had tried to run a trace on the phone number, but were quickly able to tell that the message had come from a prepay cell phone.

We sat in Monique's car waiting for my house to be checked for intrusion as Ruben entered the house with his gun drawn. Fear had me in a vice grip. I had decided to leave the children at my parents' house because I feared for their safety. I knew my parents would make sure they got to school the next day.

"We should have called Justice. She would have come back to the restaurant and waited with us," Monique stated.

Justice worked at Detroit Memorial as a nurse and had to

work a double shift starting at five in the morning. I shook my head. "No, it's already after one. I'll call her tomorrow."

"Are you sure you don't want to stay at your parents' house with the kids or at Alicia's or at my place tonight?" Monique had already asked me that twice before, and I had declined.

"No. Ruben is staying the night. I feel safe with him. I'm not sure who sent that text or what kind of person they are, but I don't want to put anybody else in danger. They stole my car from a public place. If they meant to scare the heck out of me, it worked." I exhaled because my chest felt labored.

Ruben came to the door and gave the thumbs up signal.

As I got out of her car, I said to my friend, "Monique, please call me when you get home so I know you made it there safely."

"You're the one that has to worry about your safety."

"Still, call me."

"I will." She waved good-bye as she watched me enter the house.

Ruben was sitting on the arm of one of my chairs when I walked into the living room. "I can't believe somebody is after you."

"I can't either. It's insane," I agreed.

"We're going to find out who's doing this," he assured me.

"I hope so. I would blame Khalil, but he's incarcerated. I can't think of anybody else who would have it out for me."

He took off his gun holster and placed it on the coffee table. "Maybe he has an accomplice. You can never tell in these types of situations. I think after you've had a good night's rest, we can try to make a list of possible suspects other than him, even if it's just people connected to him."

"You're probably right." I rolled my neck. Fatigue settled over my body. "Ruben, you have no idea how grateful I am to you for staying here tonight. You have been way too accommodating. I almost feel like I'm taking advantage of your kindness. And I really wish things could have worked out between you and my sister. I already feel as close to you as I do my brother."

"Some relationships work and some don't. I wanted to be with Alicia, but she made a different choice."

"You mean Phillip? As if that was meant to work out. They don't have anything in common, and he's not even half the man you are. You are a rare breed. She messed up when she let you go. Trust me, I rallied in your corner, but Alicia can be unreasonably stubborn." I was rambling because I was tired, but I wanted him to know that he was one of the good guys in every sense of those words.

Ruben got off the arm of the chair and sat on the sofa as he took his shoes off. "Thanks, Celia, for the compliments. It's too bad your sister doesn't share your sentiments. I hope you don't mind if I get a little more comfortable."

"Of course not. As a matter of fact, let me get you some towels and a blanket."

I went into the bathroom and took out the prescription bottle of Ambien that was given to me weeks ago by my doctor for the insomnia. I swallowed two extended release capsules with a swig of water from a gargle cup. Collecting a face cloth, bath towel, and blue picnic blanket, I brought them back to Ruben. My head was thumping like a marching band, and I was dead on my feet.

"I hope this blanket will be good enough, I don't have any others here. I usually keep the temperature set at around seventy. I'm going to sleep. Once again, thanks." I headed back to my bedroom and kicked off my shoes. I closed the door and lay across the bed fully clothed. I thought about Tyrese and missed his presence. He should have been here. I wished he was in Detroit instead of Houston. I wished I was in Houston instead of Detroit. I didn't want to go through all that was happening without him.

I heard the rustle of trees against my windowpane and it made my heart jump. I got back up and opened the bedroom door wide. I was entirely tired and fearful at the same time as my head hit the pillow. Sleep won out.

CHAPTER TWENTY-TWO

ALICIA

The sign read Regular Unleaded: $3.29 as Alicia shaded her eyes against the sun. "What is up with the gas prices? President Obama was supposed to hook us up. Does he have stock in the oil companies too?" Alicia balked at the Petro gas station up the street from her Eastpointe home.

Getting into her Nissan Milan, she turned on her car and watched the gas hand move to the line right past a quarter tank. That would get her to work, but not anywhere else. She glanced inside her ash tray where spare change was kept. With more copper than silver coins jammed in the small compartment, Alicia shoved it closed. She tapped her fingers against the steering wheel as she stared at the Villa Pizzeria restaurant across the street.

"I've heard of penny pinching, but this is ridiculous. I just shouldn't be this broke," she told herself. In her mind, Alicia cursed Eric for stopping child support payments after a sixteen year court free arrangement. She had a mind to go down to the Friend of Court and request that her monthly payments be reestablished. Eric didn't know how much it cost to raise a kid. He assumed all he needed to do was buy clothes and birthday gifts. He had another thing coming if he thought she was going to stay with that program.

Heading down Gratiot Avenue, Alicia decided to make a detour and go borrow a hundred dollars from Celia. It was a forty minute drive from Gratiot to Ramblewood Club Drive, but worth the trip not to be broke. A little extra cash would keep her from stressing over money until payday the following Friday.

When Alicia got home that night she would have to rethink her budget. Maybe she didn't need to spend four dollars on a Mocha Latte from Starbucks every morning. But then again, if she didn't have her coffee first thing, she would be snapping at everybody in her department. She could possibly get her hair done twice a month instead of going to the salon for weekly deep-conditioning treatments. Alicia didn't know if she could make that sacrifice either.

Alicia called her job to let her supervisor, Manning, know she was running late. He didn't have a problem with it. Dialing Celia's cell number, her call went directly to voice mail. Alicia got on I-696 and headed west anyway. Celia had to be at home. The clock on the dashboard read 8:27 A.M. Caleb and Kaleia would be dropped off by now, and Celia never worked at the office on a Friday.

Betrayed, jealous, hurt . . .

A thousand emotions seeped through Alicia when Ruben opened the front door of Celia's home in a wrinkled gray T-shirt, unbuttoned pants, and bare feet. If she didn't know better, she would have thought somebody was taping an episode of Maury Povich's talk show; the episode in which a sister found out that her identical twin had been sleeping with her ex-boyfriend behind her back.

"What are you doing here? No, don't answer that," she raged, pushing him back with her hand pressed to his chest. "How could you do it? Or better yet, how long have you been doing it? And with my sister of all people? What . . . of the many women available out here, you couldn't find one that I wasn't related to? Or since you couldn't have me you decided to get with the next best thing? My twin . . . really . . . my twin? How could you be any more scandalous?"

She shot questions at Ruben like bullets in a war zone as she poked her finger in his chest while they stood in the hallway. Alicia didn't know who she should have been more upset with, Ruben or Celia. Both of them needed to be blasted out for what they had done. And the kids must have just gone to school, so they had to know Celia and Ruben were together. She was surprised that Kaleia hadn't told her about their escapades when she spent the night last weekend.

"It's not what you think." Ruben held his hands in the air innocently like any other explanation would make sense.

Faking innocence instead of confessing and apologizing only infuriated Alicia. She wasn't trying to hear his excuses. She had hoped he was better than that. Although she didn't trust any man completely, deep down she still wanted to believe Ruben was the sweet, caring, highly moral individual he claimed to be. The supremely nice guy she'd dated, and until that moment, regretted letting go. Just by opening the front door he had fallen into the cesspool status with every other lying, cheating, and dishonorable male walking the face of the earth. That, as far as she was concerned, consisted of ninety percent of the population. It never ceased to amaze Alicia what a man would lie about. The truth could be standing right next to them singing guilty in soprano and a man would swear the sound was an apparition, or better yet, fake ignorance. When all else fails, deny, deny, and deny.

"It's not what I think? Oh, yeah, that one's classic, Ruben. Don't insult me. Is Celia still in bed? Did you wear her out?" Alicia stormed past Ruben through the living room. Her heels clicked rapidly against the travertine kitchen floor like a percussive tap dance. Before she made it to her sister's bedroom, strong arms lifted her in the air and pulled her backward.

"Chill out!" Ruben demanded. "She's already had a rough night. She doesn't need you adding to it."

Alicia was astonished by his aggression and swiftness.

Ruben didn't place Alicia down until they were back in the living room, where he dropped her on the sofa. "If you stop jumping to conclusions and listen for a minute, you can find out what's going on." Spurts of red flushed his tan face. An angry scowl stretched across his forehead. He was breathing heavily.

Alicia didn't know what to think, but she calmed down.

"Her car was stolen last night."

"Oh."

"And somebody threatened her. The same person that took her car sent her a message on her cell phone. They said she could be missing too. She called me because she didn't feel safe. She stayed at my police station until I got off work because she was scared to go home and scared to go anywhere else."

Guilt over her assumption and impulsiveness hit Alicia. "Oh."

He was incensed, his Spanish dialect became thick. "Oh? That's all you're going to say? You had plenty to say a minute ago when you thought I was sleeping with your sister. Gosh, Alicia, you have got to stop jumping to conclusions about people and thinking everybody is out to do wrong."

"It was an easy assumption. I mean, I come over to my sister's house first thing in the morning, and my ex answers the door half dressed. What was I supposed to think?" Alicia reasoned.

"You should have given me more credit than that. You should have given Celia more credit." Ruben sat down next to her and rubbed his forehead.

"I can't believe she slept through my shouting a minute ago. She usually is a light sleeper. Do you think she's okay?"

"Yeah, she's fine. I saw a full bottle of Ambien sitting on the bathroom sink. She must have taken a pill or two."

"Why would somebody threaten her? Why would somebody steal her car? Celia isn't the type to make enemies easily. If they have her phone number, it must be somebody who she knows."

Ruben put his black socks back on. "Oh, it's personal. That, I don't doubt."

"I'm still in shock. We see stuff like this at the station all the time, but it's a completely different thing when it hits home." Alicia briefly thought of Larika's response to Jaquan being arrested. Separate situations that brought all kinds of frustration.

"Morning," Celia croaked. Her long hair was matted and the clothes she wore reminded Alicia of a Michigan road map. "Ruben, did you call Alicia over here?"

"Wasn't me," he replied.

"Did Dad call you?" Celia asked.

"I didn't know what happened until I got here. Why didn't you call me?" Alicia responded.

Celia gnawed at her bottom lip. "It didn't cross my mind to call you."

Sympathy tugged at Alicia. "Are you okay?"

"No." Celia scratched her collar bone. "I'm going to go take a shower real quick if you don't mind."

"Sure. Go ahead." Alicia wondered how she could have considered for a moment that Celia would sleep with Ruben.

"We will be here." Ruben placed his hands on his knees.

"Where are Kaleia and Caleb? Did you take them to school?" Alicia asked after she heard the shower running.

Ruben leaned back against the sofa and rubbed his head again. "No, they spent the night at your parents'. I don't know if your folks took them to school or not."

"I know my dad has got to be going out of his mind over this. I'm surprised he let her come home."

"I doubt that he knows everything. I think Celia only told them that the car was stolen, not the part about the threatening text message."

"That kind of information shouldn't be hidden from them. They need to know if one of their children is in danger. Celia can get secretive at the wrong time. It's just like when she left Khalil. It took awhile before she decided to explain why she left him, and by that time, he had smooth talked our mother into his back pocket."

"Could be that she thinks omitting information will protect them."

"Sounds twisted up to me. Celia thinks she is Superwoman and can conquer the world by herself."

Ruben shrugged. "I should throw something together for breakfast. Do you think she would mind?"

"Probably, but do it anyway."

They both went into the kitchen. Alicia set her purse down and opened the refrigerator while Ruben searched for pots.

"We have eggs beaters, turkey ham, shredded cheese, green onion, and milk. All the makings for an omelet."

Ruben placed a skillet on the stove's eye. "What about butter?"

"Celia doesn't use butter. She is anti-trans fats. You won't find much of anything in here to clog your arteries. If you check that cabinet behind you, there should be some extra virgin olive oil."

He pulled it out and set the bottle on the counter.

Celia came out of the bathroom as they placed the food on plates. She was dressed in a dark green turtleneck sweater and black slacks. Her face was freshly scrubbed, and her long hair pulled back in a ponytail.

"Come eat with us." Alicia pointed to a plate with a small square of omelet. She knew Celia didn't eat when she was upset, but she hoped her sister would try to digest a little bit of food.

"Thanks." Celia pulled out a chair and slid into it. The brown globes of Celia's eyes looked distant as she glanced at Alicia.

Ruben began to talk as they sat around the table. "I was thinking last night that we should write down all the people who know you are looking for Desiree and another list of individuals that have your cell phone. Through a process of elimination, we should be able to narrow down our potential suspects."

Celia cleared her scratchy voice. "I'm home based. I use my cell phone for business and personal calls. Quite a few people have my number. On the other hand, very few know that I've been asking about a missing child. Our parents, staff at Kettering High School and the Board of Education, Mr. Carpenter, Monique, Justice, and the three of us. Then there's Khalil. I just saw him four days ago at the prison. He wasn't happy that I questioned him about Desiree. He could have hired somebody to shut me up. He may be locked up, but he still has resources."

Alicia felt out of the loop. Celia hadn't told her that she

was even thinking about going to see Khalil. She would have tried to talk her sister out of making contact with that lunatic. Alicia had few kind words to say about Khalil. "I don't see Khalil being that sloppy. Especially if you just saw him. The obvious road would be back to him. If he didn't like you asking questions about Desiree, he sure wouldn't have a message sent to you referring to her in any way. I may call him sick, twisted, and perverted, but I can't call him stupid."

Celia shook her head. "Prison changes people. He may not be as sharp as he used to be."

Ruben's fork clinked against his porcelain plate. "Alicia, you do have a point. Celia, due to your history, if he weren't locked up, he would be the main suspect. Drawing unwanted attention to himself doesn't sound logical though."

Alicia balked, "We're placing logic and Khalil in the same sentence? Well, I hope that both of you are right."

Celia got up from the table leaving her omelet square perfectly formed and untouched. "Let me start writing down the list of contacts in my phone." She returned less than a minute later. "Have either of you seen my purse?"

"You didn't leave it in your car did you?" Alicia inquired, finishing her omelet.

"No, I had my purse at the police station while I was waiting for you, Ruben. My cell phone was in it, because that's how they tried to run the trace on the text message. I can't remember where I placed it after that." Celia turned and searched the room with her eyes.

Ruben suggested, "Maybe you left it with your girlfriend."

"You know, I think I did leave it in her car. I need to call Monique."

Alicia's purse sat on the kitchen counter. She reached in it and pulled out her cell phone. Handing the phone to Celia, she remarked, "I was wondering why you didn't answer your phone this morning."

"I was a mess last night. I would have lost my head if it weren't attached to my body," Celia admitted as she began punching digits on Alicia's phone.

Ruben remarked to Alicia, "There is no way to stay in a right mind when somebody is threatening your life. I'm just glad that I could be around to make sure this house was safe. I'm going to try and keep tabs on Celia and the kids until we find out who is responsible for stealing her car and threatening her.

After talking with Monique, Celia had another request. "Would one of you mind driving me to Monique's job? She was going to bring it by the house after she got off work, but I want to get started on that list. She only works about twenty miles from here."

"I'm running on fumes right now. That's why I came by. I needed gas money." Alicia hated to admit that, considering the circumstances. "I wish I could take you, but we wouldn't get very far."

Ruben stood up from the table and offered, "Celia, I don't mind taking you over there. Alicia, if you want to ride with us, I can stop and get you some gas money."

Alicia was appreciative of his kindness. He didn't have to do that, especially after her accusation. The more she was around Ruben, the more she regretted how badly she'd treated him during their break-up.

CHAPTER TWENTY-THREE

KALEIA

"What is the Great Wall of China?" Grandma Pat blurted out.

Kaleia sat between her grandmother and Caleb sulking. Her grandfather was in a recliner laid back asleep. Her plans were being ruined as she was forced to watch *Jeopardy* at her grandparents'. It was the first game of state championships for Montgomery, and she'd promised Tevin that they would go out afterward. She had to break that promise.

The first night Kaleia had to stay there wasn't so bad because she and Caleb had both worn uniforms. It wasn't like people would know she had the same clothes from the night before and her grandmother had washed their things. Two nights at her grandparents' was too much, and it only made Kaleia more miserable that her friends were having fun without her.

She was desperate enough to ask her grandmother to take her knowing that Grandma Pat would sit next to her the entire game. But at least then she wouldn't be stuck in the house. Kaleia's mother had called earlier to tell them they would have to spend another night due to her car being stolen. Celia had picked up a rental car, but wanted to make sure it was safe for them to go home. Kaleia asked Celia if she could spend the night at Aunt Alicia's house, but she was told her aunt had limited funds and needed her money to get back and forth to work next week. Over an hour ago, Kaleia had sent a text message to Taija begging her cousin to come rescue her, and she still hadn't heard back. Taija had a habit of not answering her phone or texts when she was with Change.

"What is Rowanda?" Her grandmother blurted out another answer at the television; that one about genocide in Africa.

Caleb sat next to Kaleia zoned out with his Nintendo DS. Kaleia sat texting all her friends in hopes that somebody would keep her from maxing out in boredom. Megan texted the score as first quarter ended. It was twenty-four to sixteen. Montgomery was in the lead.

The smell of freshly baked cookies drifted into the family room. Her Grandma Pat stood up to go check on the cookies.

Kaleia jumped up too. "Can I help?" she eagerly asked her grandmother. Anything was better than sitting in front of the television watching Alex Trebek give trivia questions.

"Of course, sweetheart."

They walked into the L-shaped kitchen, and Grandma Pat stuffed her hands into a pair of kitchen mittens.

As the cookie sheet was placed on the black granite kitchen island, Kaleia's taste buds salivated. No one could mix a batch of chocolate chip cookies like her grandmother.

Snapping a paper towel off the wall dispenser, Kaleia set it alongside a glass platter. She picked up the spatula and began loosening sweet spheres from the cookie sheet and gently moved them to the platter. "Grandma, why do you like watching *Jeopardy?*" she asked.

Grandma Pat fixed her gray eyes on Kaleia with amazement. "It sharpens my knowledge of world events and history. It also makes me feel extremely smart."

Her grandmother smiled, and Kaleia could see the strong genes her mother inherited. Except for the exotic grey eyes, her mom and Aunt Alicia looked just like her. The only thing that they had gotten from Grandpa Otis was the brown in their oval eyes.

"*Jeopardy* is one of the longest running game shows on television. I've been watching *Jeopardy* since your mother was that tall." Her grandmother held her hand about three feet from the ground.

"I mean, what's the point of that information?"

Her grandmother proudly answered while pouring a glass of milk. "Learning is fundamental. Don't they teach that in school? The world is full of interesting knowledge that should be absorbed. Even when you get my age you should still want to learn new things."

"Yeah. I guess I understand," Kaleia said, with very little confidence.

The glass of milk was placed in front of her.

"At your age, you are probably into that Hannah Montana or *High School Musical*. I bet you're interested in those teen movies."

"Hannah's all right. I wouldn't buy her music or anything. I'm more into activities like the basketball championship at my school tonight."

"Kaleia, I would have taken you, but the game ends after my bedtime, and I wouldn't have wanted to drive back here tired. As you see, your grandfather is already asleep, so neither one of us could have stayed with you. Once your mom gets this thing straightened out about her car, I'm sure she will make sure that you get to the rest of those games."

"Grandma." Kaleia bit into another cookie. "You don't hate Daddy as much as Mom does, do you?"

Kaleia didn't know what made her decide to ask the question. It must have been at the back of her mind.

"I don't know if your mother would approve of this conversation. She is very particular about your dad." Kaleia noticed that Grandma Pat seemed to pick her words carefully.

"Maybe not, but you don't dislike Daddy?"

"No, I don't. Your dad is just as much a part of this family as you are. I love him because I still consider him my son-in-law, and I think for the most part, he is a good man."

Kaleia was relieved to hear that. "Did you know that Caleb is allowed to get letters from Daddy and send him things, but I'm not?"

"Yes. Your mother believes she is protecting you."

"But I don't need to be protected. He is in prison and can't hurt anybody. It's not fair that Caleb can communicate with him, but I'm not even given the option."

"Maybe that is something you should tell your mother."

"She doesn't want to hear me; she just wants to fix me."

"What do you mean, *fix you*? What's wrong with you?" Her grandmother frowned as she placed three cookies on a saucer.

Kaleia wanted to bite her tongue. Her grandmother didn't know about the cuts, and that wasn't something she wanted to share. "Nothing. She just doesn't understand me."

"Well, I'll let you in on a secret." She leaned toward Kaleia like she had something topnotch confidential to share. "I didn't understand any of my kids when they were teenagers, and I really don't understand the things they do now. Alicia is a true mystery to me, but I love her just the same. And I'm sure that goes the same for your mother with you."

"If I gave you a letter I wrote to Daddy, would you make sure he gets it?" Kaleia had written many letters since his incarceration. Most of them she'd ripped up before her mother could find them, but there was one that she kept.

"I wish I could, but there is enough tension between your mother and me about Khalil, and I don't want to add anymore." Grandma Pat picked up the saucer and glass of milk. "I'm going to take this to your brother before his cookies get cold. Did you have anything else on your mind, because I can come back into the kitchen if you want?"

Kaleia was dejected about the letter, but didn't show it. "No. That was it."

"Sweetheart, you should talk to your mother. Celia isn't as bad as you think she is."

Of course Grandma Pat would say that. Kaleia just didn't agree.

Kaleia's cell phone chirped. Trina had texted her again. Second quarter had ended. Tevin had four three-pointers. The score was forty-eight to thirty-nine with Montgomery still winning.

Kaleia could imagine the excitement in the auditorium. She was missing out. It wasn't fair. It just wasn't fair.

CHAPTER TWENTY-FOUR

ME

All that remained of my vehicle was a charred hub left in a scrap yard near the Detroit River.

Officer Jackson was a short, lanky man the color of a coconut shell who was kind enough to walk me through the area where they had my car towed.

"Looks like they stripped out the catalytic converter, motor, transmission, battery, and radiator. They took just about everything to make it tick before it was burned out. More than likely, the parts were sold on the black market," the officer told me.

I had received the call about the Jag being found a week and a half after I reported it stolen. I was at the office conducting a training seminar for initiating global marketability with the release of our new mini-spy cams. I, along with several other staff from SecureTech, had been trying out the prototypes at our houses for months and found a glitch in the sensors.

"But I had a state-of-the-art alarm system. There is no way they should have been able to steal this car as easily as they did. And it was in a parking lot in broad daylight. People were coming in and out of the restaurant the entire time we were sitting inside. Plus, windows faced the parking lot. I don't understand how somebody didn't notice a thief carrying a LoJack," I explained to Officer Jackson.

"It had to be a professional job. Thieves nowadays don't necessarily care about LoJacks. They've upgraded to laptops that can deprogram your car. Once they are inside your vehicle, nobody notices that they are stealing it. Why would they? It's terrible that you got the shaft in all of this, but the truth of the matter is there is a serious market for stolen parts."

My brown shoes crunched against the pebbled gravel in the scrap yard. As I circled the heap of metal that used to be my means of transportation, I felt violated. "I can see stealing it, but why destroy the whole car? Why set it on fire?" My question was hypothetical. I knew why. The culprit wanted me to know that not only could I be made to disappear, but my charred unrecognizable body could be left behind too.

"Yeah, I don't see a lot of that. I'm not sure why they decided to set the car on fire."

Before I made myself ill thinking about the charred hub, I explained to the officer, "I've seen enough. Thank you for letting me see the car. I truly wouldn't have believed how bad the damage was if I hadn't seen it with my own eyes."

I left the scrap yard in Taija's Honda Accord. I flipped my cell phone open and called Tyrese.

"Hello, beautiful, I'm glad to see your number come across my screen." He sounded cheerful.

I smiled at the sound of his voice. We'd only talked several times a week since he'd left, but I missed him a little bit more each time we spoke. "Hey. How are things going with your project?"

"We're behind schedule with the renovation, and there have been additional labor costs that weren't expected. But I'll cut corners where I can and get things done. What's going on there?"

"They found my car," I said solemnly.

"That's great, right?"

I wished his cheerfulness could rub off on me.

"Not so great." I sighed. "It was stripped and destroyed. The officer believes thieves sold the parts on the black market. I barely recognized it. Tyrese, how could people be so cruel and disrespectful?"

"Some people weren't raised with appropriate values, and let's face it, the economy is bad. People are desperate."

"I suppose." I hadn't told him about the text warning. He would have halted his project to see about me, and I was still undecided on what I wanted us to be in the future.

"Are you still driving your rental car?"

"Yes. The insurance company processed my claim, but it was for a lot less than I expected. I haven't decided what kind of vehicle I want to buy with the money. I've test driven a few, but haven't found one that is affordable and that I love. I'm certain that it won't be another Jag. I may use the money as a nice down payment and end up with a car note. I've been thinking that maybe I need something that's a little more family friendly, and I have to consider Kaleia. She's got her permit and soon she will want her own vehicle. I can't do two car payments on my income. Kaleia and I may end up sharing my next car."

"I can get you a car if you want one. You don't have to share a vehicle with your daughter."

"No, because then I would feel like I owe you. I can handle a car purchase."

A crackling noise vibrated from his background.

"What is that sound?" I asked as I headed home.

"I'm on the construction site. That is a jackhammer you hear. Listen, I need to go over a blueprint. Why don't I call you tonight?"

"Okay, I'll talk to you then." I prepared to press the button on my Bluetooth.

"Hey, Celia?" His voice stopped my hand.

"Yes, Tyrese?"

"I love you." That was the first time he'd said those words since he left. I could hear him waiting for my response. I knew he was anticipating what my response would be.

I bit my bottom lip. "Okay. We'll talk soon." I cared. I cared so much that it scared me, and because of my fear, I couldn't bring myself to say 'I love you' back.

When I got home I pulled the two lists that I had created out of a notebook in my dresser and set them on the bed. In less than an hour I would have to pick up the kids from school, and I hadn't put a lot of energy into narrowing down names. Probably because I was sure that Khalil set things up to scare me, and my list probably had little relevance.

Immediately I slashed through Alicia, Monique, Tyrese, Ruben, Justice, and my parents' names. There was no way that my closest family and friends had anything to do with stealing and destroying my car. Scrolling my finger down the list, I stopped at Mr. Carpenter's name. I circled it. I couldn't say with all certainty that he didn't have anything to do with his daughter's disappearance. I would hope not, but stranger things had happened.

The only people left were the staff members at Kettering High and the Board of Education. I had spoken to so many people at the school, when I was trying to gather information, that I wouldn't remember all their faces, let alone names.

Setting my ink pen and notebook down, I bent over the edge of the bed and pulled the metal box from beneath it. On top was Desiree's missing poster. I set it aside and dumped out copies I had made of all the other pictures before I turned them in to the police. I scrambled them on my bed like I was figuring out an intricate jigsaw puzzle. Categories were created by poses. I searched for details in the pictures, such as similar backgrounds, ages, and looks. I rearranged photos by the color of the girls' complexion. Desiree's picture was placed with other young ladies with deep chocolate skin. There weren't that many. Only four appeared to be in her category. The rest shared many hues of brown, yellow, and tan. I saw just as many faces of Latino descent as I did African American.

"Besides being in this box," I asked the faces, "what do you have in common?"

If I found that answer, I truly believed I would find out what happened to Desiree.

CHAPTER TWENTY-FIVE

KALEIA

The pendulum on Dr. Malawi's desk swung to the left, and then it swung to the right. Kaleia's eyes followed the thin stick like she was mesmerized. Really she was avoiding conversation with the psychiatrist as she waited for her time in session to end. Unlike times before, when Dr. Malawi would allow her to do her homework until it was time to go, Celia had taken Kaleia's book bag and cell phone from her until after the meeting. This was the third session.

During her initial meeting, Kaleia refused to say anything. She had spent the hour staring out the window at a blue sky, silently playing hip-hop songs in her head to pass the time. Occasionally, Kaleia would hum to a tune she created, but she refused to talk. On the second trip to Dr. Malawi's office, there was a list of questions she was requested to answer. She was asked what her favorite color was and if she could be anywhere else in the world right at that moment where would that be? Of course she answered purple and Egypt amongst a bunch of other things. She supposed it was to get her comfortable, because Dr. Malawi didn't ask her to explain her answers. Dr. Malawi didn't request that she say much of anything out loud; only write it on the questionnaire. That session had gone by quickly.

This session Kaleia got to choose what she wanted to talk about. She chose her preferred subject. "People always talk about Cleopatra as the Queen of Egypt, but Nefertiti was just as powerful and beautiful a queen. There were statues of her all over Egypt, and she was known to be fiercely smart and fascinating. It's like women are supposed to be submissive and weak, but she wasn't. She ruled the kingdom alongside her husband."

"You like Nefertiti because she was strong?" Dr. Malawi placed her hands on the desk.

Kaleia smiled. "Yes. She wasn't defined by her husband or controlled by him. I like her because she was strong and mysterious. Nobody knows for sure her family heritage or when she was born. And nobody is sure how she died, but there is this great period of time between birth and death where she left her mark on a country. Nefertiti was known for her importance and her independence. That's why I like studying about her."

"Is that the kind of woman you want to be, strong and mysterious?" Dr. Malawi posed another question.

Kaleia thought about Taija and how her world revolved around Change. She thought about how Taija's attitude shifted when he came by. She adored her cousin, but knew she didn't want to be like her. Taija's attitude looked like a weakness, something Kaleia could never be happy with. Taija was so different from Aunt Alicia. Alicia had a fierceness that probably kept men from trying to misuse her. To Kaleia, her aunt was just as smart and brave as Nerfertiti.

Kaleia thought about church and how she heard one of the ministers preach about submission. The minister had said that wives were to cater to their husbands' needs, but he didn't say that husbands should cater to their wives. Kaleia thought that catering or submitting to any man other than God was wrong, because a man shouldn't be allowed to have control over his wife. Marriage should be equal. When her parents were still married, things looked equal between them. Khalil didn't control Celia. Kaleia didn't understand submission, and she didn't want a husband if she had to follow that rule of the Bible.

"I think so. I don't want to be controlled by rules and regulations or stuck on pleasing some boy. I want to be free to live however I choose."

Dr. Malawi was quiet. It appeared like she was waiting for Kaleia to say something else, but Kaleia had begun to focus on her surroundings.

Kaleia didn't like Dr. Malawi's office. It reminded her of Sister Agnes's paddle room in elementary. The place misbehaving children were taken to for punishment. It was where spankings were allowed. Kaleia only saw the paddle room when she was brave enough to peek inside with one of her friends, but she never had to be punished in there. That was a different story for one of her classmates in the third grade. Dwight Riggs went to the paddle room on a regular basis. He got in trouble for throwing spit balls, making faces behind the teacher's back when she was writing on the chalkboard, and using his boogers to create artwork on the textbooks. Kaleia used to think that he liked going to the paddle room, because he went at least once a week. With the beige plain walls covered in plaques, dark wood furniture, and leather chairs, the psychiatrist's office was too formal and unwelcoming. At least it was for a teenager.

"You don't feel free?" Dr. Malawi asked as she tried to keep Kaleia's attention.

"No. I live in a prison like box created by my mother. Caleb,

my mom, and me . . . we all live in it together. My mom believes
we will be safe if we stay in that box."

"What is that box made of?"

"Rules. Too many rules. Way too many rules." Kaleia brushed
her hands over her hair before changing the subject. "Did you
know that Nefertiti had six daughters? One of them died, but
she didn't have sons to pass down the kingdom to. And that
was around the time she disappeared. Her husband and king,
Akhenaten, married their daughter, Merytaten. It was acceptable for a father to marry his daughter."

Kaleia watched Dr. Malawi to see her reaction. She expected her to be shocked or disgusted like her mother, but the
blank gaze on the psychiatrist's face stayed.

"Kaleia, what do you think about a father marrying his daughter?"

"I don't think it's as terrible as people make it out to be.
I mean, it's wrong, but I don't know how wrong. There are
different ways to love somebody and show affection. My dad
loves me differently than some other dads love their daughters.
He used to tell me that our love was special." She felt herself
opening up. She felt the need to get it out. The less she felt
judged, the more she wanted to talk.

"Do you regret that your father went to prison for loving you?"
Dr. Malawi asked yet another question.

"Yes. I feel bad that I'm the reason he was sent there. I wanted us to love each other without him touching me like he did. I
thought my mom would be happy because she took the whole
thing very hard, but I didn't want him to go to prison," Kaleia
admitted.

Kaleia remembered her father sitting in the stands at her
swim meets. He always wore the same gray sweatshirt that
said 'We Rule' in blue letters. When she won, he would give

her a hug, and when she lost, he still gave her that hug. And afterward they would go to McAllister's Frozen Treats for two scoops of mint chocolate chip ice cream in a sugar cone. She felt protected by her father. She felt loved, and even though he showed that love differently than some other dads, Khalil was the best father he knew how to be. Khalil Alexander had been a constant in her life, and now that was no more.

"Kaleia, why do you think you cut yourself?" asked Dr. Malawi out of the blue.

There it was . . . the golden question that had been beaten around and jumped over for the last few sessions.

The first time she cut herself was on the day of her father's sentencing. Caleb wasn't allowed to go. Kaleia particularly had to beg for the last chance to see her father. There was a snowstorm. Wet flakes pelted the windshield. Celia didn't want to be late to court, but drove extra slow through the ice patched streets. The entire way there her mother kept telling her how proud she was of Kaleia for doing the right thing and how she was a role model for other girls that had gone through the same experience. Kaleia wanted to believe what her mother was saying, but she felt this emptiness that grew bigger as they got close to the courthouse. And when her daddy looked at her after they ruled seven to twelve years, Kaleia felt intense sadness and a variety of other emotions she didn't understand. She wanted to scream, but she couldn't. She wanted to cry, but she couldn't. Instead, she went into the bathroom and sat on a toilet. It was in the bathroom at the courthouse where she pulled out the pack of razors she used to shave her legs before a swim meet. That's when she learned a new kind of relief.

Dr. Malawi repeated the question. "Why do you think you cut yourself?"

Kaleia shrugged her shoulders feeling herself shutting down, no longer interested in talking."I don't know."

"Do you feel good or bad after you do it?"

"I don't know." She wished there was a clock on a wall, so she could see what time it was. The session seemed longer than an hour.

"How long have you been practicing that?"

"I don't remember."

Defiance demanded Kaleia keep her thoughts intact.Dr. Malawi tried to tap into her recesses, but Kaleia wasn't ready to let her.

"Don't you want to find another way to do things that won't hurt so much?"

"I suppose."

"What do you think will happen if you actually shared your thoughts with me?"

Kaleia felt a sting within her that made her decide to answer that one. "I think that you will tell my mother, and she will want to send me away, just like she wanted my daddy to go away."

Dr. Malawi stared at Kaleia with unblinking eyes. "Why do you say that? Where would you go?"

"To a white fluffy room where they wrap you in a nice little jacket so you can hug yourself all day." Kaleia placed her arms around herself and squeezed hard in imitation.

Dr. Malawi asked, "You think your mother wants to have you committed?"

Kaleia tilted her head to the side and thought that over before answering. "No, I think she wants me to be a perfect angel that has no problems. But since I can't be that angel, since she can't fix me, she would have me committed."

Kaleia said it with no hesitation, because she believed it wholeheartedly.

"Can I share what I think for a moment, Kaleia?"

"I guess." Kaleia shrugged her shoulders again with indifference.

"I've met moms that don't care. Your mom doesn't come across as that type. I think that if your mother really wanted you committed, she wouldn't have brought you here. Therapy is to prevent that from happening. I've talked with your mom, and she wants what is best for you. It's not easy being a parent. They make mistakes. You believe that your dad was being the best father he knew how to be. Wouldn't that also apply to your mother? Could it be that she is doing all that she is capable of?"

Kaleia hadn't really thought about it like that. She knew her mother tried to be understanding, but growing up, Kaleia always felt closer to her father. Her mother worked a lot of hours and traveled, so that didn't allow for them to spend quality time together. When they did do things as a family, including bowling, trips to the movies, and skating, it had to be scheduled around her mother's work hours; even their family vacations were scheduled six months to a year in advance. Everything was scheduled with her mother. Not to say things weren't arranged with her father, but he seemed to be the fun parent that was always accessible. Kaleia could call him at work and he would give her his full attention. Before her mother started working from home, Kaleia would call her at the office, and the receptionist would put her on hold, sometimes for ten minutes while her mother tried to wrap up conversations on other calls. It didn't make Kaleia feel like she was important or that what she called for mattered.

"I just don't feel close to her. I want to be, but I finally accepted that we wouldn't have the same kind of relationship like I did with my father."

Dr. Malawi leaned forward in her chair, "Now Kaleia, I am going to ask you another question, but I want you to give me your most honest answer without thinking too hard about it." There was a pause as Dr. Malawi stared into Kaleia's eyes, almost demanding her full attention. "Because you speak so highly about your father, do you think his actions are more forgivable than your mother's? Or to phrase the question a different way, are you more willing to forgive your father for not being perfect, because you get along better with him?"

Kaleia wrinkled her nose as if she had an itch. She fidgeted in her uncomfortable leather chair before answering. "Yes. I think I do."

Sighing with relief, Dr. Malawi placed a hand under her chin as she smiled. "See, Ms. Kaleia, I think we are making progress."

The session hadn't turned out like Kaleia expected, but somehow she felt better about talking with the psychiatrist. Suddenly it didn't feel like therapy, but instead like a regular conversation. She might be able to endure the sessions after all.

CHAPTER TWENTY-SIX

ME

"Would you be willing to go with me to speak with Shayla? I want to talk to her without her mother. I think she might be holding back information, because she doesn't want to get in trouble," Joseph Carpenter requested as he sat across from me inside Bistro, the little restaurant we decided would be the halfway mark meeting place between his home and mine. Mr. Carpenter and I had spoken on several occasions, but this was the first meeting since I initially showed up at his house to ask about Desiree's disappearance. Yesterday he called to tell me that he had something important to discuss with me, and he would rather talk in person.

"Desiree told Shayla about everything she did. The two of them never made plans without consulting one another. They were extremely close. I don't believe Desiree disappeared without at least giving some vague idea of where she was going. Maybe my daughter had a boyfriend she was seeing or possibly she could have been into something else. I'm not sure, but I want to try and find out. Too many years have gone by without any answers."

"Why do you need me there?" I asked, picking up a roasted almond from a little tray.

"Because I'm a man, and I'm Desiree's father, both of which can be intimidating." He clamped his hands on the edge of the table. "I think she will feel more comfortable with another female present. I was hoping that you could bring that other picture of Desiree with you to show Shayla."

He looked desperate; his eyes were pleading. I knew I couldn't tell him no in good conscience.

I swallowed the fear from the threat on my life when my car was stolen. I was the one that re-opened the door on Desiree's disappearance. I had been impassioned about finding out what happened to her. I had put a lot of my energy into going around asking questions about Desiree's character, her interest, and her activities. And most importantly, I had given Joseph Carpenter a grain of hope. Therefore, I needed to see things through despite the consequences. I prayed constantly and continually that God would protect me from any harm.

"When are we to meet her?" I felt myself choking as a sliver of almond became lodged in my throat. I frantically coughed as I got my airway passage free. "Whew."

"Are you okay?" Mr. Carpenter asked.

"Yes. There was an almond that seemed to go down the wrong pipe. Mr. Carpenter, I need you to understand that this isn't just hard for you. I also have a lot at stake." I had to think about my own children and how my investigating could cause more harm than good for them and for myself.

"Please call me Joseph. We should stop being so formal."

I nodded. "All right, I'll call you Joseph, and you can call me Celia." I felt a commonality between us. Both of us were single parents. I wondered if he felt like less of a parent because his child was missing.

"It must have been challenging to raise a daughter on your own. My son just hit puberty, and I'm at a loss on what to tell him about being a man; you know, about grooming himself. I can only assume you had to deal with that same difficulty," I said in sympathy.

A chorus of claps erupted from a booth nearby. A staff of five waitresses began to sing Happy Birthday. Joseph and I turned our heads to watch a man in his sixties get serenaded. The senior citizen blew out one candle atop a crowning bowl of ice cream cake while the younger woman, seated next to him in the booth, gleefully cheered.

I wondered if that was the old man's daughter. A pained look crossed Joseph's face as he turned to me. He probably wondered the same thing.

Joseph pulled off his work jacket. "Desiree had already started her thing . . . the um . . . cycle when Iris died. I was fortunate in not having to give her advice about that. All I did was keep maxi pads in the house. One time I brought tampons instead of the pads, and instead of telling me that I got the wrong thing, she left the unopened box on our kitchen counter. That next morning when I woke up it had a note on it that read 'Can't use these, please get a refund and buy Kotex.' She could have told me that I bought the wrong thing instead of leaving the note, but I guess she was embarrassed, or maybe she thought it would embarrass me, since I didn't know the difference in sanitary items. I made sure she had the right thing when she came home from school, but we didn't talk about it. Unfortunately, we weren't that close. Kind of like ships passing in the night."

It sounded like me talking about my children. Caleb, Kaleia, and I all had separate lives despite residing in the same home. If I didn't force them to be together at meal time or family activity night, both my children would be content hibernating in their individual bedrooms. When we went bowling several weekends back, they only got through one full game before I called it a night. It was like they were enduring torture. Kaleia even dropped her ball into somebody else's lane.

"I can relate," I replied.

"When she was home, I was at work, and when I was home, she was at school. It didn't leave a lot of room for conversation. We could have done things on the weekends, but I usually found one project or another to work on for those weekends. Most Sundays she went to church with her grandmother, Hattie. After Iris died, Desiree became pretty independent. I didn't think she needed me around for a lot."

It appeared that Joseph was feeling guilty at not being more active with Desiree. I knew that no matter how hard we tried to raise our children the right way and with the right influences, it would never be enough. We would regret all the things that we could've done better.

"You know, when our kids are little and cuddly, you never think that they will grow out of that phase of needing our constant attention. My son, Caleb, used to follow me around the house when he was a toddler. Whatever room I went into, he wasn't far behind. I remember having to use the bathroom one time and I saw him coming, but I shut the door anyway. He screamed so loud that I was certain I had slammed his fingers in the door. I quickly opened it and Caleb wrapped his chubby fingers around my leg. He did not want to let go." I chuckled to myself in memory of his Kung-Fu grip. "Now . . . if I can get his attention away from his Nintendo DS for more than ten minutes, I count myself lucky."

Joseph admitted, "I wish I could say Desiree was a Daddy's girl, but truth of the matter, I wasn't a very active father. I worked long hours and let Iris take care of Desiree. Once in a while I'd fall asleep on the lounger in front of the television and wake up to Desiree lying next to me. She had to be five or six, but those times were few and far between. Now Desiree and Iris definitely had a special bond. I regret not spending more time with my girls. That picture you saw of us, the one taken in the Bahamas, was the only vacation we had ever taken. I took both Iris and Desiree for granted. I took the time we shared as a family for granted. If I could go back, I'd do things differently."

"If only we could live retroactively, life would be grand. I've thought the very same way more times than I'd like to admit. We can't go backward though. We can only learn from the past and recover from our mistakes. I'm still learning to do that. The learning never seems to end."

Suddenly that hope I recognized when I first met Joseph showed on his face. "You are right, and when we find my daughter, I'm going to cherish every moment from then on."

A slow smile crept across my face. I tapped his folded hands with mine. "Now that's the spirit."

He smiled and the warmth reached his eyes. "Celia, how about now?"

I didn't understand what he was asking. My eyebrows scrunched in confusion. "How about what now?"

"Let's go talk with Shayla.It is barely noon. She has her last class period right now. By the time we get back across town she will be heading to her job at Burgers and More."

"How do you know her work schedule?" I asked, concerned that he knew so much about Shayla's daily activities.

Joseph put his work jacket back on before confessing. "I called the school and they gave me her school schedule. I kinda watched her this past week and noticed that Shayla went to work about the same time every day."

I couldn't hide my dismay. "That scares me that you were following her for a week."

Joseph nodded his head in acknowledgement. He was clearly embarrassed by his own actions. "I know it was wrong, but I don't have ill intentions. I just wanted to build up the courage to ask her more questions about Desiree. Celia, not knowing what happened to Desiree is killing me. I desperately need for us to talk with Shayla today."

"Considering what time it is now, that's cutting things close Mr. Car . . . um, Joseph."

"I promise that we won't be long."

"I have to pick up my son at a quarter 'til three and my daughter shortly after."

But with me working night hours, this is the only time we would be able to talk to Shayla in person. I think that if you show her the pictures and explain about your husband, maybe that will jog her memory. Or at least get her to tell us more than what she already has."

"I guess we can go," I stated. By agreeing I realized that I was placing my life at risk and for the briefest moment I wondered if my determination to find Desiree would cause my demise.

Burgers and More on Woodward Avenue had a truck stop diner feel with its white square tabletops and red vinyl backed chairs. The smell of deep fryer grease greeted me at the entrance. It rushed my senses like a linebacker at a field goal line. I could almost feel my arteries expanding with cholesterol as I fought back a queasy ting in my stomach.

"You sure you want to do it this way?" I asked Joseph, pulling out a chair with my back to the door. "We really should involve her mother in this."

I was worried that we were overstepping our boundaries. I didn't like going behind another parent's back to get information. I would have been furious to find out Kaleia had been approached in a similar manner. It could have been that I was a little scared, but the deeper I got into the search for Desiree, the more I felt like the police should be completely involved. Whatever information I did find out, I planned to share it with Ruben. My life had been threatened. I couldn't overlook that despite my passion for finding Desiree.

"Here she comes," remarked Joseph as the door opened behind me. A fair skinned girl with a shoulder length bobbed hair style, dressed in a green fitted shirt and white knickerbockers, walked past our table typing into her cell phone.

I gazed up, but I didn't want to seem obvious. She was oblivious to Joseph and me as she rapidly typed. I almost felt like a stalker providing unwanted attention. It was too easy to watch a person and learn their habits without them being none the wiser. Watching Joseph stand up almost on cue, I felt like I should have been alarmed that Joseph knew Shayla's schedule as well as he did, but I was tired of being suspicious of every man I came in contact with.

As Joseph brought Shayla over, I thought about what I could say that would make a difference.

"Shayla, this is Ms. Alexander. She wants to talk about Desiree."

The girl sat down at the table, and I noticed the sprinkle of freckles across her nose. "Hello," she said, looking from Joseph to me and back to him.

"Hello," I replied with a nod of my head.

The box of pictures was in my lap under the table. I placed the box in the middle of the table and opened it. I didn't want to waste time as Shayla would have to clock in soon, and I would need to go pick up Kaleia and Caleb.

"I'm not sure what Joseph told you about me, but I'm certain my ex-husband knew your best friend. I was hoping you could take a look and possibly give some clarity. Do you recognize the man in this photo?" I pulled out a family picture with Khalil, me, and the kids that I used to keep in my wallet when we were still married. It was a keepsake for the children. I had taken it out of the photo album at home and put it in the box this morning when Joseph called.

Shayla stared at my family smiling gleefully in our matching blue jean outfits. She shook her head. "He doesn't look familiar to me."

"What about this picture? Do you know when Desiree had this picture taken?" I slid the photograph of Desiree in her bikini next to the one Shayla had just looked at.

I watched Shayla chew on her bottom lip. "Um . . ." She seemed hesitant to reply.

"Please," Joseph begged. "It's very important."

"She had our friend Jeremy take it with his digital camera. Desiree said she was submitting it for an Internet modeling job with a local company. She did meet a man about the job, but I wasn't with her, so I don't know who he was or what he looked like. Desiree thought she was going to make a lot of money." Shayla paused as she continued to gnaw on her lip.

"There is more. What aren't you telling us?" I asked calmly.

Shayla turned to Joseph. "Mr. Carpenter, I really don't want to get in trouble over this now. Desiree told me to never tell anybody, and I don't think her job had anything to do with her disappearance."

He assured her, "You won't get in trouble. I promise you that. I need to know anything that you may have forgotten or was afraid to tell three years ago."

"YoungLuv. That was the name of the Internet company she was working for. I remember the name because I thought it was unique and ironic. It wasn't a modeling job like Desiree thought. It was more of a chat room where men had to pay to talk with girls. Desiree was paid a small fee for the number of men she spoke with."

"Was it like a sex chat line or a porn site?" Joseph asked, and I could see the anger beneath the surface. He was trying not to show it.

"No. I went on there with her a few times. The men would sometimes ask what she was wearing or the color of her nail polish, things like that. But she never uploaded nude pictures that I know of. It seemed pretty harmless."

"Harmless? What if she ended up meeting one of those men and that ends up being why she's missing? Chat rooms can be dangerous." Joseph rubbed his forehead like he had a migraine.

Shayla further explained, "They had safety rules with her job. The first rule was to never meet anybody from the site in person. It was grounds for automatic termination. Desiree told me that there were people hired with access to all the conversations. She called them chat monitors. They also had things that you weren't supposed to say that would let the men know where you lived at or went to school or worked."

"And you didn't tell us this back then?" Joseph said appalled. He was trying to keep his emotions in check, but was having a difficult time doing it.

Shayla profusely apologized. "Mr. Carpenter, I am sorry. So, so very sorry. I honestly didn't think it was important. I thought Desiree would be found. I thought she would come back home."

I listened to the hurtful truth from Shayla, and it validated the one thing I was certain of. It was the stories that were untold that could do the most harm.

CHAPTER TWENTY-SEVEN

KHALIL

Khalil sat at the back of the room that was used as a multi-denominational church. He listened to bits and pieces of the sermon by Chaplain Moore. He couldn't get over the conversation he had with his attorney an hour earlier.

"The appeal was denied by the parole board," Harvey Creed had told him.

Kaleia's testimony and the web cam video were the overall reasoning behind the denial. Over twenty thousand dollars sank into the toilet in attorney fees and for what? Nothing They had to go back to the drawing board. The next step would be to take the appeal to federal court.

He had the smell of freedom lingering in his nostrils up until that conversation with Harvey. His hacienda in Comala, Mexico was already paid off and ready for him to re-invent himself. It was the one opportunity for Khalil to live in a location that wouldn't classify or stigmatize him. It was where his criminal background wouldn't exist.

He had been hopeful and was told that if he stayed on good behavior, they would at least consider paroling him. Due to the overcrowding of prisons, the state was looking for reasons to release individuals. Khalil hadn't expected a denial. He didn't think he could endure four more years at Kinross.

He bent over with frustration and wrung his hands as he tried to think up a new plan. The first thing he would need to do was find an attorney that would assure better results.

"Freedom up here is half the battle." Ezra pointed to his temple, right below his fading hairline as he sat on the pew in front of Khalil.

Unbeknownst to Khalil the room had started to clear. "What?" Khalil questioned, sitting back up.

Rarely did he find himself in the company of Ezra. A self proclaimed prophet, Ezra seemed to always be the first one in the church and the last to leave. On many occasions, Ezra would be left in charge of the prison ministry by Chaplain Moore. Once in a while Khalil led the prison group in prayer, but he tried to stay to himself as much as possible.

"I heard you on the phone earlier. You didn't get your appeal hearing."

"The least the parole board could have done was allow me to state my case." Khalil felt if the opportunity availed itself, he could show that he wasn't a threat to society.

"How much time do you have until you're officially up for parole?"

"Four years, but I don't deserve to be here that long."

"You talk to any man in Kinross and they will tell you that they don't deserve to be here," Ezra stated humbly. "And I'm telling you again freedom in your head is half the battle. True deliverance is releasing yourself from your negative thoughts."

Khalil asked Ezra, "What are you in for?"

"Seven counts of robbery. I've been here eleven years. Got fourteen more before I'm up for parole. Me and four other cats used to rob people's homes. We hit exclusive neighborhoods all over East Michigan. We stole everything electronic that wasn't bolted down, plus jewelry, toys, and clothes. I didn't consider it stealing. It was called taking property. The word 'stealing' made me accountable, and I wasn't interested in being accountable. We kept a few things for our own homes, but made a fortune in our neighborhood with the sale of boosted items. Things were going great until one of my guys got shot during a sting operation. Salem was leaving out of the patio door of a home he had broken into when he was killed by the owner of the house. They had come back early from a vacation and caught us off guard as we scrambled to get out of there. The police matched us by association to Salem and hidden cameras at the home that caught our faces on tape. The police matched me and two of the guys with crimes we committed back in the eighties when we were doing sloppy work. Salem's sister, Dayna, had turned us in. She testified against us. We all grew up together. It was like being shot in the face by your best friend."

As Khalil listened to Ezra, he remembered the day the police showed up at his house after Kaleia called them. He couldn't believe she had him arrested, and he was even more shocked that she had taped it. When she testified against him it broke a part of his spirit. They had a special love and on that witness stand she denounced that love. It wasn't that Khalil didn't acknowledge that their affection was in some ways wrong, but it was affection he received from his own mother after the death of his father. It was consolation during grief that forever bonded him to his mother. Even after she left him to be raised by an aunt, Khalil still remembered his mother's closeness. It was a bond that he couldn't help but share with Kaleia.

Ezra continued talking. "I came in at thirty-two years old. The first couple of years were rough. I had to fight through the bitterness of being here and being angry with Dayna. There is nothing worse than being held in bondage by someone else's action. I started reading and got my GED. When I joined the prison ministry I began reading Bible scriptures and writing them down. One day I saw my name in there. I didn't realize my purpose until I read the books of Ezra and Nehemiah. When I took the focus off why I was here and how long, I discovered my purpose and peace of mind. You have to learn to do the same thing."

"Fighting to get out of here is what keeps me going. I didn't realize it would be this hard to get an appeal. I have the money to fight this, but things aren't working out."

"But if you know you did it, why reverse the decision?" Ezra inquired.

Khalil looked across the pew and didn't have an answer. What he thought was a good reason didn't sound right or feel justified.

CHAPTER TWENTY-EIGHT

ME

Walk on through the wind, walk on through the storm,
though your dreams be tossed and blown . . . Walk on and you'll
never walk alone.

When I read that, I automatically visualized the "Footprints"
portrait my parents had in their guest bathroom. Although
I felt alone, I knew I wasn't. God had never left my side in
spite of my frustration. I reminded myself of that each time I
became discouraged.

I settled the inspirational quote of a bookmark inside the
fold on page 199 of *Saving Grace* by Ryan Phillips as I closed
the book. I had borrowed the book from Justice on the night
Joseph and I met with Shayla. I had gone to Justice's house to
tell her what I learned at the meeting. She listened, but she was
worried about me, especially after the car incident. I could
readily admit that my passion for Desiree overshadowed the
fear for my life, but I downplayed the risk I was placing myself
in. Justice felt I needed to place my attention elsewhere. She
told me the story was well written and had a beautiful message
between its pages. I liked *Saving Grace* thus far, found it hard
to put down, but felt somewhat saddened. The main character seemed to have a disdain for her mother that confirmed
the fragile nature of mother-daughter relationships.

My mother and I weren't nearly as close as we should be. I used to go over to my parents' to help can apple preserves and shoot the breeze with my mom. We used to shop at the farmer's market on weekends before making those preserves. When I was growing up, she was closer to me than my sister. I was the favored twin because I stayed out of trouble. Alicia liked to test the waters and didn't seem to mind giving our parents heartburn with her adventures. I, on the other hand, followed the straight and narrow path. Our mother gave me accolades for all my accomplishments, even when they were small enough not to notice. I never thought anything could come between my mother and me. The sad truth was that she still adored me. I was the one with the problem. I couldn't get past her unwavering love for Khalil. It wasn't that I disliked my mother; instead it was the ache of knowing she took the side of a man who created great pain for all of us. She loved Khalil like she had given birth to him. We couldn't have a civil conversation where he was mentioned without it causing tension. My poor father stayed out of it, but I knew he didn't care for Khalil.

And with Kaleia it seemed I could do no right. Her quietness at times was a loud defiance and a painful indifference. If she didn't care about most things, like she tried to portray, the scars wouldn't be on her legs to contradict that.

I closed my eyes and listened to the seagulls squawking from the sky. That, combined with the crashing waves from Lake Erie, calmed me every time. I found the sound to be hypnotic and therapeutic despite my emotional upheavals. I lay on a blanket in the grassy picnic area and absorbed the rise of water on warm sand. The sun beamed on my back as I opened my eyes and watched Caleb playing volleyball with two of his friends that I had brought to the Sterling State Park with us.

Kaleia sat on a beach towel next to me in a pastel pink sundress with an iPod in her ears and her eyes closed. Her leg had completely healed since she had been released from the hospital. I had tried to keep a better eye on her since finding out that she liked to cut herself. Kaleia didn't appreciate my attentiveness, but I knew I had her best interest in mind.

I reached over and pulled the plug from her left ear. "What are you listening to?" I turned toward her and leaned on my elbow.

"Keri Hilson," Kaleia replied.

"Who's that?" The name didn't sound familiar to me.

"She's kind of new, but has written a lot of songs for other artists like Usher, Britney Spears, and Ciara."

"Is her CD good?"

"It's not the actual CD, but I like all her songs that I downloaded from Limewire."

"How many songs do you have on that iPod?" Although, I had purchased the Apple iPod Nano for Christmas, I didn't know much about it. It was the one thing for the holiday that Kaleia was determined to have.

Kaleia held up the small device with its purple aluminum finish. "I have about four hundred songs on here, but it is capable of holding twice that amount of downloads. Nobody I know buys CDs anymore."

"Music distribution changes like every ten years or something. When I was young there was the vinyl album, then came cassette tapes, and CDs replaced the tapes. Now it looks like a CD is obsolete."

"Rarely will you find a CD where all the songs are good. Why buy the whole thing if I don't have to? It is much easier to download what I like. Limewire has all free downloads."

The Internet with its unlimited ability, I had discovered,

was more popular than the microwave and telephone. Our computer was in the living room. Both of my children used it mainly for homework, or so I thought. I had mini spy-cams all over the house, but hadn't realized I might need spyware for the computer as well.

"Do you use Internet chat lines like MySpace or Facebook to talk to people?" I inquired.

Kaleia recognized that I wanted a real discussion and pulled the other plug from her ear. "I have a MySpace account, but I don't go on it too often. I like talking with my friends in person or by phone. I never really got into the MySpace hype. I'll probably use it much more when I go away to college, so I can keep up with my friends. Why did you ask me that?"

"Because people lie about who they are on those sites. You can claim to be anybody on there and who would know? I read this story the other day about a fifteen-year-old girl in South Dakota who was abducted by a registered sex offender. He had told her he was a twenty-one-year-old college student at Northern State University. He was actually a thirty-eight-year-old financial consultant from Colorado. They had been corresponding for five months when they made arrangements to meet. She had been missing for over a week when they found her roaming around a Sears parking lot in her underwear. Apparently, he had abandoned her there and told her not to draw attention to herself or he would kill her. He threw her out the car in her panties and bra. How did he not think attention would be drawn to her?" My stomach churned at the absurd nature of a child molester. "Fortunately, she was able to remember where he lived, despite being blind-folded, and took police to his residence. They found her clothes in the trunk of his car. He is facing a slew of charges."

"That's terrible. I'm glad she is okay." Kaleia looked off

into the water as if she were thinking about something, but didn't want to share her thoughts.

I hadn't mentioned Desiree's disappearance to Kaleia, because I didn't want her to think I was blaming her father for a crime. Not until I could prove it. "Some parents don't ask questions about what their children are doing or who they are talking to. That can be dangerous. That girl's parents never assumed that their child would be on any social networking site, let alone did they expect that she would meet somebody from the Internet. You can never be too careful."

"I would never meet somebody in person from the Internet. That's creepy. I guess it can be exciting meeting people you don't know, but I have enough things going on that I wouldn't do that."

"What about Caleb? Have you seen him on one of those sites?"

"Caleb?" Kaleia scrunched up her nose. "Yeah, right. He is a video game addict. Caleb isn't interested in anything that's not interactive. He couldn't care less about MySpace or Facebook. I could be wrong, but I doubt it. Mom, if you're not sure, you should ask him."

I watched my son laughing as the volleyball hit his friend in the face, and I dismissed his possible use of social networking sites.

Since speaking with Shayla, I had researched the variety of chat lines to discover cases where children were abducted because of their use of the social networking sites. I found that there wasn't as much information about Internet predators as I thought. When I tried to enter YoungLuv.net the access was denied. It required a membership, but didn't specify how that membership was obtained. I had talked to Ruben, and he told me they had somebody in his department that could break into the system without a password. He planned to get back to me if he found any kind of link to Khalil.

"You probably think I take things to the extreme, but everything I do is to protect you," I explained to Kaleia.

She opened her mouth and closed it again like she wanted to share what was on her mind, but didn't think I wouldn't be able to handle her answer.

"Go ahead, tell me what's on your mind. I can take it." I sat up and nudged her.

"Nothing."

"You sure about that? I've told you before that you can talk to me about anything."

"It's nothing, Mom. Really."

Before I could push any further, Caleb came running over with sand kicking up under his feet.

"Hey, Mom, can we go on the other side of the pier and get some ice cream?"

"I suppose. Am I paying for everybody?" I picked with Caleb.

He pulled out the pockets of his swim trunks. "I don't have any money."

I chuckled at my precocious son.

"I want something too. See if they have the strawberry frozen yogurt, although I'm not really in the mood for that. I want some chocolate, but I shouldn't. I don't need it." I debated with myself as I dug my wallet from the orange floral beach bag.

"Mom, you analyze too much. It's only ice cream. Live a little," Caleb chimed as I handed him a twenty dollar bill.

I agreed. We were at the beach to have fun and a chocolate treat would top off the day. "You are absolutely right. It is only ice cream. Get me the Rocky Road in a waffle cone. Kaleia, do you wanna walk on the wild side with me and get that mint chocolate chip you used to like in a sugar cone?"

She seemed surprised that I remembered that even though we hadn't bought it in years. Mint chocolate chip used to be her favorite. Lately, she stuck to vanilla bean.

"No. Vanilla bean will be fine. One scoop in a cup," Kaleia requested, and I felt like I was pigging out alone.

"Caleb, see if they will give you one of those drink cups to place my ice cream in just in case my waffle cone starts to drip. And don't forget the spoons."

"I won't. Can we get chili dogs too? I think they are like two dollars. Oh and an order of large fries. Miles and Simeon can share those with me." Caleb's food list expanded.

Boys seemed to be bottomless pits. My son was growing, but I couldn't tell where the weight was going. I found some comfort in knowing I wasn't the only one pigging out. "How are you going to bring all that food back? You only have two hands."

"We'll eat the chili dogs there, and then order the ice cream," Caleb said, waving his friends to the sidewalk.

I searched my wallet for a ten dollar bill. "Fine. Bring back my change, and don't take all day to bring back my Rocky Road."

As Caleb headed off, I turned to resume conversation with Kaleia. Her ear plugs were in her ears and she lay on her side with her back toward me. I guessed that was the end of our bonding experience.

I picked up the book I had been reading and let the sounds of the crashing waves nearby soothe me as I engaged myself in the pages.

CHAPTER TWENTY-NINE

KALEIA

"Are you sure you want to do this?" Kaleia asked as Taija folded, then unfolded a clinic brochure.

"Yes . . . no." Taija's eyes stayed lowered as she ran her index finger down the crease of the paper.

"We can leave. It's not too late," Kaleia offered.

"I have to do this." A determined scowl set upon Taija's full face.

Kaleia looked around the small lobby at the other patients of Alternative Options. There was a woman in a tan suit reading *In Touch* magazine, while a young couple who appeared to be in their twenties whispered to each other while they held hands. Kaleia reached over her chair and pulled a birth control pamphlet from the wooden information capsule against the wall.

The diaphragm, condoms, IUD, Depo-Provera, and Mirana were considered good birth control methods on the tri-fold. Brief historical overviews and a description of each method's effectiveness were listed. Abstinence was highlighted in bold as the safest way to avoid an unwanted pregnancy.

Kaleia read all three sections of the pamphlet before placing it back on the capsule. She had no interest in having sex. It wasn't worth the trouble, and Kaleia didn't even like being kissed. She wondered if Tevin would pressure her into doing it if he became her boyfriend. He called her all the time, and it felt like they were already a couple. But Kaleia was losing interest in Tevin. She had liked him because he dealt drugs. She had thought drugs could replace her cutting herself. Since talking with Dr. Malawi about the things on her mind, getting high didn't seem like such a good idea. Kaleia would have to stop seeing Tevin before things got too serious. She didn't want to think about having sex.

Kaleia dismissed thoughts about sex and Tevin from her mind. She turned to Taija and declared in an upbeat tone, "I can help you take care of the baby. You don't have to raise him or her by yourself. If Change doesn't want to be a daddy yet, then don't worry about it. There are a lot of teenage moms who do it. I can be the godmother, and I'll even get a job so we can buy diapers and formula. We both could get jobs, and you could work up until it's time for you to have the baby. Dollars and More is hiring. We can leave here and go fill out applications. Wouldn't it be fun to work together?"

"You live in Farmington Hills, while I'm in Eastpointe. We don't live close enough for us to work together," Taija remarked in a low voice, staring at the receptionist area.

"But I can spend the weekends at your house and go to work at the Dollars and More near you. I don't think it will be that hard to figure out how we can make this work." Kaleia was optimistic despite feeling terrible about Taija's situation.

"Of course it will be hard. Babies are hard, and I'm not ready to be a mom. I'm only sixteen. That's too young to be somebody's parent. I don't want that responsibility and Change doesn't either. He is going into the Managers in Training program next year. The company he works for will be sending him to Atlanta for a year. He wouldn't even be here for the birth, and you are going to Stanford University. You can't help me raise a kid from California. I want to go to college too. I may not know where yet, and it will probably be local, but I don't want that opportunity taken from me. I don't want to be one of those people in a welfare line struggling to make ends meet, or stuck at home while everybody I know is out having fun. I get sick just thinking about this." Taija rubbed her still flat stomach. "I don't know how I got so caught up."

"You made a mistake. We all make mistakes."

"But this is a big mistake. Huge. Colossal. It doesn't get any worse than this. I wish I had been safer. My mom made sure I had birth control pills, but they were making me sick. I probably should have told her that instead of throwing the pills away. I thought condoms would work just as good as the pills. I don't know what I was thinking. I shouldn't have trusted the condoms. Change's mom said that's why she doesn't go bungee jumping. She said she doesn't trust her life with anything rubber. She wasn't mean when we told her about the baby, but she was right. It is a risk like bungee jumping. The rubber breaks and your life is over." Taija sighed and refolded the brochure in her hand.

Kaleia had gone to Walgreen's with Taija and sat in the bathroom of the drug store while all four sticks from the pack turned fluorescent pink. It was news that devastated both girls. They stayed in the stall for close to an hour crying together. When Taija came for her initial appointment to confirm the pregnancy and have the procedure, Kaleia hadn't been present. Taija brought Change and his mother with her. Her mother or father was required to sign a consent form according to state law, because she was a minor. The clinic wouldn't perform the surgery without a parent's written consent. Kaleia knew that Aunt Alicia didn't know about the baby. Change's mom gave the clinic permission for services, and then signed Aunt Alicia's name on the form. Taija had told Kaleia that she cried so hard during that initial appointment, the nurse scheduled her to come back. The nurse thought Taija needed time to think about her decision.

"When will Change be coming?" Kaleia asked, feeling like a stand-in at the wrong time. They rode the bus across town on that Saturday morning after telling Aunt Alicia that they were going to the home of one of Taija's friends, and then they were all heading to the mall. Alicia offered to drive them, but it was a nice sunny day, and Taija said she wanted to enjoy the weather. Kaleia felt the same as she had when they were at the hotel. She kept backing up one lie after another, and it was getting to be too much.

"His mom has the car. He told me that he expected her back soon and would call when he was on the way."

"Maybe you should reschedule for a day that he can come with you. He should really be here from beginning to end."

"I can't reschedule. I won't have the nerve to do this if I leave. He will be here. He wouldn't let me down," Taija said confidently.

"What if that's your conscience telling you not to go through with this? What if you are carrying the next President Obama or Tyler Perry or Tyra Banks? What if you're carrying greatness inside of you?" Life was valuable even when it was unexpected. Even though Kaleia had harmed herself, she would never kill; not herself or another human being. She didn't want to judge Taija, but she didn't want to keep quiet about the baby's potential.

"What if I'm carrying a serial killer like Dennis Rader or Jeffrey Dahmer?" Taija had a book about well known serial killers and found the subject to be fascinating and terrifying. She wanted to be a Criminal Justice judge. "Or what if my baby's like that guy who shot all those kids at a bus stop? Twisted people usually have problems with their parents, and there are enough crazy individuals in this world. I would rather end this now instead of torturing some kid and making him or her become a horrible individual because I didn't want 'em. Unwanted children make miserable adults."

"That's not always true. Emory's mother is pure evil, but he is the sweetest child." Kaleia mentioned the little boy that lived down the street from Taija. They had seen his mother beat him with an extension cord in the middle of the street for feeding cookies to a stray dog.

"We don't know what kind of man Emory will be once he's grown, and I still wouldn't want to be that kind of parent."

"Taija, you aren't mean spirited. You would be a good mom."

"I will be a good mom someday, but not now. I don't want to be a mom right now. Not until Change and I are able to get married. Can we stop talking about this?"

Kaleia shrugged.

The woman in tan was called back by a nurse in a doorway next to the receptionist area.

"What time is your appointment?" Kaleia asked.

"Eleven."

Doctors never seemed to see their patients at the time they were scheduled. Kaleia wondered why that was the case. She looked at the clock on a wall behind the receptionist. "Are you sure that Change is coming? It's eleven-twenty."

Taija pulled her cell phone from her purse and checked the screen. "He hasn't called back yet, but he'll be here. His mom knows how important this is, and he knows I don't have any money to get back home."

Kaleia wasn't convinced at Change's reliability because she didn't know him that well. She didn't want to make Taija feel any worse than she already did, so she sat in her chair and held her tongue while they waited.

Twenty minutes later Change still hadn't shown up despite Taija's eight calls to him. He wasn't answering his phone. The nurse came to get Taija.

"Please come with me," Taija pleaded as she looked at the open door.

Kaleia didn't want to go back with Taija, but she stood up. Her imagination was running wild with pictures of the horrific procedure. There were some things that cousins shouldn't experience together. Certain family boundaries shouldn't be crossed. "I don't think that's a good idea. I don't think I can handle it."

Taija grabbed Kaleia's hand. "I need you," she pleaded with fearful eyes.

Kaleia obliged.

After Taija got to the room and changed from her clothes to a hospital gown, she laid on the table while a nurse prepared a tray. Taija pulled at Kaleia's fingers as her chair was placed right next to the table. They mashed their hands together, Kaleia's right with Taija's left, and when the doctor came in, their eyes stayed locked on each other throughout the whole procedure.

Kaleia felt like it was her on that table and everything was breaking up on the inside. She didn't cry. She held it together for Taija.

The procedure lasted an hour that felt like a long excruciating year. Taija had asked to go to the bathroom immediately afterward, while Kaleia waited in the room.

"Are you driving her home?" asked the nurse.

"I don't have a license. We rode the bus," Kaleia told the nurse.

The nurse ripped off the paper sheet Taija had been lying on and threw it in a hazardous waste bin. "We can't release her unless we know somebody can drive her home. Do you have somebody you can call?"

Kaleia couldn't think of one person that Taija would want to know her business. She knew Celia would have a heart attack. There was no way she could call her or their grandparents. And since Change wasn't answering his phone, Kaleia thought her Aunt Alicia would be her best option.

"I'll call my aunt."

"Okay, do you need to use the phone up front?" the nurse asked.

"No, I have a phone. Can I call in the hallway?" Kaleia didn't know what else to do.

"Just let us know what you decide."

"I hope Aunt Alicia understands," Kaleia mumbled to herself as she walked into the hallway. Her stomach did flip-flops as she dialed. She wanted to cut into her own skin and relieve herself of Taija's burden. Kaleia hadn't felt that kind of relief in close to two months. Not since she was hospitalized. The desire rose up in her as she recalled Taija's anguished face on that table. It had been a horrible experience. Kaleia felt sick as she pressed her fingertips to the phone keypad. She tried to convince herself that Aunt Alicia was the cool twin and that she would handle the news better than her own mother would.

CHAPTER THIRTY

ALICIA

"Got a meeting in the ladies room, I'll be back real soon. Oh, oh, oh, oh, oh, oh." Alicia swayed her hips back and forth in the kitchen as she blasted an 80's R&B song.

The gentle pressure from her hand wiped the chemically treated grime away that had settled beneath the stove racks. Alicia placed the yellow sponge in hot sudsy water and wrung it out. She hadn't cleaned the stove in months. It was one of her least favorite household chores. Juices from a pan of baked pork steaks had spilled at the bottom of the stove the night before, and it forced her to clean it.

"Got a meeting in the ladies room, I'll be back real soon." She waved the sponge as she sang.

The stove shined like new when she turned the stereo down and heard the house phone ring. Removing the pair of latex disposable gloves, she tossed them in the garbage can under her sink before answering the kitchen console.

"Hello," Alicia answered with the phone in the crook of her neck.

"Aunt Alicia, you are going to be really mad, but I had to call you." She could hear desperation in Kaleia's voice. "Taija's in trouble."

"Please tell me Taija wasn't arrested," Alicia groaned. She

imagined her daughter being held in some small back room of a department store being interrogated by a security guard who probably couldn't pass the police academy physical but wanted to play cops and robbers. What about her criminal record? Taija's job potential could be destroyed? Thank God she was a minor. A larceny charge would be placed in a sealed record after she turned eighteen. The boys at the precinct would have a field day with her daughter being arrested.

Kaleia whispered inaudibly to somebody in the background.

Alicia sat on her kitchen stool. "Which store did she get caught in?"

"She didn't get arrested. We're at Alternative Options," Kaleia responded, whimpering.

"Alternative Options?"

"Yes," Kaleia's voice was so low that Alicia had to strain to hear her.

"Did you say, Alternative Options?" Alicia repeated the question hoping that her hearing had been impaired from playing the music too loud.

"Unh, huh."

The truth settled on Alicia like dynamite detonated at the Berlin Wall. She almost fell off the stool as the metal legs rocked beneath her.

"No. Heck, no . . . oh heck, no," Alicia moaned.

From the sounds of it, Taija had to be pregnant. Why else would Kaleia be on the phone instead of Taija? A baby. Taija couldn't take care of a baby. Taija couldn't take care of herself. Alicia's thoughts ran to the smell of dirty diapers and being awakened at two A.M., three A.M., or four A.M. with wails from a newborn that would end up being just as much her responsibility as Taija's.

Alicia stood from the stool not wanting to hear anymore over the phone.

"Aunt Alicia?" Kaleia asked.

"Yeah, I'm still here." Alicia was already searching for her purse and keys before Kaleia could say they needed a ride. There was only one Alternative Options in the city, and Alicia knew exactly how to get to the clinic. In fact, that was where she took Taija to get signed up for birth control pills when she first started seeing Change eight months ago. There was no reason why Taija should have allowed herself to get knocked up.

"But Aunt Alicia—" Kaleia pleaded before getting cut off.

"Don't say nothing else. I'm on my way." Alicia hung up the phone. She grabbed her purse and keys from the entertainment center in the living room. She slipped her feet into a pair of tennis shoes and tried to wrap her mind around the image of becoming a grandmother.

Her ride to the clinic was thirty-five minutes longer than she expected due to construction on Interstate 75, Brush Street, and Woodard Avenue. Alicia felt like she was driving through a maze with all the detour signs. The clinic was closed when she got there. She found the girls sitting on a wall partition a block and a half away from the clinic. Taija had her head on Kaleia's shoulder. Their legs swung against the brick wall.

Alicia pulled up to the curb. "Get in," she said.

Kaleia jumped down first. She held her hand out to Taija who seemed to brace herself on Kaleia's forearm as she practically slid down the wall partition.

Alicia wanted to holler out the window for her daughter to stop being a drama queen because that wouldn't get her a sympathy vote, but Alicia held her tongue. She gave Taija an evil stare as she and Kaleia got into the car. "Oh, girl, I can't believe you," Alicia hissed as she began to drive.

Taija cried into the collar of her black shirt.

"Why did you go and get yourself pregnant? What happened to that packet of birth control pills we picked up at that same clinic? That's what I get for not keeping track of your periods. I thought you were being responsible. Do you even know how much it costs to raise a child?" Alicia didn't wait for Taija to answer as she jerked the wheel around the corner of West Grand Boulevard and Woodward Avenue. "Of course you don't. Why would you know something like that? You don't have to pay for anything. At least two hundred and fifty thousand dollars. That's the cost from birth to adulthood. Do you have a quarter of a million dollars? Of course not. You probably don't have two dollars and fifty cents. You don't have a clue what it takes to be a mother. You had it easy. You can forget that. And don't think I'm going to be a ready made baby sitter. I will have none of that. If you're grown enough to get caught up, then you are grown enough to deal with the consequences. A baby having a baby; if that ain't cliché." Alicia turned onto Brush Street. Her rant seemed non-stop as she went off on Taija.

"There is no more baby," Taija said with tears running down her face.

"Wait one minute. What do you mean there is no more baby?" Alicia stopped at a red light and shifted in the driver's seat so she could look at Taija more clearly.

"I got rid of it," Taija mumbled.

Alicia's head went to Kaleia in the backseat. "Did I hear her right? As in . . . she just had an abortion? I know I didn't hear that."

Kaleia's head bobbed up and down. "I tried to stop her, but she wouldn't listen to me."

"You had an abortion?" Alicia's throat burned with irritation as she turned her attention back to a quietly heaving Taija.

"I got rid of it," Taija confirmed. She said it like she had tossed a candy wrapper into a garbage bin.

"Oh, no." Alicia felt like all the blood in her body had pooled at her feet on the floor and brake pedal. She didn't notice the light had turned green. A car horn honked behind her. Alicia placed her head out the driver's side window and screamed at the red Suburban behind her. "Wait a doggone minute or go around." Alicia turned on her emergency flashers. She didn't care that she was holding up traffic in the right lane.

A stream of cars went flying past as they tried to beat the light turning red again.

"What the heck made you decide to do that?"

"I don't want a baby and neither does Change." Taija sniffed.

"Change?" Alicia searched her car with her eyes. "I don't see Change in this car. Obviously, Change didn't go with you to the clinic. I don't see how he could have such a strong opinion about your body and your baby." Mentioning an absent Change only infuriated Alicia more.

Taija hiccupped as her lips trembled.

Another car honked at Alicia. She again shouted out the window. "Dang, are you blind? Don't you see the flashers? I'm not moving; go around."

The driver shouted back for her to call a mechanic as they passed her window.

"Shut up," Alicia hollered back. She had enough anger building up inside her that if another driver honked their horn at her, they would see what true 'road rage' was.

"Why didn't Change go to the clinic with you? He is oh so helpful any other time. What did he do, drop you off and leave Kaleia to handle his responsibility?"

Taija didn't say anything as she wiped tears away with the collar of her shirt.

Kaleia piped in. "We rode the bus, Aunt Alicia."

"The bus? He didn't even have the decency to drop you off at the clinic. You had to take the bus. Did he have to go to work? That better be why he didn't go with you."

"No, he had today off." Taija's brown face had tear streaks.

Alicia was adamant about knowing Change's excuse for not being there. "Why wasn't he there? If he told you he didn't want a baby, why wasn't he there when you got rid of it?"

"He said he was coming," Taija explained.

"Aunt Alicia, Change wouldn't answer his phone. He was supposed to pick her up, he never showed," Kaleia replied.

"What? See, men or boys, are just the same. Unh, unh." Alicia shook her head vigorously. "He does not get to treat you like that. Where does that boy live at?"

Taija protested. "Mom, don't do that. Please don't go over there. I'm not feeling good. Can't we just go home?"

Alicia turned off the emergency flashers and shifted the car gear into drive. "Give me his address before I really lose my temper."

Taija reluctantly obeyed, and the car almost hydroplaned down the street.

As she drove, Alicia had flashbacks of being in her hospital room alone with a newly delivered baby girl. She recalled that the pain of natural delivery was nothing compared to the pain caused by Eric's reason for his absence at Taija's birth. He picked that time to decide he wanted to marry somebody else. It was a disregard and disrespect that could never be acceptable. Change's actions were no better. He didn't care enough about Taija to be there when things got rough. To give life and take it away should never be a man's option. They didn't have to deal with the suffering or repercussions after birth or death if they chose not to.

Change was outside cutting grass when they rolled into his driveway. Alicia wanted to hit him with her bumper as she screeched to a halt.

"Mom, please don't do anything to him," Taija pleaded again as they watched Change turn off the lawn mower and come toward the car.

Alicia ignored Taija as she jumped out of the car and stood in front of Change. "You're out here cutting grass on the most traumatic day of my daughter's life?"

He tried to look inside the car, but Alicia was blocking his way. "Is Taija okay?"

"You don't need to see in there. I'm talking to you. And no, she's not okay. She just had an abortion. She took the life of your baby."

"Ms. Evans, I didn't mean for her to be there by herself. I was waiting on my mom to come back with the car," Change explained.

Every time his head went to the side as he looked over her shoulder, Alicia moved over an inch to obstruct his view. "Oh, that's your explanation? Why didn't you jump on a bus like they did?" she asked.

"Ms. Evans, don't be mad at me. I really was going, but I had to wait for my mom to come back. I told her that I needed to meet Taija at the clinic, but she had to run some errands. I gave Taija all the money I had so she could get it taken care of."

"Your mother knew Taija was pregnant?"

"Yes."

"Funny, because I didn't." Alicia turned toward the car. "How is it that his momma knew about this, but I didn't?"

Taija wouldn't even look their way as she stared at the garage door. Kaleia had her window rolled down as she listened to Alicia.

"You know what? It don't even matter that I didn't know, because I know now. And I don't care if you had to ride that lawnmower to get there, you should have been by her side. What kind of boyfriend leaves his girl in a clinic by herself?"

Change pulled on his dark gray shorts. "But she had Kaleia. She wasn't alone."

"Kaleia is not her baby daddy." Alicia stepped so close to Change that their noses almost touched. She spat into his face. "That wasn't Kaleia's place to be there. That was your job and your job alone. And if the truth be told, both of you should have been smart enough not to end up in this predicament where she had to make a choice like that."

"My bad. We tried to be careful." Change shrugged his shoulders and pulled at his shorts again.

His indifference set her off. Alicia grabbed him by the neck and dragged him toward her car. She pressed his face against her partly opened window.

Taija turned and stared at Alicia and Change as his forehead bumped the glass.

"Look at her. This is what your being careful has got you. I bet you didn't show up because you didn't give a care. It wasn't you that had to get up on a table and get vacuumed out like car upholstery. You threw some money at her, and it no longer was your problem. I heard that you weren't answering your phone. How many times did you ignore her calls? Huh . . . huh? How many times?" Alicia didn't realize her own strength as her nails indented Change's neck to the point that he couldn't move his head.

"Can you let me go?" he asked, straining against her hand.

"Heck naw, I can't let you go. I want you to feel what Taija feels. Uncomfortable and hurt. You looking at her face, right? You see her wet face? Those aren't tears of joy. See what you put my daughter through? I used to like you, Change. That was before I learned that you were just as sorry and trifling as the next brother."

"What are you doing to my son?" A voice came from down the driveway as Change's mother got out of her car with a plastic bag of groceries in one hand. She had parked on the street.

"I'm teaching your son about respect, because obviously you didn't," Alicia responded. Change's mother, a short, stout woman, dropped the bag of groceries on her hood and stumped up the driveway. "You better let my son go."

Alicia reached her free hand beneath her purse flap and took out her stun gun. "I suggest that you step back before I try to sterilize the boy."

His mother took two steps back, but started rolling her neck as long black weave bounced down her back. "Who do you think you are? You better not hurt my son, or you will regret the day you pulled into my driveway. You are lucky you have that stun gun, or else."

Alicia shouted as her grip tightened on Change, "Or else what? Woman, I will pull those tracks out of your head and create a weave basket. You don't want none of me. You think I have your son hemmed up, but you can get it too. I am not to be messed with." Alicia raged like a mad woman.

The other woman's eyes looked like saucers. "I'm calling the police. You are on private property. I will have you arrested."

"Call the police. Heck, I have them on speed dial. I can call some people too."

"Mom, please stop making a scene. I'm really, really sick. I just want to go lie down. Please Momma, please," Taija pleaded from inside the car as she held her stomach.

"Lying down is what got you here." Alicia saw her pitiful

looking daughter and lost some of her steam. She released Change and shoved him from her car.

"Your momma is nuts," Change shouted at Taija, rubbing his neck.

Alicia took a step toward him with her stun gun raised. "I can show you a woman that's nuts."

Kaleia begged from her window. "Oh my God. Aunt Alicia, please stop."

"I better not ever see you at my house again. Do you hear me? Not ever. This is the preview. I can give you a show. Remember that," Alicia warned as she got in her car.

It was like history was repeating itself, and all she could see was red. Alicia needed a few glasses of super potent alcohol to calm herself.

CHAPTER THIRTY-ONE

ME

"Caleb, what time did you say the Bar Mitzvah starts?" I searched for my calendar book behind the computer stand in the living room. I thought I left it there, right next to the keyboard yesterday when I was online searching for cars. Alicia had picked up Kaleia to spend the night at her house right when I logged out. My memory must have been going bad. I had left a pack of veal cutlets out to thaw last night, ordered Thai chicken, and the veal was still sitting in the sink when I went to make coffee this morning. Or maybe it wasn't my memory going bad, but rather my convoluted thoughts after watching the international child sex trade news broadcast on MSNBC. My brain was in overload between watching shows about pedophiles, searching for information about Desiree, and trying to maintain a decent family life. Also, I missed Tyrese. Each day I seemed to miss him a little bit more. We spoke frequently, but the difficult reality of being in a long distance relationship had set in. I wondered and worried about us staying together.

"Too many thoughts in too little space," I murmured to myself as I reached my hand around the computer wires.

Caleb hadn't responded. I could see his figure cross his room from the open door.

"Caleb, did you hear me? What time am I dropping you off at the Bar Mitzvah?" My voice rose several octaves as I stretched my arm behind the heavy wooden base while in a kneeling position.

"I said four thirty," he responded like he had told me that already.

"Are you sure?" Caleb wasn't very punctual. He would have us late or early to every place; never on time.

We shouted back and forth from our separate rooms.

"Yes, Mom," he said.

"But I thought you told me five the other day."

"I did. The Bar Mitzvah starts at five, but you are dropping me off at the Rosenburgs' at four thirty, and I'm riding with them."

"Oh, that's right." The previous conversation was coming back to me.

The Rosenburgs only lived three blocks away, but I wanted to drive Caleb there.

I could feel the tip of the leather calendar binder wedged under the computer stand. I curved my index finger around the metal rings, but couldn't get a good grasp.

"Caleb, sweetheart, come here."

He was standing above me in his U of M shirt and matching blue shorts. "Yeah."

"Can you lift this corner, while I pull my calendar from under here? I don't know how I got it wedged here."

After he obliged and I had the leather binder in my hands, I looked at his clothes again. "Which suit did you decide to wear?"

"The olive green one," Caleb said, heading back to his room.

"The olive green one that needs to go to the cleaners?" I followed him.

"It doesn't need to go to the cleaners. I didn't get it dirty when I wore it to church that one Sunday."

My son never ceased to amaze me with his hygiene challenges. I walked into his room and picked up the short sleeved polyester shirt and matching pants off his bed. "First of all, this is not a suit. And it may not look dirty, but it is if you wore it. There are dead skin cells and particles all over this outfit. Your body sheds skin like a reptile, you just can't see it. I told you about wearing stuff more than once without getting it cleaned. Someday you are going to end up with a rash from putting dirty clothes on."

"Mom, I'm not going to get a rash. I'm a boy. Boys can wear stuff more than once. Troy wore the same underwear for a week and he didn't get a rash."

I didn't know Troy, but assumed it was one of his classmates. "How would you know about that boy's underwear?"

"In the locker rooms you know things. We crack jokes that Troy only owns one pair of boxers."

"Oh my goodness. Still . . . you know better." I threw the suit over my shoulder. "Wear the navy blue suit. It's clean. And pick out a tie."

"But Mom, it's a party for thirteen-year-olds, not church, and I'm going to be hot," Caleb groaned at my request.

That stopped me at the door. I turned back around and said, "It is a Jewish ceremony where a boy is introduced into manhood. That is a serious religious tradition. A rite of passage. I want you to look right. Now get dressed, we have to leave in about an hour."

I pointed at the clock before leaving his room. I planned to drop him off and get back home to finish the novel I had started. I wanted to give Justice her book back.

Caleb made an appearance from his bedroom half an hour

later smelling and looking impeccable. A smile spread across my face as I took in his tailored suit and moussed dry short curly hair. "You always look so handsome dressed up, Caleb. I love you in a suit."

The only thing wrong was the slight tilt of his gray and blue striped tie. I got up from my seat on the couch to fix it.

"Mom!" he protested as I loosened his tie and created a perfect knot.

"Hush." I tucked the tie against the navy blue shirt in his suit coat and stared at my son. He looked so much like Khalil that it used to unnerve me the older he got, but I came to the realization that Caleb was the best of our union. A beautiful gift I could never regret.

Caleb suddenly frowned. "Can I ask you a religious question?"

I ran my fingers down his lapel before going back to the couch. "Of course. What's on your mind?"

"If Joshua believes in God, and we believe in God, what makes our religion different? Is one belief better than the other?"

"Wow." I wasn't expecting that question. I explained as best I knew how. "Joshua's family is Jewish, and they believe in Judaism. That means they have thirteen principles of faith that exalt God or the Creator. They also believe strongly in the laws of Moses. While we obviously are Christians, and read the New King James Bible in our church, they have a different kind of Hebrew Bible called the Tanakh, which is similar to the Old Testament of the Bible."

"Joshua doesn't believe in Jesus like we do. We don't talk about it much, but I overheard his dad say he didn't believe in Jesus. But that doesn't make sense because Jesus was a Jew." Caleb pulled the tie out that I had just tucked in as he sat on the couch.

"Jesus was a Jew, but people still have doubts about Him. I really can't say why Jewish people believe what they do or Islamic people believe what they do or Buddhists believe what they do. I can't thoroughly explain somebody else's religious background. I just know that Joshua's dad has an opinion just like anybody else. And his opinion is based on how he was raised. Caleb, there are many religions in this world, just like there are many nationalities. We all may be different, but you should stand by what you believe, and at the same time, respect the differences of others. If you believe in Jesus, then that's what is important."

"So you're not going to tell me which one is better?" Caleb looked confused.

"If I tell you that you are better than Joshua because of your religion, would that change your friendship?"

"I don't think so."

"Son, I don't want you judging people solely because of their religion, race, class, or age. There is enough division going on in this world. I want you to appreciate others for their character. Has Joshua's dad or Joshua ever said mean things to you because you are a Christian?" I asked.

"No."

"Has anybody in Joshua's family ever encouraged you to change your beliefs or become Jewish?"

"No," Caleb stated.

"You are going to the Bar Mitzvah to support your friend in celebration. It doesn't mean that you are Jewish or that you're trying to be something you are not. If somebody were to ask you about Jesus, then you proudly tell them why you are a Christian and that you believe that Jesus died for you, but you don't need to get into an argument or debate about religion. You don't need a superiority complex to prove you love God.

You honor Jesus and God, by doing great things and loving all types of people. Does that make sense?"

"It does," Caleb responded.

I stood up ready to leave. "Good."

I dropped Caleb off at the Rosenburgs' and made small talk with Joshua's parents before heading home. On the way back to the house, I received a call that made me pull over into a Chuck E Cheese parking lot. My mother was telling me that Alicia had just spoken to our father. Alicia was upset, because Taija had an abortion earlier in the day. The details were sketchy, but they wanted to ride over to Alicia's for answers. I told my mother that I was already driving and could meet them there.

CHAPTER THIRTY-TWO

ALICIA

Alicia twirled the rim of the empty brandy pint sized bottle with her fingertip. "Unbelievable," she said to herself. "Un . . . freaking . . . believable."

The news of Taija's pregnancy and abortion had her floored. Literally. Alicia sat on her bedroom floor against her bed frame wallowing in misery. She cursed Taija's boyfriend, Change, for taking her daughter through a worse situation than she herself had been in with Eric.

Men were sorry. Men were unreliable. Men were losers. Every perception, opinion, or thought about the male population was confirmed. Never trust a man. That was a philosophy she drank in just like the alcohol she consumed. To trust a man was to set yourself up for a lifetime of disappointment and misery. She should have taught Taija better. No, teaching Taija wasn't enough. Alicia felt like she should have tasered Change's behind with her stun gun the first day he came over with that stupid little lovelorn grin on his face. That is what she should have done; zapped both him and Taija. She should have zapped them right into reality.

The police-issued X26 Taser gun laid on the floor next to her. She knew it could incapacitate a person in less than ten seconds; have them on the ground twitching and foaming at the mouth. Only law enforcement personnel were supposed to have that particularly stun gun, but it helped that Alicia worked there, although her office clerk position didn't require a badge. Preston, one of her police friends, gave her his old model when upgraded models with drive stun capability became available. All the officers at her precinct had to be shocked with a taser before they were allowed to carry one. Trainers at a stun gun safety session explained that if used incorrectly it could cause long-term serious injuries or stop the heart from beating. She didn't want to kill Change, but she would have been satisfied killing his ability to reproduce.

Kaleia poked her head into the bedroom and looked down at the floor where Alicia sat. "Um, my mom, Paw-Paw, and Grandma Pat are here. They are in the living room waiting for you."

"Humph. They came together. I might as well get ready for the crucifixion." Alicia hoisted herself up with the bed post. That's what she got for calling her daddy to tell him about Taija. She had to call somebody before she caught a charge. Her father was the only man capable of calming her when she got to that level of madness. The kind of mad that wanted to go back to that boy's house and do more than scare him. Of course, her father would tell her mother, who would turn around and tell Celia. They were like a family mod squad.

Alicia's insides were warm as she stood agile, anger heated her stride. The pint sized bottle hadn't put a dent into her irritation. It only elevated her rage. She had stopped at the liquor store on the way home and picked up the bottle of brandy, along with a gin and juice mix, as well as a bottle of Hynotiq. She didn't know what she wanted to drink, but her mood dictated having several options.

Kaleia stood in the doorway waiting like Alicia's ally. That was one assurance that Alicia had. Regardless of anything she said or did, Kaleia always looked up to her.

"Let's get this family meeting started," Alicia said. Even growing up, a family meeting was a result of a leak. Otis Jr., Celia, or Alicia told one parent something, and according to what that something was, the other parent called a family meeting instead of addressing any of the children. Because she was the main topic of many family discussions, Alicia felt like a kid about to be reprimanded again.

Alicia didn't know if Taija was in her bedroom or in the living room. On the ride home she had found out that Change's mother forged her signature on the consent form at the clinic. That information didn't help things. It wasn't his mother's place to make a decision with such finality for Taija. It irked Alicia that Taija felt more comfortable telling her boyfriend's mom that she was pregnant than her. Taija trusted somebody that obviously didn't have her best interest in mind. That no account woman with her no account son could illegally sign a piece of paper for Taija's abortion, but they couldn't make sure that she got to the clinic or back home safely. Alicia couldn't believe Taija listened to advice from Change's mother. The way it happened was stupid crazy. Taija's decisions seemed to be stupid crazy. As she drove home listening to her daughter's explanation leading up to that day's events, the words filtering in Alicia's brain were far from pretty wrapped in a bow. She could have cut Taija to shreds with all the thoughts running through her head, but the damage was done, and she was far angrier with Change and his mother than she was with Taija.

Alicia walked into the living room and saw that her daughter was missing from the group settled on the three pieces of her sectional sofa. She turned to Kaleia who was still by her side. If there was going to be a family meeting, then everybody involved would be present. "Go get her." Alicia watched Kaleia disappear down the hall. She adjusted her shirt and cleared her throat.

"Baby girl, baby girl," Alicia's father exclaimed, shaking his head. That was his nickname for both his daughters. He rarely called Alicia or Celia by their individual names, but somehow they always knew which 'baby girl' he was referring to.

The disappointment and shock were tense in her living room. Her parents and sister looked at her like she was the one that had the abortion.

"Let me just start this by saying if you all came here to have a bash Alicia fest, we can end this right now. I have heard enough bad news today," Alicia stated, her defenses rising as all eyes locked on her.

"See, your attitude is part of the problem. I—" Patricia scowled as she dropped her handbag on the coffee table.

"Pat, stop," Otis Sr. interjected, calmly holding up his hand. His eyes looked weary as he began talking again. "We are not here to make you feel bad. You called me because you were upset. Baby girl, I know how you respond to stress."

"You think drinking solves everything," Alicia's mother interrupted again.

Alicia rolled her head and folded her arms as she ignored her mother's comment.

"Now Pat, let me speak!" His stern voice kicked in as his eyes roamed from Alicia to his wife.

Patricia pursed her lips and folded her hands in her lap.

Taija came into the room with red, puffy eyes. She stood in the hallway right behind Alicia alongside Kaleia.

"Go sit down," Alicia instructed as she leaned again the wall. "Both of you can go sit down."

Both girls shuffled to the sectional and found spots to sit

in the curved sofa. Celia's hand rose over her mouth as she whispered to Kaleia. She tilted her head toward her mother's voice, then nodded.

Otis Sr. slid over slightly as Taija squeezed between him and Patricia. "Alicia, you had to realize we were coming. Your mother and I already discussed this on the way here. In the past few years, you and your sister have both brought issues that I never thought I would encounter. There was that whole thing with Khalil touching Kaleia and his being sentenced to prison. We thought that would be the worst thing to happen to this family, but now we hear that Taija was pregnant and had an abortion. We don't know what's going on over here with Taija and how all this came about, but we are going to work through this. We are going to work through this as a family." His eyes shifted until he made contact with all five females in the room.

"Taija, I just don't understand why you are having sex at sixteen. I mean, there are other things you should be doing at your age. You should be doing productive things like playing sports or cheerleading. You don't cheerlead anymore?" Patricia asked Taija.

"I'm still a cheerleader, Grandma." Taija stared disconnectedly at the wall next to the entertainment center.

"But you spend a lot of time with that boy. Most of your time is spent with that boy from what we hear." Pat's words sounded like an unsavory accusation.

"I love Change. I don't want to spend my time doing anything else," Taija replied.

Listening to her daughter only infuriated Alicia more. Taija's head seemed to be stuck in a cloud. "Taija, you are acting flighty. When are you going to realize that Change is not thinking about you?"

Otis Sr. turned his attention to address Kaleia and Taija. "Both of you girls have a lot of living to still do. The last thing you need to do at your age is invest too much energy into a boy. You have to allow yourself time to grow up mentally and emotionally. Just because you are physically capable of doing grown folks things, doesn't mean you are ready to do them. Boys will use you if you allow it, and then they move on to the next girl. Love is not just about what your heart tells you. Your heart will deceive you and cause tremendous pain. That is a biblical fact. Girls, I can't pick your boyfriends for you. I can't do that no more than I was able to decide who your mothers gave their hearts to, but a boy that leaves you stranded when you need him the most, doesn't sound like a good catch to me."

Patricia reached into her purse and retrieved a pack of tissues as a tear rolled down Taija's face. "Baby, your Paw-Paw is not trying to hurt your feelings." She dabbled at her granddaughter's cheek. "And I'm sorry, but I still don't understand why you are having sex at sixteen. Just because you have a boyfriend doesn't mean you have to sleep with him."

Alicia thought her mother was out of the loop with the twenty-first century; living in a glass house, unaware of what was really going on in the world. "Mom, sixteen-year-olds have sex. Most teens are having sex these days. Asking her why is not going to stop her from doing it. That's why they created birth control."

Celia didn't agree. "Every teen is not having sex. Taija has the freedom to do what she wants, because you allow it. We can't be our kids' friends. They need guidance and boundaries with limited freedom. Kaleia's not having sex. Are you?" Celia turned to Kaleia and put a spotlight of attention on her.

"No." Kaleia pulled at her ponytail.

Alicia didn't like Celia's insinuation. "Are you saying that because your daughter isn't having sex that makes you a better parent than me?"

"Not at all. We both learn as we go, but I think that we shouldn't allow our kids to act grown so early. And as parents, we sometimes see things but don't pay attention to them or let things slide when we shouldn't."

"Oh, so you're including your own errors with Khalil, right? Obviously your vision wasn't that clear about him or his parenting skills." Alicia felt that if somebody's head was going to be on a chopping block, it wouldn't be just hers.

Celia winced. "Don't go there. This is not about Khalil. And because of Khalil, I pay more attention to what my kids are or are not doing."

Alicia remarked seething, "Don't play around with what you really mean. You think you are a better mother than I am. But Kaleia wouldn't tell you if she was having sex. She would come to me before she went to you. And it's not about being their friend, it's about understanding her. I don't own a pair of rose colored glasses or keep my head hidden in a cushion. I understand both girls, and I remember what being a teenager is like. And yes, I let my daughter have a little freedom. And yes, I took her to get birth control pills, because it's hard to avoid temptation. I didn't want her to get pregnant, so I gave her all the information I could to prevent that. I think I'm a smart parent."

"If your parenting methods were smart, then we wouldn't be here right now." Patricia pointed at Alicia. "Your daughter is a reflection of you and what you have allowed."

Of course her mother would attack her parenting ability. Patricia had been attacking everything Alicia did since she was five years old. Alicia stopped seeking her approval a long time ago. "I did what I was supposed to do. I knew she should be protected if she were having sex. You can lead a horse to water, but the drinking is a whole different matter. And we can go around and around about what I should have or could have or didn't do. But nobody will make me feel guilty about taking preventative actions for my child. That was Taija's choice to be foolish. That was Taija's choice to have sex, and that was Taija's choice to get an abortion. I couldn't stop none of that."

Patricia's voice elevated as she stood up. "But if you didn't spend so much time drinking, maybe you could have paid Taija better attention. Maybe she would have made better choices."

Alicia unfolded her arms and pushed herself away from the wall she was leaning on. "Nothing I do is acceptable to you. It wouldn't matter if I were drinking or not. I'm the demon seed, and Taija's bad because she's mine. But if Taija's a reflection of me, then I wonder who I'm a reflection of?"

"Don't be getting smart with me. I didn't come here for you to be disrespectful." Patricia snatched up her purse.

Otis Sr.'s hands went out like he was trying to fan away a fire. "All of this needs to stop right now. Arguing is not going to solve anything. Pat, we talked about this before we came."

Patricia went toward the door and swung it open. "We are leaving. I will not have Alicia talking any kind of way to me. Her head is as hard as bricks. We are wasting our time here. I'll be in the car."

Otis Sr. rose up like he was defeated. "This is not the way it should be. This is no way to solve a problem. I guess emotions are too high, and we need to talk about this another time, but

I meant it. We are going to work through this as a family one way or another."

After watching their father leave, Celia asked, "Do you mind if Taija comes over to the house with me and Kaleia?"

"Oh, and do you want to finish raising her, too, since I'm doing such a bang-up job?" Alicia returned a question.

"Alicia, you need to calm down. If I thought that you were an awful parent then I wouldn't let Kaleia stay over here with you like she does. Taija needs some time to recuperate, and since I work from home, I can look out for her. And when she feels up to it, I'll make sure she gets to school. I just want to make sure she is okay. That's all I'm suggesting."

Taija had balled herself up in the corner of the sofa. Kaleia was planted on the cushion next to her.

Every time Alicia looked at Taija she wanted to go off about Change. It was probably in Taija's best interest that she let her go to Celia's house.

Alicia knew she needed to cool off. "Kaleia, help Taija pack some clothes. Celia, she is not to see Change at all while she's at your house."

Celia assured her. "That shouldn't be a concern. We will sit up watching movies and eating cheesy popcorn tonight. I'll find ways for us to stay busy the rest of the week."

"Fine. Let yourselves out." Alicia left them in her living room. She went into her bedroom and closed the door. She removed the bottle of Hypnotiq from the bag that lay on her mattress, stared at the silver labeling, and slowly dropped back to the floor next to her stun gun and empty brandy bottle. Alicia thought about the times somebody she loved complained about her drinking. She remembered how she broke up with Ruben because he wanted her to stop the rendezvous with alcohol. She recalled Phillip standing in her driveway, a wobbling, foolish mess, declaring his affection for her. He looked stupid. He looked worse than a bum on the street. Alicia held the neck of the Hypnotiq in her hand. She decided that alcohol was no longer serving its purpose, and just like Phillip, it needed to go.

CHAPTER THIRTY-THREE

ME

When Kaleia and Taija were small they would make squares for hop-scotch on the sidewalk with pink and yellow chalk. The lines of the squares were crooked and uneven, but they each took turns hopping within their creation. The girls also swapped toys with each other. Taija liked Kaleia's Cabbage Patch doll. Kaleia wanted Taija's Barbie with the purple corvette. They played with Easy-Bake ovens just like Alicia and I did when we were growing up. Kaleia and Taija did all the normal things that little girls enjoyed. I never imagined that their transition into maturity would involve molestation, self-mutilation, teen pregnancy, and an abortion.

I knew that I could never be expected to imagine such things, especially when my own childhood was average and uneventful. Our most traumatic events were centered around Alicia's rebellious escapades, like when she skipped class to go to a senior skip party. We were freshmen in high school and technically not invited; not that Alicia cared about invitations. She made it back to school before the buses came to transport us home, but for two hours, I was scared out of my mind that she would get herself into trouble. Or the time Alicia almost burnt down the guest bathroom in our great-aunt's house when a cigarette she was smoking caused a fire in the wastebasket. Alicia didn't mind stirring up trouble every now and again, but nothing to the extent we were dealing with now.

Upon bringing Taija to my house, I resorted to love with every ounce of kindness I could muster. It didn't help. Taija stayed sullen and depressed throughout the night, which carried over to the next day and the next. After three days of watching my niece wallow in misery, we decided that maybe she should get back to school. I thought being around her peers would help Taija feel better, but the same dreary face she wore when I dropped her off at school was still there when I picked her up.

I began to pray in my living room. "Lord, you know what I am standing against. The enemy is attacking us on all sides. I need you to deliver some healing for this family. I am not able to handle this battle without you. I need you to cover us in your anointing. I desperately need you to cover us and heal us. You are able to—"

The doorbell's ringing jarred me from my prayer.

"We've found matches for some of these pictures you have," Ruben told me, holding the metal box as he came through the door.

"Really?" I responded distracted, following him. That wasn't why I called him over, but it was good to hear the news.

For the first time in months, I was more concerned about my niece and sister than the investigation. Alicia had been heavy on my mind since the weekend. I had called to check on her Sunday morning before I attended church service by live stream on the Internet. I had wanted to go to the actual church house for some spiritual rejuvenation, but Taija's stomach was cramping, and I did not have faith that she wouldn't try to get Change to come over while the kids and I were gone. Alicia was snappy and irritable. She didn't want to talk. She said she needed time to herself. I waited until Tuesday to call her again at her job, but after brief words, she suggested that I back up and give her more space. She told me that she was working some stuff out of her system, but she wouldn't elaborate. Five days after we left her house and she still wasn't talking to me.

Ruben sounded ecstatic as he explained, "Seven of those pictures from Khalil's stash matched profiles for girls on YoungLuv.net."

"Oh my." That got my full attention. I was stunned.

"Our computer technician was able to decode the Web site access. Not only that, but we were able to pull personal information."

"Were you able to find Khalil on there?"

"No. But we did find the home addresses for the girls." Ruben opened the manila envelope and one at a time set paper on the table with a picture clipped to the front.

The sun from my sky light beamed down on the glossy photos.

"Liberty O'Reilly, age 14, from Cleveland, Ohio. Passion Cooper, age 13, in Chicago, Illinois. Olivia Marks, age 15, in Milwaukee, Wisconsin. Maria Santa Cruz, also age 15, in Grand Rapids, Michigan. Only two of them are from the Detroit area. Sabrina Anderson, age 16 and Jasmine Jones, age 14."

"Incredible." I soaked in the faces like it was my first time seeing them.

"Do you notice something about all these pictures?" Ruben asked, tapping each paper.

"They are all sixteen years of age or under. If the pictures I have are at least three years old, these girls had to be in middle school when the photos were taken." The girls had been like babies. Children barely out of grade school or puberty.

"Yeah, and what else?" He was intent on making me guess.

"Milwaukee, Chicago, Cleveland, Grand Rapids, and Detroit. All are major Metropolitan areas. YoungLuv is based in the Midwest."

Ruben seemed pleased that information was coming out, but there was also irritation on his brow. "Not only that. They all live in impoverished areas of these cities. It's like the creator of the Web site purposely targeted girls from low-income neighborhoods."

My stomach churned like it always did when I received horrible news. "Girls that were easy prey."

"Exactly," Ruben confirmed.

"Ruben, are any of these girls missing like Desiree?" I dreaded those pictures being some kind of trophies, like in the stories I had heard about serial killers, who took things from their victims. I prayed that Khalil wasn't a serial killer or associated with one.

"Fortunately, no. Officials have been in contact with the families. All seven are alive and accounted for. Detective McAngus has been communicating with the families and officials in each of those states. Three of the girls, Passion, Maria, and Sabrina still have active accounts on YoungLuv. From what McAngus told me, one of the parents actually condoned her daughter's little side job. Passion Cooper's mom was like a walking advertisement for YoungLuv. She said the site was safer than some other jobs and that YoungLuv.net kept her utility bills paid. The police in Chicago confiscated her web cam because she had a live feed streaming from her daughter's bedroom. Men could watch her kid sleep."

My mouth dropped open with disgust. The despicable

things that people taught their children. No wonder the world's undeniably corrupt. "That's a step above pimping the child out on a street corner. It never ceases to amaze me the extent people will go to for self-gratification. I don't know which is worse. The mother that sells her offspring to the highest bidder, or the degenerate that takes her up on the offer."

"The sad thing is that they couldn't arrest the mother for producing child pornography. Passion was fully clothed, and the officials in Chicago couldn't prove that the chats and live feed were with adults instead of other teenagers, which is completely legal."

All I could do was shake my head at blurred laws. "Speaking of officials, what is up with McAngus? Why didn't he look deeper into this case years ago?"

"His partner had been on leave after being shot in the line of duty. McAngus was left alone to handle a stack of missing persons files, and from his own account, Desiree seemed to be a kid that ran away following the death of her mother. The case didn't seem suspicious. He didn't have information about the pictures or YoungLuv.net. When you brought those pictures to the other precinct, they didn't bother to contact him about the investigation. Things fell through the cracks," Ruben admitted.

"Somebody dropped the ball on Desiree." Even with the current findings, I didn't have comfort, because of the mismanagement of information.

"Yes, somebody dropped the ball. But since learning about YoungLuv, the missing persons team has spent the past two weeks overturning every rock they can to uncover what happened to Desiree."

"Are one of those rocks named Khalil? There is no denying his connection to all this now. You guys should have enough to implicate him on something."

"I can only assume so. Missing persons in not my division. I'm only involved by your request and McAngus's coopera-tion."

The process was going too slow to please me. I had to re-main patient. Soon they would close in on Khalil, and he wouldn't be able to lie to them like he lied to me.

CHAPTER THIRTY-FOUR

ALICIA

Eight days into sobriety, and Alicia was ready to give it up. She had dumped out all the bottles of liquor in her house, but the taste of alcohol seemed stuck on her tongue like an unrelenting desire. Alicia woke up thinking about having one glass, one shot, one swig. Not drinking was making her irritable and almost intolerable.

As she entered her supervisor's office she knew Justin Manning didn't want to chit-chat. The discussion would be centered around her disposition.

He twirled a pen as Alicia sat down across from him. "Are you that unhappy in your position that you think it's okay to send out nasty e-mails?"

Alicia pursed her lips and shook her head. She knew when she accidentally hit send to the entire department that a backlash would follow. Her e-mail highlighted her and Shannon's job description in bold letters and explained how she refused to proofread any more reports placed on her desk by incompetent badge holders with the reading level of third graders.

"Justin, I don't dislike my position. My job isn't the problem. It's the being taken advantage of that I don't like. It's like we are the paper dumping ground. Some of the officers don't take the time to read over important details before they hand them to us."

"You don't think you could have found a more appropriate way to demonstrate your frustration?"

Alicia didn't need a second to answer. "No, I don't think I could have. They expect Shannon and me to clean up the reports. I thought it was the officers' job to type up their reports, but Officer Sanders has gotten comfortable enough to hand Shannon his notes from a leaf pad. Justin, what brand of lazy is that?"

Shannon didn't like to speak up for herself. Instead she complained to Alicia, which was fine before Alicia got fed up with them being used.

Justin had frustration written across his face. The pen he held drummed against his desk. "Alicia, you can't send out nasty e-mails insulting your coworkers."

Alicia usually kept a professional demeanor at the office, but her cup of irritation ran over, and the attitude could no longer be suppressed. "It was justified. There are stronger words I could have used. I mean seriously. These are policemen who spend their days chasing murderers and hog tying criminals. When did they become sensitive to my word choices? No disrespect, but whoever complained should take a word hit and keep on ticking."

Justin's eyebrows arched, then furrowed as he went from being shocked to insulted by Alicia's comment. "I'm the one complaining. There have been whispers since you sent it out, but not one person has mentioned the e-mail to me. I suppose I'm the one that needs to take a word hit and keep on ticking."

Alicia wanted to figuratively take her foot out of her mouth and kick herself in the behind. From the look on Justin's face, she knew she had vented too much. She didn't know what he was going to do, but she was certain that as her supervisor, he wouldn't let her action pass without a good work ethics lecture.

"For the past few days you have been blithe and argumentative. I wasn't bothered by it because you are a great employee. Nobody can complain about your quality of work, but you sent out a completely unnecessary e-mail, and I can't allow you to behave in such a rude manner." Justin pulled out a pink pad from his side drawer.

Alicia glanced at her supervisor marking on the sheet. Justin was writing her up. Alicia should have expected that, but still she was surprised. She couldn't believe he was actually writing her up for one e-mail. Alicia had been with the precinct for nine years, and not once had she received a written reprimand. A reprimand that would hinder her raise next year.

After Justin finished scribbling on that pink piece of paper, he ripped it off and placed his folded hands on top of it. Justin didn't like being the disciplinary type. "What's going on with you, Alicia? It's not just the e-mail. You've been a demon in heels this week."

Justin wasn't just a boss, he was a friend. They ate lunch together on a regular basis and hung out during happy hour after work. "I'm having a few personal problems. Things going on with Taija. I'm trying to work it out. I didn't mean to bring a poor attitude to work." She truly meant that, but it had been hard to separate work from home without a drink to take off the edge.

She thought about her daughter. Taija had come back home yesterday, and Alicia had to confiscate her mobile phone within hours. The phone had dropped on the floor leading downstairs to the laundry room when she went to wash her school clothes. Alicia had picked it up while Taija was still in the basement. She scrolled through the call log. There were a series of calls between Change and Taija for each day she was staying at Celia's house. The majority of those calls were placed after ten at night. Most likely when Taija thought her aunt was asleep.

When Taija came back up the stairs and saw Alicia with her phone, she had the nerve to say that she was told not to see Change; calling him hadn't been mentioned. Alicia had explained that since Taija didn't have a job and was on her T-Mobile family plan for the phone, it no longer belonged to her. Taija was thoroughly informed that she'd better not get caught using the house phone to call that boy either.

The world seemed to be coming to an end as Taija sulked her way to her bedroom. Alicia used that opportunity to promptly dial Ruben's number. They had been getting along great since they saw each other at Celia's, and Alicia knew that he would do just about anything for her. She requested that he and his partner make a police visit to Change's house for a harassment talk. The little boy obviously didn't take her last warning serious. She needed Change to understand that the law was on her side. Any more contact with Taija would result in him getting hit with a statutory rape charge. Ruben delivered the message without hesitation. Alicia wished she could have seen Change's face when they pulled up to his house. But as long as Change got the message, police siren loud and clear, that was all she cared about.

Alicia heard the scrunching of paper and snapped back into her current conversation. Justin was balling up her pink slip. She sighed. It was like a get out of jail free card.

"Consider this your warning. The one and only warning that I'm going to give you. I've worked with you for five years now, and we have a good relationship. I don't want your personal problems to cost you a job. If you need to take time off to get your head clear, then do so. If you need to use the Employee Assistance Program to blow off some steam with one of our counselors, then do so. But under no condition will the rude and disrespectful conduct be tolerated," he explained.

"It won't happen again," she assured him.

Alicia noticed the glances as she left his office. She fought the urge to say something snappy to the eyes following her back to her desk. With her head held up, she resumed her work duties.

She sipped lukewarm coffee and mumbled to herself. "One day at a time . . . one day at a time."

CHAPTER THIRTY-FIVE

KHALIL

Khalil knew things were getting worse for him when the prison guard told him that there was a visitor waiting for him, but didn't take him to the visitor room. Instead he found himself inside a square twelve by seven space alone, being interrogated by a man who introduced himself as Detective McAngus from the Detroit Police Department.

"What's your affiliation to YoungLuv.net?" probed the detective. His starchy looking suit rubbed on the edge of the table. Steel blue eyes settled on Khalil and instantly made him uneasy.

There was only one chair in the room, and Khalil was sitting on it.

It sounded like a baited question. A dig for information that Khalil didn't necessarily feel inclined to offer. *He's bluffing*, Khalil thought. The detective couldn't have anything on him. He was blowing smoke like a cigarette junkie on a lunch break. Khalil had gone to painstaking efforts to insure that no part of YoungLuv be linked to him. All association was under several alias names, including the offshore accounts. That was the beauty of the World Wide Web. Like pin needles in a barn, it was easy to get lost.

Khalil folded his arms and settled back in confidence. "If

you haven't noticed, I'm incarcerated. Internet use is restricted. How would I know anything about that particular site?"

Detective McAngus inched a little closer to Khalil. His baritone voice registered low. "Mr. Alexander, you're a pedophile. I wouldn't expect you to be honest. If you want to play dumb, we can sit here all day. I'm on the clock, but I assure you it won't get you anywhere."

"You came here to ask me questions. I think I'm well within my rights to ask some questions back."

"Since you aren't going to make this easy, how about I share what I know about YoungLuv.net. We have the names of several girls that appear to be current and former employees of yours. Adolescent women all across the Midwest have identified you as the man who interviewed them three years ago for your . . . um . . . Web site opportunity. Evidently, when you started your little business you did all the leg work yourself. I guess you met a lot of little girls that way. Some of those girls recognized a picture of you that we had. Still want to play dumb?" Detective McAngus's knowing glare knocked the smugness off Khalil's face.

He felt sweat circles form in the armpits of his orange jumpsuit. He kept his arms folded as wetness stuck to his skin. His foolproof business plan had a glitch. Somebody had to dig deep to uncover that information.

Khalil thought about Celia's visit only a month before and how she'd had a picture of Desiree. She had mentioned the other pictures he used to have hidden. She was able to use those pictures against him after all. He assumed that nobody would listen to her after three years. Who would have known that the police would decide to take her seriously after all the time that had passed?

"That Web site you have is pretty advanced. It took quite

the effort for our computer technician to decode your system. I bet you've made a few shiny pennies since you started your little business. With two thousand members at nineteen ninety-five per month, that's what? About four hundred eighty grand? That's a nice income, isn't it? You would be living like a fat cat if you weren't locked up." The detective inched close enough to touch Khalil's chair with the tip of his right shoe, until Khalil could feel hot breath graze his cheek.

Swallowing a golf ball-sized lump in his throat, Khalil replied, "Get to your point."

"People like you are eye sores on society. A man that uses children for profit in the enjoyment of other depraved minds should never be able to see the light of day. I wish the State of Michigan could give people like you the death penalty. Or instead of closing down Guantanamo Bay, they should isolate all you freak crazy, child molesters, and murderers on that Cuban island without food or water. Maybe let you feed off each other's flesh like cannibals." Disdain and venom spewed from Detective McAngus's mouth.

Khalil never proclaimed to be a saint. Nor did he expect the detective to understand his career choice. "I'm sure your dislike for my kind didn't bring you out here to Kinross. What do you want from me?"

"Desiree Carpenter. She appeared to be an employee of yours just like those other girls I mentioned. Her family wants to know where she is at. Dead or alive, they deserve to know her whereabouts. We can get you on at least seven charges of child solicitation, but I'm sure an arrangement can be made to lessen that if you have beneficial information about Desiree."

Her name pecked at his conscious like a wild bird on a birch tree. Khalil never intended for anyone to get hurt. He never expected a child to disappear simply from association with him. That was why they had safe links on his site. That was why he had chat room monitors who did random checks on the conversation content between members. It was a 'look but don't touch' site.

"I think I want to request my attorney be present." Khalil refused to say another word until he had representation.

CHAPTER THIRTY-SIX

ME

When I learned of Desiree's death, I was at a Thursday night prayer meeting. There was no pre-empt that could have prepared me for that news. It was only by God's grace that I was in that meeting when I found out.

Having missed two months in a row, I had relished the fellowship and instantly felt in sync with Taylor, Monique, and Justice, my group of faith filled sisters. The discussions helped fuel me with extra positive energy until I could get to church service on Sunday. On that day I had brought Kaleia, Taija, and my mother along to the meeting. Caleb was staying the night with Joshua. I wanted the females in my family to experience what I did when in attendance. Alicia was invited, but declined. She told me she wasn't ready for that type of thing, and all I could do was plant the seed and trust God to water it. My hope was that in time, Alicia would come around. Since admitting her efforts to stop drinking, I saw how hard it was for her to handle the struggle. I knew the group would be a great support for her, would pray for her in unity, but since she wasn't ready for that, I had to support her in a different way.

"I had a come to Jesus moment at work yesterday," Taylor declared at the prayer meeting after reading her scripture card on judgment. She worked at the Department of Human Services in Dearborn and admitted her struggles as a social worker. "You all know how my job challenges me and lately I have a not so nice disposition when I step into the building. Yesterday, I felt like I had food stamp applications growing out of my ears by noon, and my phone would not stop ringing with one complaint or another. It's like you can only carry so much of other people's *stuff* before it weighs you down."

I understood completely where she was coming from. I thought about Desiree and her father. I thought about Alicia with her drinking, Kaleia with her cutting, and Taija with her abortion, and all that was going on in my family. The past few months had me bending like a willow tree in a hurricane. Life and situations could break a person that wasn't rooted.

I looked at my mother with her study Bible in her lap and my lips tilted upward. After her reaction to Alicia on the day of our family meeting, I confessed to her the things I had been dealing with concerning Kaleia. I didn't want her thinking that I was better than Alicia or that my parenting trials weren't as hard. I made bad decisions just as easily as Alicia had. The good daughter versus bad had to stop. Alicia and I weren't Cain and Abel. My mother admitted that her favoritism wasn't fair and that she needed to stop persecuting Alicia. For her to say that meant we were moving our family as a whole in a better direction.

I brought my attention back to the conversation.

Taylor was saying, "So one of my clients came in for a review. She only had her three children listed on the application but I knew that her boyfriend had been staying with her and that he had a job because my younger sister stays in the same apartment complex."

Monique stated like she knew what Taylor was going to

say before the words came out her mouth, "She was trying to scam the system, wasn't she? Her boyfriend was probably laying up in her place, eating her food and not contributing a darn thing."

"That was my instant thought, but there's more to the story." Taylor paused as she took another glance at her index card. "When I saw the client's boyfriend's name missing from her application, I started asking her all kinds of questions. And honestly I was already biased before she answered because I see cases like hers all the time. But instead of hearing a bunch of lies, she pulled dog tags from around her neck and explained that he was in the Army. The client said that last week he had been deployed to Afghanistan for a two-year tour. I felt awful for assuming that her boyfriend was no good and that she was trying to commit fraud. And I was convicted on my lunch break while reading a daily devotion. It was about courage in leading a people, from the book of Esther. Between that devotion and this scripture I just read, I've been convicted on my thoughts. I need to implement the courage of Esther in my life."

Monique confessed, "That means I need to repent for assuming the worst too."

"There is such a bad connotation associated with public assistance that it's easy to assume everybody is getting over on the system. To be honest, a lot of people do take advantage of our services, but it's not everybody. I have to keep reminding myself of that."

"Who is Esther?" Kaleia asked from her seat on one of the blue card table chairs placed in the circle.

I hadn't realized she was paying attention to our discussion. My hope had been that they would listen, but considering how she and Taija had been whispering to each other since we got there; I was thrown by her inquisition.

Justice filled her cup with sparkling juice and explained, "Esther was a queen in Persian Empire before Christ. She'd been born a poor Jew. When Esther became royalty she didn't forget where she came from, and she didn't judge her people for not having what she had. She risked her life to save the Jewish people in her empire from being slaughtered by her husband. She was known for her mystery and beauty, but more so for her courage."

"Really?" Kaleia seemed genuinely interested. "I don't think I've read about her before. I think I would like to find out more about Esther."

I made a note to take her to the bookstore to find the complete story of Esther for her.

"Kaleia, we can go to the store this weekend to search for books if you want," my mother offered as if reading my mind.

Taylor also addressed Kaleia. "There are a lot of amazing women in the Bible, but Esther does rank as one of my favorites. I needed to get my attitude in order and remember that everybody's situation is not like my situation or within my realm of understanding. Sometimes I have to pray before work, during lunch, and when I leave that place just so I don't lose my purpose. I have to remind myself that I became a social worker to aid a people not judge them."

I looked at Taija who remained quiet. I would have to include her on that trip to the store and maybe I would find someone from the Bible that Taija would enjoy reading about.

We discussed Taylor's work situation some more before it was time for another member of the group to pick a scripture that helped to deal with life.

"I'll go next." I pulled a scripture index card from the stack on Monique's round table and held it. I read aloud, "Mine is from Ephesians 1:17 and 18. *The God of our Lord Jesus Christ,*

The Father of Glory . . . give to you the spirit of wisdom and revelation in the knowledge of Him, the eyes of understanding being enlightenment. Well, let me see. That can be interpreted in a multitude of—"

The ring tone with J Moss began to play. Ruben's number came across my screen. He had told me that Detective McAngus was going to visit Khalil, and I hoped he had some information about that meeting to share with me. I held up my index finger. "Excuse me, ladies, but this is important."

I quickly rose and headed to the bathroom right off the living room. I waited for good news. But what I heard Ruben say, I wasn't expecting. I couldn't prepare for it and didn't know how to absorb his words.

He began with an apology. "I hate to tell you this over the phone."

"Hate to tell me what over the phone?" I felt an ever insulting twinge within my stomach as I slid down to the rim of the toilet seat.

"Celia, Desiree's dead. Her remains were found in a plastic bin inside a rental storage unit outside Dearborn about an hour and a half ago."

"What? . . . How? . . . Who?" The thoughts in my head conjoined like blood clots. I didn't know if I meant who found her or who killed her. Numbness pelted down from my head to my toes like cold raindrops. In that moment I could have stepped outside my body and watched the conversation continue.

Ruben told me, "It's a long story, but McAngus got a confession from her murderer, which led to the recovery."

Recovery, not rescue. It was too late to rescue Desiree.

"Did Khalil kill her?" I braced for him to confirm that my ex-husband was not only a child molester, but a murderer.

"No. Khalil didn't kill her, but he led us to the murderer who happened to be an active member on his Web site. He showed our investigators records of conversations between Desiree and others using a monitoring system. Khalil had it connected to his Web site. He could track all e-mail correspondence on YoungLuv.net. It was supposed to be a safety measure to monitor the pedophiles. One man seemed especially suspicious and had a personal connection to Desiree. It was her band teacher's husband, and he confessed. His name is Michael Mellon. Evidently, Desiree went to the Mellon home for help with preparation for a Christmas recital. Mrs. Mellon wasn't at the residence when Desiree got there. Mr. Mellon was there alone, and he recognized Desiree from YoungLuv. net. Desiree recognized him too. He had been corresponding with her for close to a year. Mr. Mellon said that killing her was an accident. That he got worried because Desiree was acting nervous. He just wanted to talk her into keeping quiet about their online conversations, but Desiree wouldn't listen. She tried to run and hit him in the head with a lamp. Mr. Mellon said he impulsively reacted. He strangled her to death. Then he used the plastic bin she was found in to transport her body to a rental space they kept for old furniture from his bachelor years. From what McAngus told me, Mr. Mellon seemed relieved to get the murder off his conscious after three years."

I recalled my conversations with some of Desiree's teachers when I first started looking for information. I remembered Mrs. Mellon, the petite brunette with a warm personality, had nothing but kind words about Desiree. "Mrs. Mellon's just like I was. Living a lie with our spouses. That's just terrible, absolutely terrible that a person could kill someone and still go to sleep at night." My throat had begun to hurt. "Does Joseph know?"

Joseph had already lost his wife, and now it was confirmed that his daughter was gone too. He had to be going out of his mind from the news.

"Yes, there were local reporters from broadcast stations all over that storage facility when she was found. Target 7, WDIV, and WWJTV were breaking their necks trying to be the first to get the story. Detective McAngus made sure Mr. Carpenter was told before it hits the eleven o'clock news tonight."

"I should call him. Maybe it's too soon." I saw myself as Joseph's friend and wanted to reach out.

"Are you going to be okay?" Ruben's concern touched my numbed heart.

"I don't know. I guess I have to be. But . . . um . . . I'm at a prayer meeting. If you get anymore information, please stop by the house tomorrow. I just really need to know all the details of what happened."

Ruben promised, "I will."

As soon as I flipped my phone closed, I felt that familiar burning in my throat like I got right before the flu or a head cold set in. But it was seventy-five degrees outside, and it wasn't the kind of sick that came from a cold. Somewhere between Monique's bathroom and her living room, my numbness began to dissipate. By the time I squeezed through a pair of blue card table chairs to get to my seat, I could no longer compose myself. All the hope I held for her to be found surfaced in pain. I stood in the center of the circle next to a coffee table with my friends and family. I let the tears from two months of searching finally roll from my eyes.

"She's gone." I cried with incomprehensible grief. "They found her remains. Desiree's dead."

A pair of arms surrounded me, then another, then another, until six sets held me as we stood.

My mother began to pray, "Though we walk through the valley of the shadow of death, we will fear no evil, for you are with us. Lord, as we stand here unified, I ask you to give comfort despite what has occurred. Allow the tears to cleanse and the pain to heal. Show us mercy and give us grace, for only through you can we prevail."

A chorus of 'Yes, Lord' rocked the walls of Monique's home. I felt God's presence larger than life. I felt Him telling me that Desiree was safe with Him, and within time my tears of pain would transcend just like Desiree had when she made it through heaven's doors.

CHAPTER THIRTY-SEVEN

DESIREE

On May 29, 2009, my home-going celebration was held. It was exactly one week to the day that my body was found. Four days after the Memorial holiday. Family and friends gathered at Emmanuel Church of God in Christ on the east side of Detroit. Emmanuel was my Grandma Hattie's church. She has been a member there for forty-two years now, ever since she was a young girl like me. On the days I stayed with Grandma Hattie, it was the place I went to for Sunday morning services and Vacation Bible School. It was where we served God together before I died.

At the front of the small sanctuary laid a pristine white casket. Four large silver easels were at the head and tail of my closed casket, two at each end. The outer shell of my earthly presence was no longer in good condition and couldn't be viewed. Instead, pictures of my childhood were displayed on those easels. They were pictures of the happier times during my life, the times when my mother and I were joined at the hip.

My father sat in the first pew. His head was bent down. I could feel his pain and wished he could feel my touch. Next to him was my Grandma Hattie dressed in a navy blue dress with a matching brim hat that shadowed her face. There were aunts, uncles and cousins I hadn't seen in years. Also in the church was my best friend, Shayla, alongside her mother.

The woman named Celia was sitting farther back in the sanctuary. She had brought a man and a girl with her. Celia's expression held grief. Although we never officially met, I knew she was responsible for the search to find me two months ago. I saw her many times talking with my father. She even offered to pay for the arrangements to my home-going celebration. My father didn't have a lot of money, and he couldn't afford the beautiful proceedings on his own. I was not quite sure why she did those things, but I was grateful for her help. I was certain my father was grateful too.

I heard Bishop Solomon McLemore, the church father of Emmanuel, as his voice boomeranged throughout the sanctuary. "As we mourn Desiree, who left us so tragically, the question often arises: Why did God allow this to happen? We know the God we serve is sovereign and fervent. God is loving and all knowing. God wouldn't allow the lives of His angels to be taken without His knowledge. But we have to remember that Jesus died tragically too. God hurt when His son gave up His life. God hurts when we hurt. God is not to be blamed in Desiree's death, and let's face it, blame can bring comfort. Whenever tragedy strikes it tests our faith. God doesn't want us to rely on negative feelings to get through pain, suffering, and mourning. He wants us to fold ourselves in His loving arms."

I watched the tears shed, the hands held in comfort, and I realized how much I was loved.

From the pulpit, Bishop McLemore continued, "Isaiah 25 says, *The Lord will wipe away tears from every cheek.* We can share all our sorrows and disappointments with Him. When we find our peace in God, when we live with God's love in our hearts, then we have peace."

My old band teacher, Mrs. Mellon, was the last person who spoke during my eulogy. I felt bad for her, because she had to find out her husband murdered me. She explained, "At first I wasn't sure if I should come here. I was ashamed of what my husband had done. I felt responsible for not being home. I felt it was my fault for picking that day to get stuck in line at the grocery store. I want to believe that I could have prevented this from happening, and I only pray that Desiree's family forgives me for allowing her to be put in harm's way. I can't change my husband's incorrigible crime, and I will live with that forever. But I had to be here to pay homage to a beautiful, bright, and creative young lady. I had to give Desiree her due." With her head held high, Ms. Mellon recounted a memory of me. "When Desiree first entered my classroom, she was so quiet that I almost didn't think that she wanted to be in band. But once I laid out some instruments I kept from the previous year and I watched her stroke that clarinet, I knew she had found her passion."

Mrs. Mellon was right. Music had become my passion. After my mom died, I had felt lost without her. The clarinet brought me joy. It had made me feel connected to something.

A broad smile spread across my band teacher's face. "Before she passed, we were practicing for a Christmas recital. She was to play 'Silent Night.' I spoke to Mr. Carpenter a few days ago and asked if that could be my contribution to the service . . . playing her song." Her voice became choked up. "He said he would be honored, and with that, I would like to share 'Silent Night' by clarinet."

The clarinet was pulled from a black case on the floor. Mrs. Mellon lifted it to her mouth and closed her eyes as she began an instrumental dedication. The nice, smooth sound of a B flat vibrated in Emmanuel Church of God in Christ.

During the third bar of the song, a group of twenty in white and blue robes with silver trim stood up in the choir stand. The choir sang in beat with the clarinet. A harmonic synchronization began to soothe the pain I saw in my father's eyes and calmed the posture of others that I held dear.

Sleep in heavenly peace, sleep in heavenly peace.

I could not have asked God for a better service in my honor. After the procession of the funeral, they took my casket to the gravesite.

It wasn't until my body was lowered in the ground at the cemetery that I saw my father's emotions completely overtake him. "Good-bye, my precious girl. Daddy will always love you."

"*I'm so sorry, Desiree. I'm sorry that I couldn't prevent this. But I'm glad you're home.*"

Celia didn't say the words out loud, but I had clearly heard every word.

The pastor finished with, "Ashes to ashes, dust to dust."

Fourteen white doves were released by the man Celia called Tyrese. It was very pretty. I'm resting now, happy that my mother's resting next to me.

CHAPTER THIRTY-EIGHT

KALEIA

In her imagination Kaleia's father had been Bruce Wayne or Clark Kent without the red floppy cape and minus the black Batman suit. Khalil Alexander had been her superhero in plain clothing. Her love for him had been unbending. But after learning that he had been running a business that used young girls for profit, she could no longer see him as her superhero. Kaleia could no longer look up to him as that one special force in her life.

Her mother had told her about the girl that had died and the pictures that led police to search for her. Kaleia had never heard about the girl until her mother's breakdown during a prayer meeting a week and a day ago. Celia had been grief stricken over the girl named Desiree. Kaleia hadn't seen Celia cry like that ever before. She always seemed to have it together until that night.

There was a memorial service held yesterday. Caleb thought funerals were creepy and decided to spend time with Paw-Paw. Kaleia asked to join her mother for the service. The discovery of Desiree's body had opened up conversation between Kaleia and Celia about life, how precious it was, and they talked about the domino effect of decisions. If Desiree had never worked for Khalil on YoungLuv.net, she would have never known her band teacher's husband was a pedophile, and she would not have been murdered by him. Khalil's Web site was shut down. Kaleia's father didn't get charged with a crime, because he led the police to Mr. Mellon, but it all was still terrible.

When they stood at the gravesite where Desiree was laid to rest, Celia cried a storm again while Tyrese embraced her. Kaleia wasn't jealous that her mother talked about the girl like she had given birth to her. It was like seeing her mother shed tears publicly made Celia seem more human, more real. Learning about Desiree had completely changed Kaleia's perspective about both her parents.

Holding Desiree Carpenter's obituary in one hand and the letter she wrote Khalil in the other, Kaleia traipsed to the living room where her mother was working on her laptop. The letter had been her secret connection to her father.

There were black folders and white paper stacked on the sofa next to Celia

"Mom, can I share something with you?" Kaleia asked as she sat in the lounge chair.

"Of course." Celia immediately set the laptop amongst the stacks of papers and gave Kaleia her full attention. "What's on your mind?"

"When Daddy went to prison, I wrote him a letter. I had wanted to send it to him, but I knew you wouldn't let me. You made it very clear that you didn't want me to have any contact with him. At that time I didn't think it was fair. Caleb got to send him stuff, but not me. Even though he wasn't the best father, he was still mine, too, and I wanted to talk to him. "

Celia sighed before apologizing. "I'm sorry that I did that to you. Maybe I shouldn't have allowed Caleb to mail his stuff, yet restricted you. I thought I was doing what was in your best interest. I still think it would have been a bad idea for you to communicate with Khalil, but maybe I should have given you the same option as your brother."

Kaleia replied with sadness. "I understand now why you did it. Daddy isn't necessarily a good person. I understand now why you don't like him."

"Kaleia, it's not that he's a bad person. Khalil makes bad choices that affect a lot of people. And it doesn't matter whether I like him or not. That had very little to do with my decision to keep you from him. I didn't want you influenced in the wrong way. But you said you wrote him a letter. You want to tell me about it?"

"Can I read what I wrote him?"

Celia nodded.

"Dear Dad, it has been three months, one week, four days, and six hours since they sentenced you. I'm keeping track because I feel like I was sentenced too. I want you to know how sorry I am for sending you to prison. I love you very much and regret that I'm the reason you are behind bars. I feel so alone without you here, and if I could be Dorothy from *The Wizard of Oz* for just one day, I would click my heels and make all of this go away. I know that I am special to you and that you didn't mean to hurt me. You are special to me. No one could ever replace you, Daddy. I promise to never eat mint chocolate chip ice cream again. Not until you get out. I hope you forgive me for what I have done, because I'm not sure if I can forgive myself." Kaleia looked up from the letter to see her mother's face. She saw the sadness in Celia's eyes that matched the ache in her heart.

"Oh my." Celia pursed her lips.

"I also wrote him a poem. Would you like to hear it?"

Her mother's head dipped once.

Kaleia began to recite her words.

Bubble gum, ice cream, and candy treats
That's what my Daddy gave to me
Heart shaped kisses and hugs a plenty
That's what my Daddy gave to me
Special attention and love for free
That's what my Daddy gave to me
Now it's gone, blown in a breeze
Now I wonder who I will be
Without what my Daddy gave to me

Tears glistened Celia's eyelashes. "That was...Wow! I don't know what to say. You wrote that three years ago?"

"Yeah."

"It's pretty deep."

"I wanted Daddy to know I missed him. I wanted him to know *how* much I missed him. But I couldn't get the letter to him. I didn't know how to send it without you finding out."

"Do you still want to send him your letter?" Celia asked almost hesitantly as if she were trying to be understanding but didn't know how.

Kaleia looked from the obituary to the letter. "Mom, now I read those words and they don't feel the same. Now I know what he has done. A part of me wants to burn it and forget I wrote it. But I was thinking that maybe I could add to the letter what I feel since I learned about Desiree. Dr. Malawi told me that it could be the cleansing. She told me that in session on Monday. She said that current events don't change past feelings and that I should acknowledge how I felt when he went to prison because I held it in for so long. Dr. Malawi thinks that sending the letter will help me heal. It will help me keep fighting the urge to cut myself. She also suggested that I talk to you about it. At first I didn't know how to come to you, but yesterday when we were at that gravesite, something changed. Just like Daddy seems different to me now, so do you."

"Well, I hope that the difference you see in me is a good thing. And I do agree with Dr. Malawi. It can be a cleansing. I know for me that I had to learn to forgive your father. Not just say it, but really forgive him. Any bad feeling I held on to had to be released. When they were placing dirt on Desiree's grave, I cleansed while I cried. I let go of every bad thought I had about your father. I allowed it to be buried so that I could move on. There is a verse in the Bible that says, *He that hath clean hands, and a pure heart; who hath not lifted up his soul unto vanity, nor sworn deceitfully. He shall receive the blessing from the Lord.* God needed me to move on. I needed me to do that so that I don't miss out on my blessing," Celia acknowledged. "And although I am sad that Desiree is no longer here, I thank God for His grace. If you want to send that letter as is, revise it, or burn it, I am behind you one hundred percent."

Kaleia smiled. "I want to revise it and send it to Daddy. Can you help me find the right words?"

"I can try."

Kaleia felt warmness inside at finally seeing her mother in a different way.

CHAPTER THIRTY-NINE

ME

The gas grill sizzled as Tyrese laid lamb chops on the iron rack.

He had invited the kids and me over for the Fourth of July. Tyrese had planned to cook for us and take us to see the fireworks later in the evening.Kaleia and Caleb were in his living room playing the word game Scattergories as I assisted Tyrese with the meal. Tyrese had also invited Alicia and Ruben to come over, but they took Taija on a trip to Canada for the holiday. Since Alicia had stopped drinking she spent more time with her daughter. Alicia's moods shifted from one day to the next, but I could see her effort to stay sober. I was glad that she had Ruben for support.

"Ginger."I had dipped my finger in a bowl near Tyrese and licked the glaze while simultaneously placing a platter of vegetable shish kabobs onto the outdoor table."I taste ginger and a citrus flavor.Is it orange juice?"

He denied, brushing the sweet concoction on those wonderful smelling lamb chops. "No orange juice in my glaze."

"Come on, tell me what it is."

"I will not.My glaze is patented and locked away in a safe like the recipe for those spices in Kentucky Fried Chicken. "

"Oh, please, KFC has enough sodium to give a race horse

high blood pressure. I don't want that recipe.But yours, patented or not, should be shared, at least with me."

"Sorry, can't help you. It was passed down by my great, great grandfather and will remain in the family. You would have to marry me to get the recipe. " He flicked my nose with the handle of the glaze brush.

"You know, that's not such a bad idea. I mean, I love you, and you love me. " The words left my mouth before I realized what I had said.

"Wait a minute. Repeat that."

I measured my words and said them again, with more emotion. "I love you, and you love me. Us being married isn't such a bad idea."

His dark gray eyes sparkled as he lowered the hood of the grill, dropped the brush on the table, and pulled me in his arms. "Say that first part again."

"What?I love you?" I said jokingly as I tried to contain my smile.I said those words like they came naturally.

His head rolled back, then forward.He kissed my forehead as joy danced in his eyes."Oh, that's like heaven to my ears. You have no idea how long I've been waiting for you to say that."

"So the 'us being married' part doesn't really count?"

"Sweetheart, I'm still trying to absorb the 'I love you' part. Give me a minute."Tyrese closed his eyes and hugged me for several moments.

The pop and sizzle of the grill played like music as I allowed my heart to completely open to him.The Berlin Wall I held inside my chest had come crumbling down.

"What brought about this change?" he asked.His arms were still pressed firmly against my back.He didn't want to move and neither did I.We fit together.

I admitted, "My feelings for you hit me hard on the day of Desiree's funeral. I was trying to be strong for Joseph, and you jumped right on it without me having to ask for help with the arrangements. You walked in humbly with those balloons and that case of doves and . . . and . . . I felt this thing . . . this strong affection for you that I couldn't deny any longer."

Tyrese's grip loosened as he looked at me with concern. "Celia, funerals make people emotional. I paid for those arrangements because I knew you wanted to and couldn't. I did it because that was the right thing to do. But I don't want you to confuse endearment with love."

"That's just it. I'm certain it's not endearment. The funeral was the capstone for me to admit how I truly feel. It was like God was encouraging me to let go of the past and move forward with a clean heart. And my clean heart doesn't want to live without you." I spoke freely and honestly.

He kissed me again on my forehead, my lips, and my forehead. "So we're going to make this long distance relationship work? Are you willing to move to Houston?" Tyrese had been bouncing between Texas and Michigan for the past two months.

"I think it would be best if we didn't make any abrupt decisions. Kaleia graduates from high school in two years, and I'm not sure if I should uproot her like that. Plus, Alicia's having a hard time remaining sober, and I want to be here as her support system for a while. Prayerfully, she and Ruben will get back together soon. Tyrese, I just wanted you to know that I'm open to loving you, and I'm open to being your wife someday."

My family had been through a great deal and was still standing. If anything we were stronger than we had ever been. Kaleia and I were becoming closer, Caleb actually left his Nintendo DS at the house and had told me that he was looking forward to all of us spending time together.

"I've been waiting a few years for you to get to this point, I guess I can be patient for a couple more years if need be." Tyrese released me. "I need to turn these chops over before they turn to lamb charcoal."

I grabbed his arm before he turned fully toward the grill. "One more thing."

"Um . . . okay."

"Your mother. I need to know your mother.In fact, I need to know your whole family. Aunts, uncles, cousins, and everybody else you are related to. I need to know the people you come from."

"That can be arranged." Tyrese chuckled in agreement to my terms. He knew that my love for a man would never make me blind again.

I had learned that faith in God would carry me through any storm, but wisdom had to be my foundation too. And after more than three years of turmoil, I could finally say, I found peace again.

READER'S GROUP GUIDE QUESTIONS

1. Celia took it upon herself to look into Desiree's disappearance. Do you think it was divine intervention or resentment toward her ex-husband that created the interest?

2. In order to cope with her emotions, Kaleia cut herself. Can you understand her guilt about her father's imprisonment?

3. Do you think Celia placed the search for Desiree above the needs of her own children?

4. Although Alicia and Celia had distinctive personalities, they both harbored anger toward their exes. Is Alicia's attitude worse because she doesn't go to church and her anger is blatant? Can you relate to either woman?

5. Celia said early in the story that she prayed for Khalil to be healed. Do you think Khalil could be healed as a child molester?

6. What do you think about Khalil's business operation? Would you blame him for what happened to Desiree?

7. Do you see any similarities between Kaleia and Alicia on addiction, religion, and/or men?

8. Do you believe in generational curses? Were there any generational curses in the story?

9. Caleb asked if Christianity was better than Judaism. How do you feel about Celia's response?

10. How does faith or the lack of faith play into the lives of these characters?

ABOUT THE AUTHOR

T.N. Williams is the author of two other novels, *Something On The Inside* and *After The Feeling*, which made Black Expressions and Black Christian News bestseller lists. She is a contributing writer for EKG Magazine. T.N. has received several awards for recognition and collaborated poetic work in the published collection entitled *Traces of the Infinite*. She graduated from Grand Valley State University with a Bachelor degree in Sociology. She currently resides outside of Charlotte, NC with her family.